Catbird Singing

Amish Horses Series
Book II

Thomas Nye

CROSSLINK
PUBLISHING

Catbird Singing: Amish Horses Series Book II

CrossLink Publishing
www.crosslinkpublishing.com

ISBN 978-1-63357-013-9

Library of Congress Control Number: 2014956128

Chapter 1

ALONE

"**A** large storm system will be moving northeast. These storm cells could be severe at times. Be prepared to move indoors into a basement or interior room. ... "

Lenny turned down his radio and looked into his rearview mirror. Dark, ominous clouds loomed over the highway behind him. He was still ahead of it.

"C'mon, Impala!" He pressed the gas pedal until he noticed his speedometer. "Oh, man, I better watch my speed." He leaned forward in his seat even though he knew it wouldn't help. Glancing out his side windows, he searched the heavens for signs of a funnel. Angry clouds filled the sky, churning and rolling. Lenny turned up his radio to listen for an updated report, but one of his favorite songs thumped out instead, momentarily soothing his fears.

Lenny looked at his rearview mirror again—this time into his own troubled eyes. He knew where he came from, he knew who his parents and grandparents were, but he didn't know where he was going. No matter how fast his Impala went, the wall cloud stayed right on his heels. He felt as if the storm were pursuing him; however, for some reason, it chose not to overtake him. A construction crew working on a bridge brought Lenny's trip to a standstill. "Oh, great! Don't these guys know we are gonna get hit with a big one?" He sat alone in his Impala, nervously looking over a railing into dark, swirling waters of a river below. He wondered what it would be like to fall into water like that—powerless in overwhelming currents. A solitary red-tailed hawk circled high in the heavens above. Lenny imagined the hawk's view: a dark ribbon of a swirling river snaking its way through wooded floodplains, surrounded by vast open prairie. Columns of sunlight broke through gaps in turbulent clouds, illuminating tracks of cultivated farmlands that lay under the shadow of an impending storm.

A flag man waved Lenny on, and he hurried across the state line into Iowa. He immediately felt better knowing he was in his home state; it almost seemed that he was getting ahead of the storm. He gave a sigh of relief and caught a whiff of hogs. The only visible signs of swine were long white buildings with huge fans at each end. Every now and then, an old barn surrounded by outbuildings came into view, standing stoically straight even though no longer in use. Like tiny ghost towns, these abandoned acreages served as a reminder that the glory days of the old-fashioned farm were over. His memory took him back to Uncle Alvin's Amish farm. Two summers ago, Lenny had spent time among the Amish, in a community where the world seemed small. Amish farms there were full of life, with families raising livestock in a bustle of activity. Those memories, on one hand, were vivid. Yet, at the same time, it seemed like a dream.

Lenny wondered if it really happened, or if he had only imagined it.

An obnoxious warning came blaring from his radio. "Errr, errr, errr... The National Weather Service has issued a severe weather alert for the following counties in Iowa..." Lenny pressed his gas pedal hard, and then retracted his foot for fear of the state police. The young man felt a twinge of guilt overtake him as he thought about how he had promised his cousin Perry that he would come back and help him farm with horses—and he hadn't kept his word. He thought about Leah; he could still see her sweet, brown eyes, a wisp of light-brown hair daintily playing across her forehead in a gentle breeze. He thought about how cute she looked when they rode home from Singings together. Those were his first dates with any girl. "Leah probably has a boyfriend by now," he said aloud. "I wonder if I would have had a chance with Leah?"

Deep inside, Lenny craved to see his Amish relatives, but it felt awkward even to think about meeting up with them at this point. He longed to ride in a buggy again; he could almost feel leather driving lines in his hands. He fondly remembered the sensation of power passing through those lines, especially when driving a big team of draft horses. He felt that if he could only drive through his Amish relative's community, it would quench his burning desire to see them again. Glancing in his rearview mirror, it seemed he had finally escaped the clutches of the monster storm that had been pursuing him for hours. Golden arches near the highway kindled his hunger, and he took the Bulltown exit off the interstate. Lenny pulled his silver Impala into the parking lot and came to a stop beside a massive, red four-wheel-drive truck with huge tires. As he hurried past advertising signs showing images of French fries, cold drinks, and huge sandwiches, he could smell food. It wasn't night, but dark clouds made it seem later than it was and caused a swarm of tiny bugs to draw near the building, unable to resist the bright lights. Lenny walked past the bugs, through the doors, and up to a plastic yellow counter. "Can I help you?" a young girl asked.

"Yeah, I'll have a number one value meal." She pushed a touch screen, and he swiped his debit card. Then she handed him a dispensable cup for his pop. While he got some ice and Coke, he noticed a small group of teenagers talking nearby. He chose to sit on the opposite side, near a guy and girl who were talking quietly in a booth.

Lenny took a big bite off his sandwich and drew a mouthful of pop out of a straw. While he did, he listened to the couple talking in the booth behind his.

"Yes, I'm sure; it was definitely positive," the girl said casually. Lenny and the girl waited for the young guy to speak.

He finally managed to say, "Well, I'm not ready to settle down yet. What are our options?"

She answered, "I'm gonna have this kid. You do whatever you want."

While he inhaled his burger, Lenny's cell phone vibrated with a text message from his college buddy Brad. "Hey, Lenny, you know what we are gonna be … sophomores!"

Lenny quickly texted back, "LOL, you know what? Prof Miller says, 'sophomore means: smart enough to know something but too dumb to realize how little you know.'"

Brad replied, "Ha ha; that's us all right!" Lenny noticed his cell phone was almost out of battery power.

He went to refill his drink and glanced at the couple that sat talking in a booth behind him. She looked too young to have tattoos, or a baby. Her dyed-blond hair was up in a ponytail, revealing brown hair growing back at the roots. He was a stubby little guy, obviously a wrestler, judging by his cauliflower ears. They both looked up at the same time. The guy gave Lenny an angry, challenging glare, and then turned it on her. Lenny hurried for the door. As he did, he overheard a woman at the counter complaining loudly, "My children ordered cheeseburgers without pickles, but there are pickles on both." Her children were crying and making a scene. Lenny took his fries and drink and headed out to his car.

It was only six o'clock, but thick, dark clouds hanging overhead made it seem much later; everything felt heavy. He sat in his car for a moment, trying to decide if he should hurry back onto the interstate, or if he could swing by Bulltown to see some Amish people. He concluded that Bulltown was only about seven miles from the interstate; he surely had time to swing by for a few minutes. He felt drawn to the Amish community like a bug to neon lights.

Only moments later, he began to see a few Amish farms; they seemed out of place along a paved road. Lenny decided to turn onto a gravel road where he knew there were more Amish farms; nobody would ever recognize him anyway. He could see that up ahead, a woman was driving an open buggy, and he had to slow down as her horse chugged over a long sloping hill. He got the sensation a person might have when crossing a time warp and traveling back in time a hundred years. Lenny enjoyed watching the horse; it made him miss Tug and Train, his favorite horses at Uncle Alvin's place. The Amish woman turned and looked back at Lenny's car as though worried she was slowing him down. There wasn't any way she could know that he was enjoying the view and didn't even want to pass.

When her horse crested the hill, it picked up speed coming down the other side, but Lenny's Impala easily caught up and raced past her horse without even trying. He looked back at her trotting horse in his rearview mirror and felt bad about her having to eat his cloud of dust. All at once, a huge gust of wind came up. Instantly, Lenny remembered the storm that had been dogging him. It seemed the storm had been lurking behind a few hills, waiting for him to let down his guard. He looked for a place to turn around and head back to the interstate; it was too late. Winds grew stronger. Lenny thought of that poor Amish woman driving a horse in such bad weather. Huge raindrops or small hail began to hit his windshield, making it hard to see. Lightning flashed followed by a heavy clap of thunder. Lenny heard a roar and felt his Impala leave the road, slipping into a ditch. "C'mon, Impala, don't let me down!" He sat helplessly, listening, as the wind moaned and shook his car, thrashing it with pelting rain, sticks, and other debris kicked up by the storm. Thunder rumbled on, sounding like voices murmuring.

In a daze, Lenny tried to see out of his windows, but his Impala was dead, and his wipers weren't clearing off the windshield. As quickly as the wind came up, it died down. Lenny pushed open a door and climbed out of the ditch. Some trees had been knocked down, and leaves and corn stalks were strewn about everywhere, covering the road. He instinctively knew that it was time to call his mom. He pulled his cell phone from his pocket and, in a moment, had her on the line.

"Mom! Hi, Mom, I'm okay … but I just went through a tornado or something … I think."

"Where are you, Lenny?"

"I'm near Bulltown."

"Bulltown, what are you doing there?"

"Sorry, Mom, I was just going to drive by there. It's only a few miles from the interstate; I should have hurried on home."

"It's okay, Lenny; I'm glad you weren't on the interstate during a storm!"

Lenny looked down in the ditch at his Impala. "Mom, my car is in a ditch, and my cell phone is about out of battery power. Don't worry about me; I'll be fine. I think I'm near Uncle Noah's place. I will go there, okay?"

Susan answered, "Good idea. Thanks for calling! I love you, Lenny!"

"I love you, too, Mom. Don't worry; I'll be fine! I will call you sometime soon."

"Okay, bye."

Aaron Burr

As Lenny put his phone back in his pocket, it began to sink in that he was alone in the middle of nowhere. He looked around nervously, trying to think of what he should do next. He remembered the woman on the buggy. He trotted back in that direction, knowing she couldn't have been very far behind him, afraid of what he might find. He looked for her anyway.

He saw wheels spinning on an overturned buggy; his heart sank. He rushed down the ditch bank, searching frantically for the woman. The horse lay there still but seemed to be alive. Lenny tied the horse's lead rope to a big tree limb that was beside it, so he could unfasten its harness. He wouldn't have known what to do if he hadn't seen his cousin Perry unharness a horse after a buggy wreck a few years ago. When he got the horses harness unbuckled, he watched it struggle to its feet, and then resumed his search for the woman. A moan gave away her location; Lenny hurried over beside her. Her black Amish bonnet covered her face, but he could see she was bleeding from her forehead. Lenny plunged his hand in his pocket and drew out his cell phone. In his panic, he couldn't even think how to dial 911. He tried it several times before realizing his phone was dead.

His mind was racing; he looked around, trying to think of what he should do. Up above them on a hill stood an Amish farm; he took off running in that direction to get help. He stopped and turned back. "I better see first if there is anything I can do for that woman." She was trying to sit up, mumbling something in Dutch. He rushed up to her. "Ma'am, are you okay?"

She struggled to get to her feet, and then stumbled; Lenny caught her before she fell. He looked up at the farmhouse. And because he was already holding her, he lifted her up, carrying her uphill toward the house. She seemed lighter than he had expected; adrenaline was helping. He cradled her like a small child. She kept mumbling in Dutch, and Lenny understood she was worrying about her horse. He tried to comfort her. "Your horse will be okay." She was soaking wet from the rain and almost snuggled into him as though trying to get warm. He carried her across the yard toward the white farmhouse where he hoped to find help. He wondered if this was her home; her husband might get angry on seeing his wife being carried by a man. It was too late to think of that; he couldn't set her down now.

Without any warning, the woman came to and seemed disorientated. She spoke loudly in Dutch, and Lenny understood her enough to know what she was saying. "Let go of me, Englisher."

He felt bad because the poor woman couldn't know what was happening. Fortunately, an elderly woman came out of the house at that moment. The older Amish woman tried to console the younger one. "Now, now, he was trying to help you. Oh my, let me look at your head."

An old man came up and joined them. Lenny thought he ought to tell him what happened. "I was coming down your road when this storm hit, and I found this young woman's buggy overturned in that ditch." The older woman took the younger one inside to attend to her wound.

"We need to get her to a doctor," Lenny said. The old man was completely calm, confidence emanating from him. That calmness swept over Lenny, and, for the first time in hours, he caught his breath and relaxed.

All old Amish men look something alike, and this man reminded Lenny of his deceased grandpa.

He said, "My name is Aaron Burr."

"I'm Leonard. I had better head back down to the road and fetch that horse of hers. Can I bring it up here?"

The old man gave a blank stare but answered, "Good idea!"

In only a few minutes, he had untied her horse and led it up near Aaron's barn. Lenny noticed a large uprooted tree in the elderly couple's yard; it was lying across one end of their clothesline. The aged man met Lenny at his barn and said, "Leonard, do you see that sliding door?" It was right in front of them. "Slide that open and you'll find some horse stalls; you can tie Stanley in there." The old man said the name Leonard with an accent on the second syllable, just like Grandpa always did.

When Lenny slid open the big doors, he immediately found horse stalls. A warm horse smell mixed with sweet hay breezed over him, and he drew in a deep whiff. While he tied Stanley, he took in the amazing sight of a huge team of black Percherons in the next stalls.

"Is Stanley okay?" Aaron asked.

"Well, he walked up here all right; I can't see a mark on him." The old man didn't respond with words but smiled. Lenny liked him immediately; however, something about the man seemed odd. He noticed that the older gentleman stood looking off into the distance instead of at his visitor. "Is there anything I can do to help?" Lenny asked. Aaron stood still for a moment. Lenny wondered if he was hard of hearing, but he soon realized the elderly man was thinking.

"You know how to harness up a team of horses, don't you, Leonard?" Lenny looked at him, not sure what to say. He wondered if the old man was blind and maybe unaware that his visitor wasn't Amish.

"Well, yes, I do."

"You'll find work harness hanging behind that big team. My wife and I want to head down the road and check on our neighbors."

"Okay, are they broke good?"

"The best," Aaron smiled. Lenny found a brush and ran it over them quickly. The horses reminded him of Tug and Train, but not quite as big. When Lenny set the harness on the first horse, Aaron Burr said, "I'll get Duke's harness; you take care of Prince." While harnessing Prince, Lenny glanced over at Aaron, who seemed to be feeling his way through, in snapping Duke's harness in place.

"Let's hitch this team on that forecart over there," he said, nodding in the direction of a two-wheeled cart with one seat. Lenny instantly knew that the old man was going to expect him to drive his horses. Lenny struggled to finish harnessing Prince because his hands were starting to shake. It had been a long time since he had driven a team of horses.

The old man stood looking off into the distance for a moment and began to speak. Lenny didn't know if the words were directed to him or not. "When storms come, remember Him who spoke and calmed the storm and sea. When troubles rise around you like a flood, keep your head above the waters and look for your deliverer."

Lenny listened but he didn't know how to respond. The elderly blind man seemed kind and sincere, so Lenny concluded that Aaron was getting old and losing touch with reality.

Aaron Burr helped Lenny hitch the huge horses to a forecart and the cart to a hayrack. They waited for the women to come out of the farmhouse and join them. Aaron's wife came out arm in arm with the young woman Lenny had carried in earlier. She had bandaged her head and put a scarf on over it.

"Shouldn't we get her to a doctor?" Lenny asked.

"She will be fine," the old woman answered. She stopped at the end of her sidewalk and looked Lenny over—first at his hatless head, and next at his face. Lenny remembered that he hadn't shaved in over a week and scratched his fuzzy chin to cover up his scruffy attempt at a beard. She turned her attention to Lenny's tee shirt with fresh bloodstains accenting the bold lettering of his favorite team: Iowa Hawkeyes. "Do you think this young man should drive?" she directed her question at her husband while helping the stern-faced younger woman up onto the hayrack.

He answered her confidently, "Oh yes, he's good with horses."

Aaron's elderly wife seemed to accept her husband's opinion and stepped up onto a hay bale next to his wagon that served as a stoop. She helped the younger woman climb up. Although the young woman seemed to be getting along better, she was clearly not herself. Lenny had yet to get a good look at the young woman's face, partly because it had been covered in blood and now with a bandage. She never returned his glances in her direction, which gave Lenny the impression she was discussed with him because he had been so bold as to pick her up and carry her. He wanted to apologize but didn't know how to put it into words without making things worse.

Aaron Burr smoothed things over by addressing the issue at hand. "We have obviously had some kind of bad storm like we've never experienced before. Let's be thankful to God for protecting us and sending this young man along at just the right time. The Lord sees when a sparrow falls; he knows how to provide for all of His children. Now, it would only be right for us to see if we can help someone else in need." Lenny nodded in agreement even though the old man couldn't see. He threw the step-up bale onto the hayrack and climbed onto his forecart seat and clucked. The huge black horses stepped forward obediently, pulling the hayrack down a gradually sloping lane toward the road. "Turn left," Aaron directed. Lenny looked to the right at his Impala, which was mired in a muddy ditch. Beyond his car, he could see the woman's overturned buggy. He could hear her asking about her horse again. Aaron calmly assured her, "Stanley is fine. Don't you worry now; Stanley will be just fine."

From his vantage point, Lenny could see widespread wind damage. Cornstalks, leftover from last year's crop, were strewn about on the road. Lenny told Aaron Burr, "Over in the distance, I can see a whole row of power lines down!"

"Really? That can't be good."

"You will probably be out of power around here for days," Lenny noted, then thought about how silly it was to say to an Amish man.

"Do you think it was a tornado?" Lenny asked.

"I don't think so, more like straight-line winds."

Junior's Boys

They rounded a curve and came upon a large herd of black-and-white dairy cows crowding the road ahead of them, mooing and bawling. Aaron Burr asked Lenny, "Do you think these cows got out during the storm?"

Lenny looked from side to side, surveying the situation. "No, there are young Amish men driving them somewhere." Lenny slowed his team of horses, but they overtook the slow-moving cattle drive.

A tall, lanky Amish guy hung back from his part in driving cows to explain what was going on. He gasped for air as he spoke, "Our neighbors … the Johnson's … are out of power! We're taking their cows … down to our place to milk them … with our generator." He stopped explaining long enough to encourage a slacker cow to catch up with her herd. "We could sure use more help ... this is more than twice what we usually milk."

Lenny noticed the young Amish fellow eye him suspiciously, but he obviously had too much on his mind to ask any questions. In only a short time, they were herding the noisy Holsteins into a long lane. A line of trees along the lane was damaged by winds and were laying to the east; however, the lane was on the west side. Prince and Duke behaved perfectly, and Lenny's driving job was easy because they had to go slowly in following the cattle herd.

Three or four young Amish men were driving the cows; none of them had beards, so Lenny deducted that they were unmarried and around his age. A set of hound dogs brayed loudly, running along with the youthful men as they jumped over fallen trees and climbed fences, whatever was in their way, to keep their cows moving forward. Lenny watched as they skillfully maneuvered the whole herd into a makeshift holding pen. Aaron Burr instructed Lenny, "Do you see that hitching rack up near the house? Tie Prince and Duke there, and you can help with milking." Lenny hurriedly tied the horses and walked through a milk-house door to see what he could contribute to their project. Once inside, he found Amish young men releasing cows from stanchions, upright metal frames used to confine cows for milking. It appeared that they were letting their own cows out to pasture, so they could start bringing in Mr. Johnson's herd for milking. Lenny knew how to unlatch stanchions because of his experience on Uncle Alvin's farm; he joined in quickly with the rest of them. The distinct aroma of cattle saturated everything. As soon as the last Amish cow was hurried out, someone opened large doors at the other end, while another young man began scooping feed into a bunk at the head of each stanchion in a clear effort to entice the unfamiliar, non-Amish cows to cooperate with their plan. Lenny knew enough to move in gliding motions—anything jerky would spook these nervous bovines.

In an effort that was astounding to watch, this group of tall, lanky Amish men outmaneuvered and outwitted each cow into submission. Some of the guys were dragging out milking units while others were still latching cows into stalls. Lenny was glad he had some experience with milking at Alvin's, but even then, it had been a few years ago, so he felt rusty. He quickly joined in, taking stainless-steel containers full of milk to pour into their bulk tank when he saw that need arise. Even during a rush, Lenny couldn't help but notice the wonderful smell of cows; it almost seemed he could smell milk, too. The Amish fellows were so busy hustling to get their huge job done that nobody was scrutinizing what Lenny was doing, which made him feel free to work hard. Not worrying about how inexperienced he looked, he rushed around doing anything he could to help. Halfway through the major undertaking, Lenny realized everyone was having fun while they worked. The young Amish men were all grinning while they hurried around, joking and teasing each other about who was slower than the other. That would have made the newcomer feel awkward, but they did it in such an easygoing way that it didn't. It seemed impossible not to like these guys. When the last cow was finally milked, Lenny was almost disappointed because they had been having fun, and he wasn't sure what was going to happen next.

All of the young men gathered in a semicircle when they were done. An older, non-Amish man stood with them, and Lenny guessed that the man must be Mr. Johnson, whose cows they had been milking. "I'm Leonard Gingerich . . . call me Lenny . . . my car is stuck in a ditch up the road."

They all looked at him with big smiles on their faces. One of the older boys spoke up. "Well, you kept up with us real good!" Lenny grinned at that.

Mr. Johnson interjected, "Boys, it doesn't look like I will have power back in the morning. Is there any chance we could . . ."

"Oh yeah, we will plan to milk your cows in the morning again," that oldest boy replied. Then he turned and looked at Lenny. "If your car is stuck in the ditch, you just as well stay on with us overnight and help us with morning milking. We will take a team of horses over and pull your car out when we're done."

"Sounds good," Lenny answered.

Mr. Johnson was grinning. "Thank you, boys. Thanks a lot!"

Sophomore

As one large group, all the young men headed up toward a huge white farmhouse standing opposite the dairy barn. A pair of hound dogs sniffed their visitor's pants as Lenny followed them. There were so many boys that Lenny had assumed they were a group of neighbors working together to get this milking project accomplished.

As they all clomped up a set of steps and in through the back porch, Lenny began to conclude that these were all brothers. It made sense; they were all lanky, big strapping fellows. None of them looked just like the other, yet they all looked something alike. As an afterthought, Lenny also deducted that they were not very far apart in age for brothers.

Each of the brothers tossed their straw hats onto a pile over the top of the heap of work boots they kicked off. They all washed up in the same sink full of water, including Lenny. He followed them into a big, open kitchen area. The brothers divided into two groups, and there, in between them, stood Abraham Lincoln. Lenny was stunned and actually stepped back a few paces. He wasn't sure if he should bow or reach out and shake his hand, not being prepared to come face-to-face with one of the greatest men of all time. Abraham Lincoln furrowed his heavy brow and said, "Hello, I'm Junior." Lenny knew deep down this was not Honest Abe, but he was caught off guard again, not expecting such a tall, imposing man to assign himself such a diminutive name. Lenny's response was delayed enough that it was almost awkward when he did finally give it. "I'm Leonard Gingerich. Call me Lenny."

"This is my wife Ruby," Junior said, motioning to a petite Amish woman who was about half his size. It seemed impossible that such a little woman could have carried and delivered that row of big strapping men. However, as small as she was, one look in her crystal-clear blue eyes—a spunk and fire were visible there—made Lenny believe that she was more than capable of rearing these sizable sons and of doing anything else she put her mind into. That very evening, she and her daughters had prepared a huge feast for her family, enough food to last most families a week. Beef and homemade noodles glistened, releasing a steamy and delicious smell.

It appeared that Junior and Ruby had been stuck on having sons for a while, and then could only have girls after that. A whole string of little women in Amish dresses bustled around their kitchen. The oldest of them looked just a little younger than the youngest son, and they went on down in age from there to a set of twins who looked to be about two. The boys clamored up to Ruby's table and, after a short prayer, dug in and dismantled the meal that had moments before looked like a piece of artwork. While the sons sat around exchanging stories about what they had heard from neighbors concerning the big storm, Lenny start wondering about the woman he helped. Lenny, all at once, interjected his question, "What happened to Aaron Burr and his wife?"

Junior, the Abraham Lincoln-looking man, answered, "While you boys were milking, they helped my wife and I clean up a tree that was down in our yard. I took them back home. That was my team of horses that you drove here. So, I was going to go down and get them this evening anyway."

"What about that woman they had with them?" Lenny had to know.

Ruby answered, "She is upstairs resting; she is gonna be fine. The roads are bad between her place and ours; we will try to take her back home tomorrow."

Lenny wanted to ask if she was a married woman, but it didn't seem appropriate. While everyone was looking at him anyway, he decided to ask about something else he was wondering about. "Was that a tornado we had today?"

His question set off a long disagreement between the group of brothers. Some of them felt that there may have been a twister inside of the storm, but they all agreed it was mostly straight-line winds. After a long, heated debate, Ruby intervened, "Well, it doesn't matter much what you call it; we know it was a bad storm. It's plenty late, and we ought to all get to bed, so we can get up early and start cleaning up the mess it made."

They prayed again and everyone got up and milled about, except Lenny—he wasn't sure what to do with himself. Ruby spoke to her son who was closest in age to the visitor, "Herbie, show Leonard where he can sleep and get him some work clothes for in the morning. It looks like his shirt got a stain on it today." Lenny looked down. He forgot about the bloodstain and wondered if it seemed odd to the others that he had that woman's blood on his chest.

Herbie led Lenny up a set of creaking steps. At the top of the stairwell, there was a wide hallway with several doors; this house was bigger than Alvin's. Herbie looked like a young Abraham Lincoln: tall, dark haired, and with honest, kind eyes. He told Lenny, "On the right side are the girls' rooms, and on the left boys." They went into one of the doors, and it looked like a dorm room with a set of bunk beds. "You can sleep on the bottom of that far bunk over there," Herbie said. Then he began to inquire, "So, are you still in school?"

"Yeah, I am going to a college in Kansas."

"What are you going to be?"

"A sophomore," Lenny was almost proud to say.

"What's that mean?" Herbie asked.

Lenny's mind went back to the text he had gotten from his college buddy. The first thing that popped into his head was what Prof. Miller said. "'Sophomore' means that you are smart enough to know something but too dumb to realize how little you know."

Herbie looked over at the other young man, confused, "That seems like a strange thing to want to be?"

"Oh, that is just a name for people that are in their second year of high school or college."

"Us Amish don't go to high school or college. So, we don't have to go through that stage in life." Herbie grinned at his own joke.

Then Lenny realized that Herbie was asking what he was studying to pursue as a career. He tried to explain, "I'm taking Gen. Ed. classes right now; I'm not sure what I'm gonna be." Herbie seemed mystified, so Lenny tried to explain it better. "If you're not sure what you're gonna be when you go to college, you take general classes, you know, about the main things like English, Math, Science and stuff. Then you can decide later what your major is…what you're going to focus on."

"Oh, I get it," Herbie's face was friendly as he nodded. "I wanna be a mechanic. If I was gonna go to college, that would be my major."

Just then, Herbie's brothers clamored into the room, talking and teasing each other. They appeared to be having fun all the time, and none of them appeared to have a mean bone in their body. Someone blew out the kerosene lantern that had been giving off a smoky scent. Everything became quiet. Lenny's mind went back to that moment when his car blew off the road; he remembered that helpless feeling. He thought about the Amish woman he had carried up to Aaron Burr's house. He had never carried a woman before, except maybe his sisters when they were young. He recalled her snuggling into him, and he imagined how happy a man would be to have a little wife like her. And then he drifted off to sleep.

Chapter 2

SURPRISED

Lenny woke to multiple crowing roosters—so many that it sounded like a rushing waterfall. All of Junior's sons were snoring loudly, unaffected by the torrent of crowing. A faint light came through a sheer curtain and rested on Lenny's face. He knew from his days at Alvin's place that it wasn't quite chore time at the first cock-a-doodle-do, so he tried to get back to sleep. It was no use. Amid the roar of snores and crows, he was wide awake. He lay in bed worrying about his car, wondering if it was drivable. He wanted to get back to River City as soon as possible to start looking for a job. He thought about a pizza place near his home and decided it would be a great place to work—he could eat pizza all the time if he got a job there. While he was pondering over a possible employment, he heard Ruby calling up the stairs, her voice booming over the sound of possibly hundreds of roosters and five chainsaw-sounding snorers. The boys heard her and all stood up.

Herbie dug around in a dresser and pulled out a pair of broadfall pants, with suspenders attached, and a blue button-up shirt and tossed them to Lenny. "Here's some stuff for ya to wear."

"Thanks, Herbie"

"You don't mind wearing Amish clothes, do ya?"

"No, I don't mind. By the way, what's with all the roosters?"

"We raise brooders."

"What?"

"Baby chicks that someone else fattens up. We have thousands of hens, so we need a fair amount of roosters in with 'em."

On their way out of the porch door, Herbie snatched up an extra straw hat. "If you're gonna dress Amish, you better have a hat, too!" Lenny put on the hat and stepped in his shoes. Herbie went out barefoot.

Once inside the dairy barn, those big raw-boned boys got right back to work in high gear, milking cows. A generator puttered outside—a pulsing sound filling the air in the barn, along with a pungent cow aroma. The brothers called out instructions to each other, throwing in a teasing comment constantly. Herbie's face appeared above the black-and-white back of a Holstein cow and asked his brother, "Henry, aren't you feeling well this morning?"

"I feel fine, why?"

"You're moving so slow it's making me sick."

Henry laughed. "Nope, I'm just moving so fast it looks like I'm standing still." They all laughed.

Lenny went to work, carrying full canisters of milk into a stainless-steel bulk tank that was almost overflowing. Lenny asked Herbie, "What happens when you run out of room in your milk tank, with all these neighbor cows here and all?"

"We will see if we can get the milk truck to make a stop here today. But if we can't, we will dump the milk."

"And just waste it?" Lenny asked.

"We gotta milk these cows, or they will get sick. We will save the milk if we can."

Lenny noticed that a few girls came into the parlor to help with this major milking project. As everyone was rushing around getting things done, Lenny hurried through a doorway and crashed into one of the girls. He looked up at her and saw she had a bandage on her forehead. She looked at Lenny with a surprised face. "Leonard?" Her face broke into a big smile, and Lenny saw a dimple sink deep into her cheek.

He looked right into her brown eyes. "Leah?" She nodded. "I didn't know that it was you in the buggy yesterday."

"I didn't know that it was you who carried me up to the house," she answered. He wanted to give Leah a big hug, and almost did, but her dimple disappeared immediately and her face went sober. She hurried back to the task she had been doing before they bumped into each other. Lenny continued on with his work, although he couldn't stop himself from looking in her direction. He fumbled with everything he did and couldn't work as fast as he had before. He kept trying to think of what he could say to her, but nothing seemed right.

When all the cows were finally milked, they all went in for breakfast. Herbie told his dad, "When we are done eating, Lenny and I plan to take Prince and Duke over to pull his car up outta that ditch."

Junior grinned, took a drink, and asked, "Where are you planning to take his car?"

Lenny and Herbie exchanged a blank look. Herbie guessed out loud, "Probably Noey's place?"

Lenny had a mouthful of food; he almost choked and looked at Herbie in amazement. "You mean my uncle Noah?"

"Yeah . . . isn't that where you were headed when you got tossed into the ditch?"

This made Lenny's head swim. He didn't know that any of them knew who he was, or that he had any connection in the area at all. He didn't want to tell them that he was just driving by to look at Amish people and farms, so he agreed. "Yep." Lenny glanced over at Leah, who was looking back at him, clearly wondering what his plans were.

"Well . . . I was on my way home from college, and I thought I would swing by my uncle's place, but then that storm hit. I don't think Noah knew I was in the area."

Junior answered, "Nope, I told him that you were here, and he was surprised. Noey seemed pretty happy about it, but I told him we needed to keep you for morning milking at the very least."

Leah looked somber, and Lenny could tell she was trying to avoid making eye contact with him. Her dimple was nonexistent that morning, except for the moment they first saw each other. One of Herbie's younger sisters told her dad, "I can take Leah home after breakfast!"

Junior eyed her for a moment, then answered, "That's a little far for you; you'd be alone on the way back."

Herbie's older brother Henry suggested, "I could go along ... to keep Fannie Ella company."

This brought chuckles out of the other brothers. Ruby cleared her throat and said, "That would be very nice of you, Henry."

Leah looked up at Lenny with a sheepish face. Junior's smallest daughters appeared to be a set of twins. Lenny watched them, amused by their Pennsylvania-Dutch jabbering and adorable teeny Amish dresses. They half talked, half sang, entertaining each other. Lenny quietly asked their oldest sister, "What are they saying?"

"I'm not really sure; they kind of have their own language."

Impala

The family polished off Ruby's huge stack of pancakes and prayed an after-meal prayer. The brothers all headed back into the great outdoors, their stomachs full but still hungry for adventure. They crossed Junior's acreage heading toward the horse barn. Lenny looked around, noticing that everything was loosely put together, unlike Uncle Alvin's perfectly manicured farm. Junior's place wasn't messy, but was exactly like Junior's sons—carefree. Apparently, one of the brothers had been driving a steel-wheeled tractor and stopped in the middle of a job, leaving it parked at an angle. Lenny remembered what it was like when he stayed at Alvin's farm, that would never "fly". If someone used a tractor, it had better be put away as soon as they finished their job. More than that, it needed to be parked straight north and south, or east and west—none of this crooked parking. A couple of hound dogs followed the group of young men. Herbie told Lenny, "My dogs' names are Tick and Blue." The newcomer was thinking to himself, *What creative names they give their dogs.* Herbie explained, "These dogs are bluetick coonhounds, so we just call one Blue and the other Tick."

The horse barn was exactly the way everything was kept outside, as if it had been thoroughly cleaned a week ago but since then had been let go. Lenny noticed an extremely large black horse in a box stall as they passed by; he stepped closer and peered in.

"That's our stallion, San Hosea," Herbie informed his guest.

"Where did he get that name?"

"He came with it."

"He wasn't born here?"

"Nope, we bought him at the sale barn a couple of years ago; he's kinda old."

"Well, he looks like a dandy to me," Lenny told Herbie.

The stallion had a massive head with a long, thick curly mane that looked like dreadlocks. A herd of buggy horses stood in a nearby corral. There were four draft horses in with them: Prince and Duke, along with an old mare and a slightly smaller mare. Herbie climbed in among the mass of horses that swirled around him and each other, some laying their ears back at the others, a few turning rumps, feigning a kick at another. Herbie didn't seem to notice that his life was in jeopardy even though he looked like a diver swimming in the midst of hungry sharks. It wasn't clear how Herbie did it, but he managed to grab hold of Prince and Duke's halters and pull them out of a pool of spinning horses.

"What about that other team of mares," Lenny asked.

"That ain't exactly a team. Our old mare, Queen, has one foot in the grave. We don't use her anymore, but she has lived here her whole life, and Dad wouldn't think of ending that. That smaller mare, Misty, is only two. We harnessed her up a few times and hitched her with old Duke, but we never have time to get her broke proper."

Lenny and Herbie harnessed Prince and Duke. They hitched them to a forecart, and Herbie told Lenny, "You can drive."

"Where are you gonna sit?" Lenny asked.

"I'll catch a ride on here." Herbie stepped up onto the tongue about where the doubletree was attached. He crouched, balancing himself by taking a firm grip of Lenny's paint leg. Lenny clucked; Prince and Duke lunged into a trot out of the long lane lined on one side with trees, many of which were lying down because of yesterday's storm. "We got a big mess to clean up across that other lane over there," Herbie noted.

"Where does that lane lead?"

"To our chicken house. Dad didn't want feed trucks going up our lane all the time. So when we built that chicken house, we put in a lane directly to it."

Lenny turned the geldings left. He had driven them from Aaron Burr's place yesterday, making it easy to remember his way back.

It was a fine morning, and seemed hard to believe that a devastating storm had occurred the previous night. Birds sang in trees that remained upright, their songs mixed with the rhythm of horse hooves, bringing back good memories in Lenny's mind. He had been missing life on an Amish farm, and being back in the Bulltown area made him realize just how badly he missed it. Soon they came up on the scene of yesterday's car and buggy wreck.

Lenny suggested, "Let's check out Leah's buggy first."

Herbie called, "Whoa," to his horses, and they stopped without Lenny pulling on their bits.

Herbie jumped off and Lenny sat holding the reins. "What about these horses?"

"Oh, just let them there; they aren't going anywhere."

Lenny wrapped their lines around a knob he supposed was there for that purpose and left Prince and Duke standing on a shoulder of the road. Lenny and Herbie flipped Leah's open buggy over. The wheels seemed fine, but its seat was smashed as well as the dashboard. They threw all the parts that had broken off on its floor, along with a few pieces of harness that were left on the ground.

"Leah was lying over there," Lenny said, pointing. They went over and examined the spot.

"It's a wonder she wasn't hurt bad," Herbie concluded, looking at the distance she was thrown.

Lenny looked at the buggy seat and said, "If she would have stayed on that seat, it might've been worse."

Herbie nodded, but he was clearly itching to look at Lenny's Impala.

They stomped through the soggy ditch down to where the silver Impala lay helpless and quiet. "Why don't you see if you can start it up," Herbie suggested.

Lenny squeezed into a door that was cramped because of the ditch bank. He tried to start it up, but there was nothing, not even a click.

"Unlatch your hood!" Lenny did and when he climbed back out, he realized that Leah, Henry, and Herbie's little sister had pulled up in a buggy.

Henry called down to them, "Maybe the battery is dead?"

Herbie pointed to the battery. "Here's your problem; a battery cable shook loose, probably when you took this ditch." Herbie called up to his brother, "You're nothing but a sophomore!"

"What's that supposed to mean?" Henry asked.

"Lenny told me that it means you're smart enough to think you're smart but too dumb to know how dumb you are!" Henry laughed but Leah looked at Lenny as though disappointed he would say such a mean thing. Herbie asked, "Leah, what should we do with your buggy?"

Henry answered, "Take it up to our place; I think I can fix that." Then he told them, "We're going up to get Stanley," motioning toward Aaron Burr's place as he turned his horse in a short circle on the road.

Herbie called after them, "Ain't that a nice-looking couple!"

Leah looked back; her eyes met Lenny's but she didn't say anything.

"Now you sound like a sophomore," Henry called back.

When they got out of earshot, Lenny asked Herbie, "Are they a couple?"

"Well, her sister Ruby and me are." He seemed pleased to admit it. "Ruby has been trying to talk Leah into taking a ride home from a Singing with Henry, but she hasn't said yes yet."

"You and Ruby," Lenny was happy to hear that part of the story. "I know Ruby, from when she was a neighbor to me at Alvin's place. She's a nice girl!"

"She was named after my mom. Her mom, Mildred, and my mom have always been best friends." Herbie grinned, but he seemed to want to change the subject. "Let's try starting this car up again."

It turned right over, and Lenny put it into gear, revving the engine, yet nothing happened. "Let's pull it out of there with these horses," Herbie suggested.

The Amish young man had his team backed up quickly and tossed Lenny the other end of a chain that was already hooked on the forecart. The city fellow tried to get it hooked but couldn't figure out where to connect. Herbie knew right away where a good spot was. He told Lenny, "Just put your car in neutral, since we don't know what's wrong with it. You better leave it running, though, so that your power steering and brakes are working."

Lenny hadn't thought of that. When he was ready, he waved to Herbie. Prince and Duke leaned hard into their collars. The big horses' muscles rippled as they dug their hooves in the soft muddy road. Lenny wished he was driving the team instead of the car. All at once, he could feel his Impala lurch forward; he steered up a slope and out of the ditch. When his car was on level ground, they looked it over again, and Herbie shared the bad news, "Your car needs a new rear end."

"Is that a big job?"

"Well ... I can do it ... but it would take some time."

Lenny's heart sank; he was hoping to get back to River City soon and find a summer job. He hated the suspense of not knowing what his future held.

Herbie advised, "Let's take it over to Noey's place and see what he thinks."

It seemed wrong in Lenny's mind for everyone to call his uncle Noah "Noey"; however, he knew it was the Amish way.

Herbie asked, "Is this your car or your dad's?"

"Mine. I bought it with money I made mowing yards last summer."

"Really? I just bought my own horse, Smoky, with money I made making hay last summer."

Lenny asked, "Do you think Prince and Duke can pull me all the way to my uncle Noey's place?"

"Oh, they can do it all right."

Herbie used some of Stanley's harness to hook the buggy on behind the car. Just as they got ready to pull away, Henry and Leah came down Aaron Burr's sloping drive, with Stanley tied on behind. Henry called out as he went past, "Are you boys having your own parade here?"

Herbie called back, "Sophomore!" Clearly, his new favorite word.

Noey and Ruth's Home

Herbie and Lenny pulled into Noey's drive with a clamorous racket and were met by Noey and his son Davy W., who looked like a young Elvis Presley. He was Noey's adopted son; he came with the name David. Noey and Ruth began calling him Davy W. because Noey's brother Alvin already had a son with the same name. Lenny was surprised to see his cousin because the last thing he had heard about Davy W. was that he had moved away and left the Amish. At that moment, he wasn't wearing a hat or suspenders, which seemed odd even to Lenny.

Uncle Noah's farm was beautifully set, like a plantation sprawling out in a long flat area of rich, river-bottom soil. The large white farmhouse, straight and tall, contrasted a picturesque backdrop of black fields. Four huge oak trees, one at each corner of Noey's home, gave his place a stately appearance. His massive barn with a stone foundation sat just far enough from the house to keep the flies and smell at a distance, yet near enough it wasn't too far a walk. The barn sat on the lowest part of the farm, with other outbuildings surrounding it, all of those tied together by a network of fences.

They stopped near Noey's house, and Lenny got out of his car and said, "Hello, Uncle Noah. I took my Impala in the ditch yesterday, during that big storm, and it's kinda broke down right now. I'm not sure what to do with it until I get a chance to talk to my dad."

"No problem, Leonard." Noey's eyes looked as blue and kind as Grandpa's always had. He pointed and said, "Let's take your car over to that corncrib. It has doors at both ends, so we can pull it in one side, and Junior's horses can go right on out the other side."

"Oh, nice," Lenny answered, not understanding why they wouldn't leave it out front.

Herbie got off his cart and untied Leah's buggy, leaving it in Noey's drive. Noey and Davy W. went ahead of Herbie's horses and slid open big doors at both ends. Herbie drove his team, pulling Lenny in his Impala, maneuvering it into place. Once Davy W. unhooked the chain, the horses walked right on out. Lenny watched as they slid both sets of doors shut; his Impala disappeared. Just like that, his modern life seemed to vanish along with it.

"Well, Leonard, we're really happy you decided to stop by on your way home from college," Aunt Ruth said with a smile. "Let's go in and have some lunch."

Herbie spoke up. "Our neighbor, Bill Johnson, is still out of power. We are planning to milk his cows at our place again this evening, and it sure would be nice if Lenny could come over and help."

"I don't see why he couldn't," Noey answered.

Lenny was happy that Herbie wanted his help. "Okay, I will plan on that then."

Herbie tied Leah's buggy behind his team of horses and clucked to them. They stepped off, trotting out of Noey's lane.

Lenny called, "Good-by," then remembered that Amish don't say good-by. The others looked at the non-Amish visitor when he said it; they seemed to understand that he wasn't one of them.

Aunt Ruth's large open kitchen was filled with the wonderful smell of baked bread; her table was set with a meal of roast beef, mashed potatoes, string beans, and canned peaches. A sturdy little white dog with black ears sat on a spotless linoleum floor near Ruth's feet, head cocked to one side. Ruth scurried about her kitchen without acknowledging the dog's presence, except that she occasionally dropped a tiny morsel of food. She did it as though by accident, yet Lenny suspected it was on purpose. Lenny noticed a plaque on the kitchen wall that read:

> *The voice of the Lord is over the waters; the God of glory thunders, the Lord thunders over the mighty waters.* Psalm 29:3

When Ruth finally sat down, they bowed their heads in silent prayer, and then began to eat. Uncle Noey did all the talking. "It's been a really wet spring around here. Was it raining a lot down in Kansas?"

Lenny had a mouthful of mashed potatoes, which gave him a moment to think of an answer. He didn't pay much attention to the weather while in college. "We had some rainy days, but I don't think it was too bad," he finally was able to say.

Uncle Noey nodded and repeated, "We've had a really wet spring here. In fact, it's been so wet I haven't been able to get into the fields at all."

Lenny didn't know what to say about that. He took a bite of buttered bread and mumbled, "Oh."

Uncle Noey told Lenny, "I've been thinking that I'm gonna need to borrow some horses and use them for my fieldwork. A man can work up a field with horses when a tractor couldn't do it without getting stuck."

Lenny asked what he thought was a smart question. "Can't you use Jim and Stone to do it?"

"If I'm gonna work up my whole farm with horses, I will need at least eight."

Lenny realized how silly it sounded that he had thought Jim and Stone could do it alone. He tried to make up for that by suggesting, "Could you borrow Tug and Train from Uncle Alvin?"

"Funny you would say that. I was just thinking about going to talk to Alvin about that very thing. Alvin's place is hillier; they are getting their fieldwork done with tractors. I'm down here along the river, and my fields are flat and don't drain that well. I have a team of crossbreds that I can use with Stone and Jim, but I still need to come up with several more horses."

"Maybe you could use Bell and Babe or Alvin's crossbreds?"

"I'm sure Alvin needs those horses for hauling manure and such ... I'll think of something."

Aunt Ruth changed the subject. "What are your plans for the summer, Leonard?"

"I'm gonna look for a summer job up in River City."

"What kind of work will you look for?"

Lenny felt his face flush hot as he stammered out, "I ... I think I might get a job at a pizza place."

Davy W. had been focused on eating, but when he heard pizza, he looked up and said, "That sounds like a good job!"

Uncle Noey announced, "After we finish eating, I'm going to go up the road and help the Hershberger family clean up storm damage. Would either of you like to come along?"

"I was planning on going fishing," Davy told him.

Lenny could see the disappointment in Noey's eyes. "I could go and help," Lenny said.

All four of them bowed their heads for an after-meal prayer. Aunt Ruth went back to work, sewing something on her treadle machine, pumping away with one foot powering the machine. Davy disappeared, clearly not wanting to get talked into helping neighbors.

Helping the Hershberger family

Lenny and Noey headed out to the barn where Stone and Jim were quietly waiting. Their heads popped up when the men came into the stalls, and Lenny felt a twinge of excitement, knowing they were going to hitch up draft horses. Stone and Jim were dapple grays—their faces were almost white with mostly black bodies, yet covered with white star-shaped splotches. These stars seemed to melt together on their bellies. From the knees down, the horses were solid black.

Noey grabbed a collar off a nearby wall. He pointed to the next collar over. "You can harness up Jim while I harness Stone."

Lenny's face was hidden from sight, so he didn't try to do away with his big grin. He talked to Jim, "Ho there. Easy, boy," while setting the collar on his thick neck. He gathered a mass of harness as Grandpa had taught him, hoisting it all up on the horse's back. He arranged everything neatly and snapped it all in place.

Noey led Stone out; Lenny untied Jim and followed his uncle. Once outside, Noey let his horse loose. Stone stood obediently while the older man snapped on driving lines, connecting the two horses to each other. There was a steel-wheel forecart twenty yards away, and Noey told Lenny, "You can drive them over, and we'll hitch them on that cart. Then we can hook onto that hayrack over yonder," nodding toward another steel-wheeled vehicle. Lenny took the lines and clucked to Stone and Jim.

A few moments later, they had everything hooked and were clattering out of Noey's lane.

They took a dirt road, a shortcut that led to the Hershberger's place. Without rock on the road, their steel-wheel vehicle traveled quietly enough that Noey could talk easily. "Leonard, I would be willing to hire you on for the summer if you are looking for a job."

"To work on your farm?"

Noey nodded. "I need a horseman to help me get my fields planted. I've been having troubles with my back, and I don't think I can sit on a plow for hours. I have plenty of other work around here that keeps me busy; an Amish farm needs more than just a man and his wife to keep things going."

Lenny immediately thought of Davy W. As if Noey had read his mind, the older man added, "Davy just isn't a horseman. I've already discussed it with him; he is not willing to farm with horses."

Lenny watched Stone and Jim trotting over a hilltop while thinking how to answer. As they came down the other side of the hill, beautiful Iowan farmlands spread out before them. Birds were singing in trees along a fence row, celebrating the arrival of spring. A rabbit jumped and ran, as Stone nearly stepped on its hiding place. Soft jingles came from the harness as the team trotted along. Everything around him seemed to be urging Lenny to say yes. Finally, Lenny tried to give an answer. "Well, I hadn't really thought about getting a farm job. I need to call home anyway. I will see what Dad and Mom say."

Noey responded right away. "Leonard, you don't need to answer now ... but if you need a job, I sure could use you here."

"Okay, I'll think about it."

The Hershberger farm looked neat and orderly, except that a large tree had been blown over onto their chicken coop during the big storm. Uncle Noey and Lenny helped limb out sizable sections of that tree, and Lenny used Stone and Jim to drag them off to a clearing where everything was cut up for firewood. Lenny thoroughly enjoyed working with the big horses. He loved the jangling of harness, hearing horse snorts and watching them dig in and pull. Little Amish children scrambled around, picking up smaller branches as though playing a fun game. The girls wore long dresses, aprons, and head scarves, all running through the yard barefoot. Boys with suspenders reminded Lenny of little horses in harness trotting here and there. Every place Stone and Jim stepped, they left hoofprints, with the ground so soft because of spring rains.

There was a pretty, dark-haired girl about sixteen years old in the Hershberger family. She threw some larger branches in a pile while Lenny was working nearby and made a point of talking to him. "I have two older sisters: one is married and the other, Rebecca, is about your age. She works at Beantown Grocery these days. If you're ever in there, you'll probably see her. Rebecca looks a lot like me, only older."

Lenny didn't know how to respond, but the girl seemed friendly, so he replied, "I'll watch out for her." He didn't like how his words came out, but it was too late to change them. When they got everything cleaned up, it was about chore time.

Noey told Lenny, "Let's head to Junior's place, so you can help with milking."

They hooked their horses on the hayrack. The Hershberger family had neatly stacked firewood on it as a thank-you for Noey and Lenny's help. Noey tried to refuse, but the Hershberger's insisted, "You helped us clean up; you ought to have some of the firewood."

Noey told Lenny to turn left when they got to the road. They came upon a little white shed near the road, and Uncle Noey said, "Turn in here. There is a phone in that shed; we can call your parents." Noey waited outside with Stone and Jim while Lenny went in and made a call.

"Hi, Lindsay, how's summer going?"

"We are still in school; high school doesn't let out as early as college," Lindsay reminded her brother.

"Oh yeah, sorry for rubbing that in! Did you hear about me wrecking my Impala?"

"Yes! I'm glad you're okay. Are you going to stay there in Bulltown for a while?"

"I'm thinking about it, but I was looking forward to hanging out with my sisters this summer. I'm on an Amish phone line, so I'd better not talk too long. Is Mom close by"?

"Yep, she is right here, trying to take the phone out of my hand. Good-by, Lenny."

"See ya, Lindsay, tell Ashley hi for me!"

"Leonard, how are things going down there?" his mom asked.

"Good, Mom … except that my car is broke down!"

"Really, what is wrong with it?"

"Uncle Noey's neighbor said that my rear axle needs replaced. He thinks he can fix it, but it will take some time. That's the other thing, Mom; Noey wants me to stay here for a bit. He offered to pay me to help him farm with horses."

"Oh, really? Would you like to do that, Leonard?"

"Yeah, kind of. I bet we would have everything planted in a few weeks. I could come home then and spend some time with you guys before I go back to college.

"You decide, Leonard. I think it would be good for you, though. Are things bad down there because of the storm?"

"Well, we've been cleaning up trees that blew over."

"On the news, they keep saying that everyone is out of power in the Bulltown area."

Lenny laughed. "Almost everyone I know down here has been out of power for a long time!" His mom laughed. Lenny told her, "Really, though, nothing changes much on an Amish farm when the electricity is out. Except that we have been helping some non-Amish farmer milk his cows because his power is off. In fact, I need to go help now."

"All right, Leonard, call me soon and let me know what you decided about this summer."

"Okay, Mom, tell Dad hi for me."

"All right, bye. I love you, Leonard."

"Love you, too, Mom. Bye. Oh, one more thing, Mom. Could you call my buddy Brad and tell him what happened. He's probably wondering why I don't answer his texts."

"Sure."

Uncle Noey and his horses were waiting patiently outside. "Sorry it took me so long," he told his uncle.

"That wasn't long; I'm glad you got a chance to talk to them."

Noey dropped Lenny off at Junior's place, and a purring generator suggested that milking was already under way. With so many extra cows, they needed to start early. As the parlor door popped open, a bustle of activity brought a smile to Lenny's face. Junior's boys made Lenny laugh just by looking at them. Not that they were funny-looking; they were good-looking guys, all tall and lanky. Lenny even thought that their Amish hats actually looked sharp on them. They made him laugh because each of them wore an ornery look on their face, always ready to laugh at anything funny. They never let up on one another, teasing and poking fun, yet in a way that didn't make anyone feel bad.

"Come on, Leonard. Wake up. You're missing out on all the fun," Howard called over.

Lenny jumped to work, carrying milk to the bulk tank. He was almost glad to be teased; it made him feel like part of the family. They worked through suppertime, so Ruby and her daughters brought out sandwiches. When they finished, Herbie said, "I'm going up to talk to Bill Johnson; I could drop you off at Noey's."

Herbie's horse, Smoky, was waiting, tied and already hitched to a two-wheeled cart. The boys jumped on, and Smoky trotted out with long, strong strides; hound dogs romped behind howling. Just as they turned onto the gravel road, a big pickup growled past. Smoky didn't flinch or even brake stride.

"Wow! That is a nice horse!" Lenny told Herbie.

Herbie shrugged, "Yeah, I like him."

The Answer

When Herbie dropped Lenny off in front of Uncle Noey's place, the old moon was his only light. He had never noticed moon shadows before. Not only did moonlight gleam off the windmill blades, but it also cast a spinning shadow on the ground near Lenny's feet. He could see shadows under Aunt Ruth's apple trees moving slowly on the ground as branches above swayed in a gentle breeze. Every breath of air was fresh. The young man looked up into the starry sky; one bright twinkling star caught his attention. He remembered Grandpa. All at once, it came back to him. Shortly after Grandpa's death, he had looked into a night sky like this one and told himself that he would remember Grandpa whenever he saw a twinkling star. A guilty feeling pressed down on Lenny's heart. He had not even looked into a night sky for a long time, much less thought about Grandpa. He didn't know if he should stay on for the summer and work for Uncle Noey. It occurred to him that maybe he should pray about it, and then he realized that it had been sometime since he had prayed, too.

He looked deep into the heart of a star-filled sky and said, "Dear God, please help me know if I should stay here for the summer and work for my uncle Noey … " He stopped praying because the answer was obvious. He walked up creaking porch steps and through a screen door that slapped shut behind him.

Aunt Ruth's kitchen was only lit by what escaped through a doorway from a lantern in the next room. Lenny could hear a steady tapping. He followed the light and sound to where Aunt Ruth was still up sewing. When he walked in, she looked at him and smiled. "Good, I am just finishing this pair of broadfall pants; try them on and see if they fit." Lenny took them. Then she pointed at a couple of shirts hanging nearby. "Try on those while you're at it."

Lenny said quietly, "How did you know that I was going to stay?"

"Noey needed someone to help him get his crops in, so I have been praying. When I heard you had come, I knew that God answered my prayers."

Chapter 3

BEANTOWN

Acock-a-doodle-do from a solitary rooster woke Lenny. He soon realized that hundreds of roosters were crowing in the background. Davy W. breathed in heavily, sound asleep. The little white dog with black ears lay curled up in a nest of blankets at Davy's feet. The dog lifted his head, cocking it to one side while watching Lenny get up and pull on his new work clothes. When Lenny opened the bedroom door, the dog jumped out of bed and followed him downstairs. A sizzle of bacon combined with the coffee aroma filling the air.

Aunt Ruth said, "Good morning, Leonard, breakfast will be ready when chores are done."

"Okay, we will hurry," Lenny said as he smiled and trotted out toward Noey's barn, with a small dog at his heels. He found Noey inside, milking a short brown cow. The older man sat on a small stool that had only one leg, a peg with a point on the end. A row of multicolored cats lounged nearby, bathing themselves with their tongues, at times licking their paws, and then using that wet paw to wash behind an ear. Lenny watched his uncle and listened as streams of milk hit the sides of a metal pail, ringing out a rhythmic melody.

Finally, Lenny asked, "What are those cats doing?"

"They're waiting for this." Noey turned his hands, so that the streams of milk shot toward the row of felines, each cat—mouth wide open—catching a milk spray perfectly aimed by the older man. When he stopped, they all went back to licking themselves, cleaning up whatever milk had missed their mouths.

"No wonder they were sitting there patiently," Lenny said laughing. Then he asked, "Do you raise brooders here like Junior's family does?"

"No. Why?"

"I woke up to the sound of a hundred roosters, just like I did yesterday in Junior's home."

"Those are Junior's roosters you hear. His chicken house is right over beyond those trees."

"I had no idea they lived that close." Lenny grinned, happy to hear it. "Uncle Noey, I've decided to take you up on your offer and help plow with horses for a few weeks."

Noey looked up at his nephew and smiled. "Thanks, Leonard."

Lenny walked over to help Junior's family with morning milking. All he had to do was cut through a few trees past Junior's chicken building. It so happened that Noah and Junior's lanes angled back toward each other, so that it was a lot further between places on the road than it was through the woods.

When Lenny came through the trees, Tick and Blue brayed their hound-dog bugle sound and came running at him. He nervously called their names as they got near. Both dogs ferociously wagged their tails and followed him up toward the milk house. Junior's sons were already hard at it, milking and teasing.

"What took ya so long, lazy bones," Howard smirked.

"If you guys were any kind of workers, you would have this job done by now," Lenny called back, and everyone let out a yahoo.

While they were still milking, Bill Johnson came in and announced in a jovial voice, "I got my power on again!" He took his hat off his bald head and wiped his round face with a hanky. "I don't know how you boys do it. We almost went nuts without electricity for just a few days."

Shortly after Mr. Johnson left, they finished milking the last black-and-white cow. Herbie made a suggestion, "Let's go get starling eggs out of the mow!"

His brothers all seemed excited about it. Lenny followed them up a ladder into their haymow where the brothers had another huge ladder leaning against a large wooden beam that spanned between walls. They took turns climbing up and raiding starling nests and made a sport out of throwing the tiny eggs at each other.

"Why would you guys kill off your birds?" Lenny asked.

"Are you kidding!?" Harvey, Herbie's youngest brother, exclaimed. "Starlings are big pests. They make manure all over everything; chase off good birds, like purple martins; and some say they carry diseases." It was all new to Lenny; he didn't know there were good birds and bad birds.

"You want to take a turn at it, Lenny?" Herbie moved the ladder and motioned for Lenny to climb up.

Lenny thought it looked kind of fun, and he wanted to have his turn throwing eggs at the others who had been throwing eggs at him. He started climbing, but, as he got near the top, he realized it seemed much higher than it had looked from the ground. He stopped climbing and reached his arm up, just barely enough to get his hand into the nest. He felt a pile of leathery bumps and called down, "Wow, guys! This nest is full of eggs!" He pulled out his handful and looked at it. Suddenly, his mind processed that it wasn't eggs he had in his hand, so he yelled, "Snake!"

He dropped his handful on Junior's boys who were watching from below. They all let out a whoop. From his overhead view, Lenny watched the serpent glide, as if in slow motion, onto Herbie's arm. Herbie flailed it from him, causing it to wrap around Howard's hat brim momentarily. Howard flung off his hat, and the snake gently flew onto Henry's back, just as Henry fell onto his belly. The snake slithered off between Harvey's dancing legs while Henry scrambled frantically in the opposite direction on his hands and knees. Time soon returned to a normal pace, and Lenny came down as quick as he could with shaky hands. The brothers were all laughing and retelling, play by play, everything that had just transpired. Much to Lenny's surprise, they all seemed to think that their city friend had accomplished a brave feat. Herbie laughed and told Lenny, "You really got us that time!"

"What was that snake doing clear up in that bird's nest?" Lenny questioned his new friend.

"I guess it was hunting eggs. You'd be surprised bull snakes can climb about anywhere."

When Lenny got back home, Aunt Ruth had a big breakfast ready, just as promised. While they were eating, Noey stated, "I think we should go visit Alvin; we need to talk to him about borrowing some horses."

Lenny had mixed feelings about it. He wanted to go see everyone; however, it was awkward because he hadn't been there for so long. He felt bad that he had promised to return last summer and help Perry farm with horses but failed to keep his word. Uncle Noey hitched his good buggy horse, Big Red, onto a two-wheeled cart. They hooked a forecart on behind it, so that Lenny could drive home Tug and Train if Alvin agreed to it.

The sky was mostly gray, reminding Lenny of a picture he had made as a small child. His Sunday school teacher told her class to tear pieces off grayish construction paper and glue them on a white one. The sky looked just the way his artwork had. Uncle Noey seemed chipper, trying to make small talk with his nephew. Lenny could only sit and worry about seeing Alvin's family. Rolling hills of Iowan farmland stretched out before them, much of it seemed familiar, especially when they drew near Yoder Feeds. Sweet grain smells spilled out of the mill, reminding Lenny of the horse ride he and Perry had taken secretly after dark. He looked at the bench in front of the auto repair shop, where he had left his hat that night, and Uncle Alvin had found it a few days later. Lenny had to hold back laughter as he thought about how Patches, the pony, had kicked at a town boy, knocking the bully off his bike.

Yoder Feeds and its tall elevator towers faded behind them as Big Red trotted closer to Alvin's farm. When they crossed the place where a road split two hills, Lenny's heart was pounding with excitement, and he started biting his lower lip. The old homeplace came into view, as picturesque as Lenny had remembered it: white farm buildings surrounding a massive barn, everything as neat as could be. Brightly colored quilts hanging on a clothesline contrasted the stark white farmhouse and gray sky. While Noey tied Big Red, Alvin's whole family emerged from a variety of places around the acreage and greeted their visitors.

"Well, Leonard," Uncle Alvin took on the role of the spokesperson, "we are all happy to see you. Sorry to hear about your vehicle mishap. Will your car be okay?"

"Oh...yeah, I think it can be fixed. It's an old car anyway."

Apparently comical to Alvin's family, they all laughed. Aunt Lydia suggested, "Why don't you both come in and have a piece of apple pie?"

"That sounds great," Lenny heard himself say, and everyone laughed again.

As they walked into the house, Edwin, Viola, and Little E crowded around Lenny; they didn't say anything but looked him over closely. All three younger children had grown up a lot over the past two years, but Perry had changed the most. He was taller than Lenny and looked like a teenager instead of a boy. Sam and David looked like men, except that they didn't have beards, a sure sign they hadn't found a wife yet. Rosie and Ruthie seemed way friendlier than he used to think they were.

Little E spoke in broken English, "Where you been, Leonard?"

A deep voice repeated what she said. "Yeah, Leonard, where have you been?" Lenny felt his face get hot. He instantly recognized the voice of his disabled uncle. Truman said it again. "Where have you been, Leonard?"

Lenny already felt bad about not keeping his promise to come back to the farm last summer and wanted to avoid that topic if possible. However, as usual, Truman repeated the most awkward part of any conversation.

Not knowing what else to say, Lenny replied, "Hi, Truman."

Truman grinned. "Hi to you, Leonard...yeah, hi to you!"

Inside the house, everything was exactly the same as it was the day Lenny left two years ago. Everyone sat quietly around a large oak table while Lydia cut pieces of apple pie. Lenny's eyes fell on the wall hanging with Leah's verse written on it. "The heavens declare the Glory of God."

Rosie took a large glass pitcher of milk from the fridge and poured some in Lenny's cup first, and then for everyone else. The whole family sat staring at Lenny as though waiting for him to speak. Uncle Alvin broke the silence. "Are you going to stay for a while at Noey's place?"

"I think so," Lenny tried to talk around a bite of pie that filled his mouth.

Uncle Noah took over, answering Alvin's question. "Actually, Leonard has agreed to stay on and help me do spring fieldwork. With this wet spring we're having, I can't get into my fields with a tractor. Leonard is going to help me till my fields with horses. Lenny continued eating pie, relieved that Noey was doing the talking. Alvin's family continued watching their cousin; they all had smiles on their faces at this point, as if pleased Lenny was going to be staying in the area.

"Do you have enough horsepower at your place for that?" Alvin asked, looking at Noah.

"No, I am looking for about four more horses. Is there any chance you could loan us Tug and Train for a while?"

Perry stopped eating and looked at his dad. Alvin took hold of his own beard and tugged on it, deep in thought. His eyeglasses blurred with reflections, preventing Lenny from reading his expression. At last, Alvin spoke, "I guess we could spare them for a while ... " and then a grin spread across his face as he added, " ... only if you take our colt along and put him to work."

"Mr. E?" Lenny asked.

Alvin nodded as he took a bite of pie, looking pleased that he had thought of such a good idea. Noey seemed to like the idea, too. "That would be great. How old is that colt by now?"

"Just two, but he's a really big colt. We've had him hitched a number of times, and he is started good. But he needs some real work to take the edge off him. I'd like to sell him. We don't have enough work for all the horses we've got."

"Well, I'm not looking to buy him"—Noey laughed—"but we could put him to work for a while."

Aunt Lydia changed the topic. "How are your parents doing, Leonard?"

"I haven't seen them for a while; I've been in Kansas going to college."

"What are you going to be?" Alvin asked.

Lenny started to say, "A sophomore," but he caught himself and changed it to, "I'm not sure; I'm taking general classes until I figure that out." Everyone gave him blank stares and seemed to be waiting for Lenny to say more; however, that was all he could think to tell them.

Truman piped up, "Maybe you should be Amish, Leonard?"

The room fell into an awkward silence as everyone tried to ignore Truman's comment.

Tug and Train

They all had their fill of pie. Afterward, Alvin and Noey headed out toward the horse barn, with Lenny and Perry following. Lenny could hardly wait to see Train, Tug, and the other horses. Perry measured out feed into their bunks while Lenny slid the large door open and whistled. Moments later, Bell came tromping through the doorway, then Babe, Train and Tug, the crossbreds, and last of all, a big colt.

Alvin and Noey stood having a conversation while the younger men slipped halters on each horse. Train let out a deep nicker as Lenny put a halter on the enormous horse. Alvin said quietly, "I haven't heard Train do that since Grandpa died."

As soon as each horse was tied, Perry handed Lenny a currycomb, and they went to work grooming them all. Perry took Bell, no doubt to be nice to his cousin, because Bell was everyone's least favorite horse. Lenny was glad to see both old mares, though. He couldn't wait to brush Train. When he stepped into the stall beside the massive horse, he was in awe of Train's beauty all over again; he had never seen any horse quite like him. Train's thick neck was always arched, with his head held high, and his whole body was bulging with muscles. Lenny spoke quietly so Alvin wouldn't hear. "Train, I've really missed you ... and you, too, Tug."

Both horses were soon decked out in harness, and Perry helped hitch them to Noey's forecart. Alvin led out Mr. E and tied him to Train's hame ring, a metal bar on the huge horse's collar. "I don't think Mr. E will give you any trouble," Alvin told Lenny. "He will be happy to follow his big friend Train."

"I hope!" Lenny said, and everyone laughed.

Lenny couldn't help but smile on the way back to Noey's. Tug and Train looked so black against a gray sky. While riding along admiring them and watching Mr. E trotting parallel to Train, all at once, Lenny had a great idea. Junior's filly Misty was the same age as Mr. E; maybe they could make a team out of them. Lenny got so excited about his idea that he could hardly wait to get home and bring it up to Uncle Noey. The young man talked to his horses while they were prancing down open roads. "Well, boys, we're gonna get a chance to work together again. Tug, Train, I've missed you both so bad!" All three horses' ears turned back, listening carefully. "I am glad to see you, too, Mr. E. The last time I saw you, you were a little baby."

The road between Noey's and Alvin's didn't seem to have a lot of motorized traffic, a relief to the inexperienced horseman. All three horses trotted briskly into Noey's lane. Tug and Train had visited many times before, and Mr. E trusted his friends. Lenny unhitched his team and drove them into their summer barn home. Once he slid shut the large door, he untied the colt. He took the harness off his big team and turned them out into a separate lot adjoining the horse pasture—Noey's plan to keep peace between horses. He had warned Lenny, "There will be some fights when horses work out their pecking order. If we let them work some of it out over a fence, we can hopefully keep down injuries."

Misty

Noey and his little white dog met Lenny as he came up from the barn. "Noey, when I was driving Alvin's horses, a thought occurred to me. Junior has a two-year-old filly that would be a perfect teammate for Mr. E."

"You're right, Leonard. I forgot about her. Let's go talk to him about that after we eat. That would give us one more horse for our hitch."

The small white dog followed them inside and took his spot watching Aunt Ruth prepare lunch, waiting for her to drop something. Uncle Noey laughed. "That little Russell is our vacuum cleaner; he picks up anything that falls on the floor."

Ruth seemed embarrassed. "Well, I don't know why I ever agreed to letting that dog in the house. My mother would never have allowed any dog to set foot in her kitchen." Noey winked at Lenny as they both saw her purposefully drop a sliver of cheese on the floor, and Russell quickly lapped it up.

As soon as the noon meal was eaten, Noey and Lenny tromped out through trees toward Junior's place without talking. When they walked past Junior's chicken house, they were surprised to find Herbie near the building with a smoking metal can. It dangled from a chain he held in one hand; his other hand was fishing through a white box. As they got near, a buzzing sound grew louder and louder. Suddenly, Lenny called out, "BEES! Look out Herbie, there are bees everywhere!"

Herbie didn't budge but said calmly, "These are my bees; I'm fine." Lenny felt his face turn hot, feeling silly for yelling. He and Noey stopped and watched Herbie pull out drawers covered with bees. Herbie calmly explained, "I have to shake these panels loose every so often, or things begin to stick together."

"Don't they sting you?" Lenny asked in amazement.

"Not too often. This smoker keeps them calm, and like horses, bees can tell if you're scared of them. Right now, I'm not upsetting them too bad. If I'm going to take honey out of here, then I wear my bee suit." Bees were in bunches clinging to his clothes; others were hovering around him on all sides.

Noey asked, "Is Junior up at the house?"

"I think he's in the wood shop with Henry."

Noey headed off in that direction while Lenny watched Herbie. In only a short time, Herbie finished with his bee work, and they headed together to join Noey and Junior.

As they walked, Lenny told Herbie, "We came to see if we can borrow Misty. I'm gonna stay around for a while and help Noey farm with horses."

"That's what I heard." Herbie smiled. "It will be good to have you around this summer."

Lenny followed Herbie into a dimly lit shop, where sweet aromas of freshly cut wood filled the air. When his eyes finally adjusted enough to see, Lenny realized Henry was working on a wood project. Both older men were admiring a beautiful china hutch, and Junior was explaining, "Henry does this in his spare time. Someday, when he gets a wife, she will be happy for it, I suppose." Junior turned to Lenny and said with a grin, "I hear you want to break my filly-colt this summer?"

"Oh ... well, I thought she was already broke?"

Everyone laughed at his response, and Henry told him, "Don't worry, Lenny, she won't give you much trouble after a couple of days of plowing. She'll be too worn out." They all laughed again, but Lenny wasn't sure what was so funny. Maybe they knew something he didn't.

Herbie and Howard put on a short rodeo trying to catch their young horse. Noey and Lenny watched, amused by the brothers' antics as they fished Misty out of a pool of swirling horses. They haltered her up and sent her off with their neighbors. Misty whinnied, pranced, and side-stepped all the way back to Noey's farm. Lenny was nervous, and the filly seemed to sense it. Somehow, they made it to the barn and turned her loose into a box stall, where she whinnied and stomped while Noey talked with his nephew.

Lenny asked, "Why did Junior call Misty a filly-colt? I thought males are called colts and a female, a filly?"

"Here in Iowa, Amish call them all colts. We call a male a horse-colt, and female a filly-colt."

"Oh yeah, that does sound familiar," Lenny answered.

"I think I'll have you take my big team over to Aaron Burr's harness shop. Tell him that I would like to have a new set of harness made for Stone and Jim. We can use their old harness on these young colts when he gets another set made."

"What harness will they wear until then?"

"We will have to get by with this really old set of work harness." Noey pointed at a pile of harness that was dull brown from years of use, with twine string replacing some sections of leather as a makeshift repair job.

Harness Shop

Stone and Jim chose to gallop up the hill of Aaron Burr's lane, as horses do when facing any steep incline. Lenny tied them at a hitching rack just outside of the harness shop and said, "I'll be back soon, boys." Even though it was early afternoon, it felt like evening inside because of being poorly lit. While his eyes adjusted to the dimness, Lenny drew in the scent of leather. There were a couple of sets of heavy work harness and some driving harness hanging on one wall. The opposite wall was covered with a collection of horse bits. Lenny didn't know there were so many styles of metal bars made for horse's mouths. There were large oval horse collars and even a few leather saddles. A wooden counter was covered with pieces of leather in a variety of lengths and colors. Another section had buckets of currycombs, brushes, and other horse care products.

"Hello, Leonard," Aaron Burr spoke.

Lenny finally saw where the old man was sitting. He was behind a sewing machine pumping a treadle with his foot, powering it himself. A dimly lit shop is not an uncommon thing among Amish. Without electricity, darkness is something that is tolerated. Nevertheless, this harness shop was darker than even Amish would normally be willing to endure. Lenny had to remind himself that better lighting wouldn't help Aaron see.

"Hello, Aaron, my uncle Noey sent me here to ask you to make us a new set of work harness."

"Did something happen to his harness?"

"No, but we are going to use a six-horse hitch to farm with," Lenny tried to explain. "Noey has two sets of harness, but we will need a third set. We decided that we want the new set to fit Stone and Jim and use their old harness on the colts we're breaking.

The old man sat for a moment as though deep in thought. He rose up slowly and let one hand run along the edge of his counter as he walked up to where the young visitor stood. "Do you have Stone and Jim tied outside?"

"Yeah, that's them."

"All right…let's go out there and size them up," he said as he walked through the door. With one hand on his hitching post, he used the other hand to take hold of Jim's lead rope, slipping his fingers up to the horse's large head. "Good boy, easy now." The old blind man looked small next to Noey's huge horses. He ran his hand down to the base of Jim's neck, where the height of a horse is measured. "Jim is close to 18 hands; I'll call him 17.3." He pulled a cloth tape measure out of his pocket and ran it down along the hame. "Twenty-five-inch collar, huh?"

"Yep, exactly."

The old man used his tape to measure Jim's girth. Lenny felt he could ask, "How do you know what your tape measure says?"

Old Aaron Burr smiled. "I have a very good wife; we've been married over fifty years."

Lenny wasn't sure what that had to do with his question, but he humored the old man. "Really? That is a long time."

"The Bible says, 'A good wife...who can find...her worth is more than rubies!'" The old man tossed his tape measure in Lenny's direction. "Feel that. Can you tell there is a line sewn on every inch and dots sewn on every foot mark? My wife came up with that idea and sewed those marks on my tape measure, so I could feel it." Lenny felt along the cloth tape, and, sure enough, there were lines and dots. "Leonard, I will tell you how to know whether a girl is the kind that will make a good wife. When you're around a girl you're interested in, shut your eyes and listen. Try to forget about her looks and listen to what she says. 'For out of the heart the mouth speaketh.' A woman with a beautiful heart will still be attractive when she is old. Outward beauty is deceitful and fading, like the Scripture tells women, 'Do not adorn yourselves with braided hair and gold jewelry but with the inward beauty of a meek and gentle heart.'" After Aaron Burr measured Stone and Jim, he pointed beyond his harness shop. "Can you see a set of buildings over in that direction, Leonard?"

"Yeah, I see a long white building."

"That is the dry goods store, Beantown Grocery. If I am going to start working on this harness, I'm going to need a spool of this heavy thread. Would you take your team of horses up that dirt road yonder to that store and get me some more of this thread?"

"Well, I guess I could." Lenny wasn't sure what it would be like to show up at that Amish store by himself, but he didn't want to say anything about it to Aaron Burr.

The old man handed Lenny his used-up spool of thread. "Take this along to make sure you get the right stuff." He also handed the young man a ten-dollar bill. "When you get the thread, pick up a Bulltown bar to eat on your way ... and bring back one for me, too!"

"Okay, thanks," Lenny replied and climbed on his forecart. He clucked, which sent Stone and Jim trotting down the hill out of Aaron Burr's lane. Gray clouds hung over the dapple team of horses; it wasn't raining but seemed it could start soon. In a short time, Stone and Jim were pulling onto a paved road, and their hooves rang out a nice sounding clip-clop as they arrived at the dry goods store.

Cars were parked out front, opposite where Lenny tied his horses. Some little English children came up and asked, "Can we pet your horses, mister?"

"Sure, but only if you stay up here by their heads. Don't go around by their feet; they could step on you while they're stomping flies." Lenny looked them in the eyes to make sure they got it. The older one was a boy, and he nodded. Lenny told him, "Make sure your sister stays up here, too, okay?" The boy nodded again, and Lenny grinned at him.

Beantown

Inside the store, Lenny saw an Amish woman who was stocking shelves; she didn't notice him as he walked up. "Can you help me please?" Lenny asked, and she turned and looked at him. His heart skipped a beat.

"Leah, do you work here?"

"Yep." Her dimple appeared for a moment with a smile, then her face went sober and her cheek smoothed out.

"Aaron Burr sent me here to buy some thread for him. Can you show me where it is?" he asked, wanting to say more but not sure if this was the right time for that. The store was full of people—some Amish, some not. He wanted to talk to her so badly, but it wasn't a good place to tell her what he really wanted to say. He was sure that an opportunity would come soon enough.

She walked ahead of him to where the thread was located and pointed, then walked back to where she had been working before. Lenny figured out which thread was the same as Aaron Burr's old spool, then went into the area with freezers and got two Bulltown bars. On his way back to Leah, he casually commented, "I hope we get a chance to talk soon." She turned, opened her mouth to speak, and looked around nervously, as if to see who would hear her if she did. She closed her mouth and gave Lenny a look that communicated she didn't want to talk at that moment. Lenny took the hint and walked to the counter to pay for his items.

A young Amish woman with pretty dark eyes and black hair was running the register. She looked familiar to him, but he didn't know for sure who she was. She told him, "That's eight-dollars and twenty cents." He handed her the money, and she asked him, "Whose the other Bulltown bar for?"

He surprised himself with his answer. "For my horse!" She laughed out loud, with a chortle that reminded him of a horse.

On his way back to Aaron Burr's harness shop, he remembered that the Hershberger girl had told him that her older sister worked at Beantown. He said out loud, "That's why she looked familiar. The Hershberger girl said that her sister looked just like her, only older, and she does." Stone and Jim perked up their ears, turning them back in his direction, listening. He laughed, remembering what he had said to the younger sister and repeated it to his horses. "I will watch out for her!"

The Bulltown bars were starting to melt by the time he got back to Aaron Burr's shop. He and the old man ate them down right away, slurping on the wooden-stick handle.

Bishop Mose

Lenny unharnessed Stone and Jim as soon as they got back to Noey's farm. The small white dog joined him in the barn and sat watching with his head cocked to one side. "I like you, Russell; you seem like a really friendly little pooch." Just as he said that, Russell barked loudly toward the house, drawing Lenny to the barn window. An older Amish man pulled up in a buggy and tied his horse at Noey's hitching rack. Lenny called Russell. The dog came to him, and he held him while they watched from the barn. A gray-bearded visitor climbed the house steps. Russell's chest vibrated with a long, low growl. Noey must have noticed the horse pull in; he stepped outside and joined the old man on the porch. Lenny had been planning to go up to the house, but he wasn't sure who this man was or what he was there for, so he took his time heading in.

Lenny thought that he had better carry Russell upstairs. Aunt Ruth had made it clear that she didn't like "that dog" around when they had visitors. He pushed the door open quietly, hoping to go in unnoticed, but it didn't work out that way. As soon as he walked in, Russell jumped from his arms and scrambled over, taking ahold of their visitor's pant leg. The dog growled and pulled. Noey's old visitor tried to shake the little pest from his pants as Lenny tried to pull the dog off.

Uncle Noey said, "Russell!"

Instantly, Russell released his grip, and Aunt Ruth told Lenny, "Take that dog out of here."

Tension filled the air. As Lenny went to leave, Uncle Noey said in a friendly voice, "Mose, do you remember Jake's son, Leonard?" The older man nodded slightly yet never said a word. There was no expression on the man's face. He seemed familiar, yet Lenny couldn't think of how he knew him. The old man was wearing his black Sunday clothes even though it was Saturday.

Lenny told them, "I believe I will head on upstairs." Uncle Noey nodded, which made Lenny feel he had guessed right.

Once upstairs, Lenny found Davy W. lying flat on the floor and almost said out loud, "What are you doing on the floor?"

But Davy W. quickly motioned with his hand for Lenny to keep quiet, and then Lenny realized that he was eves dropping on his dad and the old man. Lenny sat on the bed and watched him press one ear to the floor and plug the other with one of his fingers. After what seemed like a long time, he got up and sat on the other bed opposite Lenny. Davy W. looked at his cousin and shook his head. "That old Mose was sure rough on Dad."

"Why would he do that?" Lenny asked in a whisper.

"'Cause he's the bishop. He stopped here to get after Dad about me; he thinks I'm not following the rules."

"Really? Is that what he was saying?"

"He was telling my dad that if I don't start wearing a hat and suspenders all the time, they are gonna shun me. He talked about you some, too, Lenny."

"What did he say about me?"

"Well, when he got done saying everything bad about me he could think of, he started in on you. He was saying that he was surprised that my parents were willing to take on trouble like you when they have their hands full with me."

Lenny's heart sank. He felt bad for his aunt and uncle, and he felt sick to his stomach that the Bishop thought that way about him. "Is that all he said about me?" Lenny asked even though he wasn't sure he wanted to know.

"He said he thinks you are probably going to take one of our girls away from the Amish. He said, 'If I hear anything about Lenny running around with Amish girls, he'll have to leave.'"

"What did Noey say about that?" Lenny inquired.

"He told him that he would make me start wearing suspenders and everything."

"I mean ... what did he say about me?"

"Oh, he told him that you were only going to be here for a few weeks and that he had to talk you into staying to help him with fieldwork." Davy W. laughed and added, "Mose wondered why I couldn't do the farmwork. Dad was stuck there; he couldn't go telling the bishop that his son refuses to work with horses."

Lenny felt terrible for Noey. He knew how much his uncle wanted Davy W. to fit in and just follow the rules. Lenny lay back on the bed wishing he could scold Davy W. and say, *"What is so bad about being Amish? You don't know how good you have it here. Just follow the blasted rules. What difference is it if you have suspenders on or not?"* However, Davy W. wasn't the type of guy Lenny could talk to easily, and definitely not scold, so he held his tongue. While they were talking, little Russell hopped off Davy's bed and jumped up by Lenny's feet, curling up.

"Davy, do you think you'll stay Amish?"

Davy W. chuckled. "There is only one way I would stick around here; that's if I could get that Leah Yoder to date me. But don't tell anyone that I said that."

Lenny's heart sank. He never would have guessed that Davy W. wanted to court Leah. He felt he needed to say something, so he said, "Leah is a really nice girl."

Davy W. answered, "Yeah. She's pretty hot, too!" None of this sounded like anything his other Amish cousins would say, but more like guys at college. Davy W. didn't stop there. "Have you seen how that girl is put together? If you look past all those Amish clothes, you'll see what I'm talking about."

Lenny's teeth clinched shut. He looked down at his own hand and saw white between his knuckles. He quickly loosened his fingers, ashamed of himself for making a fist. For Noey and Ruth's sake, Lenny kept quiet and didn't say anything more about it.

Chapter 4

FLY IN CHURCH

N oey's rooster crowed on Sunday just like every other day; a backup choir of Junior's roosters chimed in behind him. Lenny woke up happy—it was finally Sunday. Hopefully, he would have a chance to see Leah and maybe even talk to her. Secretly, he hoped Leah would find a way for the two of them to ride home from the Singing together, like she used to do, a few years back. Even so, at the same time, he knew it would be better if she agreed to ride home with Davy W., so his cousin would stay Amish.

Chore time was not nearly as complicated at Noey's place as it was at Alvin's. Noey milked his one cow; Ruth fed chickens and gathered eggs; Davy fed stock cows and fat cattle—which left horse chores for Lenny. Noey told Lenny, "Let's not tie all our horses this morning. Just put grain in every feed box and tie the standardbred horses. You can brush and harness Davy's horse, Lightning, and my horse, Big Red. Let Nelly, my wife's old mare, go back out with the draft horses."

Lenny was disappointed that he wasn't going to brush Tug and Train or Stone and Jim, but he consoled himself by remembering that he was going to be working with those horses every day for the next few weeks. After tying up the standardbreds, he took a few minutes to look over his herd of draft horses and enjoy the sound of all those horses eating grain at one time. Mr. E and Misty looked nice together. Lenny thought about what it might be like working with young inexperienced two-year-olds until he realized he was biting his lower lip. He then decided not worry about that until the time came. One by one, the draft horses finished their morning grain, exiting the barn at will, while Lenny used the gate to sort them into two pens again.

He got to work brushing Lightning and Big Red. Lightning was a rich, dark brown horse with a black mane and tail. He seemed to have Davy W.'s personality, stubborn and rebellious. Lenny had dealt with buggy horses when at Alvin's farm, yet he had never gotten comfortable with them. Lightning was one of the worst. He stomped impatiently while tied, never stood still while being harnessed, and had a nervous habit of chewing on his lead rope. Big Red, on the other hand, seemed friendly enough; he lived up to his name in size and color. He was as tall a buggy horse as Lenny ever remembered seeing and a deep red sorrel. Even his mane and tail were red, but he had tall white socks and a bold white strip from his forehead to his nostrils. Russell joined Lenny in the horse barn and sat watching with his little head cocked to one side as though trying to figure out why this guy was struggling with buggy horses. When Lenny finished harnessing horses, he headed over to help Noey. Little Russell trotted ahead, anticipating where Lenny may be heading. From behind, the small dog's chunky body looked exactly like a little white piglet. They found Noey was done milking and Davy W. and Ruth were already in the house.

Breakfast was quiet. Davy W. always seemed sullen despite Noey and Ruth's lighthearted friendly ways. Ruth made fried eggs and toast on the stove. Lenny had almost forgotten that Amish didn't have toasters, one more thing that needed electricity. Ruth's toast was better than any Lenny remembered eating, partly because it began as homemade bread. While they ate, Noey suggested, "Why don't you ride along with Davy? You will find that more interesting than riding with a couple of old people." Lenny smiled but inwardly disagreed, being sure he would rather visit with kind, older folks than with Davy W.

Aunt Ruth called Lenny aside after breakfast. "Here, Leonard, I thought you might as well have something fitting for Sunday." She handed him a newly sewn set of Sunday clothes.

"Thank you, Aunt Ruth. I wasn't sure what I was going to wear to church."

Ruth smiled and said, "Well ... I'm glad you like them."

Noey helped Lenny hitch Lightning, but Davy W. still hadn't come out of the house. The older couple got into their buggy and headed off to church. Lenny paced back and forth while Lightning pawed at the ground. He couldn't imagine what was taking his cousin so long. After waiting for what seemed like an eternity, he went back inside and found Davy W. sitting on a couch reading from an old newspaper.

"Shouldn't we be on our way to church?"

"Yeah, pretty soon. I don't like to get there early; church is way too long as it is. Besides, Lightning will catch up to Big Red anyway."

"Oh, okay, I guess you're right."

Lenny wanted to get there as soon as possible; he kept thinking about seeing Leah. Finally, Davy W. got up and sauntered out to his waiting horse, with Lenny following. Lenny barely got seated before Davy W. let Lightning take off. He didn't call to his horse or cluck; Lightning was so keyed up. All Davy W. had to do was stop holding him back, and they were gone. Lightning tore out of Noey's lane, lurching as they turned onto the gravel road. Lenny wanted to take ahold of something and hang on but resisted the urge. He pressed his feet on the buggy floor, as if pushing on a break.

Davy W. told his cousin, "Lightning came off a racetrack in Indiana. I was told he used to win a lot of sulky races."

Lenny was curious. "I wonder why they quit racing him."

"The guy I bought him from said that he was just too hard to handle." Davy W. laughed as though proud of that. Lightning trotted way faster than Lenny felt any horse ought to go. It seemed Davy W. barely had his horse under control, as if at any moment Lightning may decide to turn into a ditch. Lenny was worried that something may spook the nervous horse, but Davy W. held loosely onto his driving lines, casually slouching and looking bored. They passed several other slower buggies before they got to the house where they were havingchurch but never did catch up to Big Red. By the time Lenny and Davy W. got up near the house, all the men were already lined up in order of age. Davy W. knew where he fit in; however, he didn't bother to help Lenny figure out where he should be. Lenny had to ask some of the young men—who looked about his age—how old they were. They were nice about helping the outsider find his place in line.

Junior and his sons came at the last moment. They walked up together, and Lenny almost had to laugh at the sight of them. Herbie and his brothers were all tall and lanky, and there was something ornery about their faces that made everything they said hilarious, even when they weren't trying to be funny. On the farm, Junior and his boys looked sharp in their work clothes, but they were straight out comical in Amish church-clothes. None of their black pants were long enough; their lengthy torsos made it difficult for them to keep their shirts neatly tucked. As a result, shirt tails puffed out from under black vests that didn't fit either. The brothers were handsome in Amish hats. However, when they took their hats off to go into church, it seemed their mother had slicked down their dark brown hair with water in an effort to make them presentable. Her plan failed.

Herbie and his brothers all divided up and slipped into the line of men and boys who were ready to walk into church in order of age. Lenny was happy that Herbie ended up right next to him.

"Our cows were out this morning," Herbie whispered. "My sophomore brother Howard forgot to tie the gate shut last night." He said it with a straight face, which made his words seem even funnier to Lenny. They both fought back laughter as they walked into the house's dark interior and past a row of sober-faced Amish elders. By the time they were seated, Lenny was feeling hot and sweaty from his effort to stifle laughter, making his new Amish clothes itchy.

Lenny watched the women come in. He enjoyed seeing the age progression in the line as the oldest women came in first and slowly transformed into middle-age women, and then young married women. As the line progressed to younger women, Lenny's heart beat faster in expectation of seeing Leah. There was no sight of her. When little girls streamed in, his heart sank, knowing that Leah wasn't there. In fact, he realized that he didn't recognize most of the faces and remembered that there were ten districts in the local Amish community. This meant that on any given Sunday, there were ten Amish church services going on in the area. Lenny tried to remember if he had seen Noey and Ruth at church in Alvin's district; he was sure he hadn't. Fortunately, when the young folks got together for Singings, there were only two youth groups, not ten— which also meant that he had a fifty-fifty chance of being at the same Singing as Leah.

German hymns were sung slowly in long, drawn-out notes that filled the house. Lenny hadn't heard this type of singing for a couple of years and had missed it. He sat and listened because he didn't know German, but he mouthed the words so others wouldn't think badly of him. At long last, everyone drew silent and a preacher rose and took his place under the threshold of a doorway between rooms. He seemed upset as his voice rose and fell; all the while, his white beard shook against his black, lapel-less suit coat. He paced back and forth enough that he could be seen by everyone even though the congregation was divided into several rooms of a very large Amish home.

Herbie seemed fidgety beside Lenny. At one point, he reached in his pocket and pulled something out. At first, it seemed he was fussing with an invisible object, and then Lenny saw that Herbie was straightening a long hair, probably from one of his sisters. He carefully made a loop in one end and laid the hair over his pant leg. The non-Amish boy fixed all of his attention on his buddy, completely mystified. Next, Herbie held his hand up just above his knee, like he was going to grab something. All at once, with lightning speed, he snatched a housefly. While the preacher rambled on and on, Herbie meticulously gathered the tiny fly between two fingers and used his free hand to loop the noose of his sister's hair around the fly's head. Lenny wondered if his friend was planning to execute the poor insect. Instead, Herbie released his victim, and it flew off, but only a few inches before it began to fly in circles, hovering over Herbie's lap. In an instant, Lenny came to the realization that Herbie had this fly on a leash, an invisible leash. The helpless fly buzzed around and around, even changing directions, but never getting anywhere.

Herbie gave the leash more slack; his sister's hair was really long. Without knowing he was going to do it, Lenny burst out laughing but caught himself instantly and changed his laugh into a cough. Almost everyone turned and looked at him as he pulled himself together.

The next preacher who stood kept saying Noah while he spoke, making Lenny think it may be something about Davy W. or himself. He listened carefully to see if he understood some of the other German words. It seemed the sermon was about Noah in the Bible, and about how Noah was the only righteous man in a wicked generation. Lenny drifted off into a light sleep; images of floodwaters filled his mind. He could almost imagine what it must have been like to live in a huge floating barn filled with big animals. He sank into a dream of a boat rocking in waves of a terrible storm. Thunder rumbled on and on until he woke up realizing that the preacher's deep rumbling voice was the thunder he heard. Church ended abruptly, and when it was their turn, Lenny and Herbie filed out with the other boys their age.

The young Amish men gathered in a group near the buggy horses' heals. They talked quietly about farming and what a wet spring it was. After a time, they all headed back to the house and were directed downstairs into a very clean basement, all painted white. Everyone had a spot at lengthy makeshift tables and given a bowl of soup. Herbie teased an older woman who served them,

"What took you so long to make this soup? Did you have to butcher this chicken after church?"

She teased back, "Yeah, that's why your soup is really warm. Hope you don't mind a few feathers in it?"

After the meal, the men and boys headed out to their horses, getting them ready for the drive home. One by one, buggies pulled up near the house and women and children climbed aboard. Lenny looked around for Davy W., finally concluding that his cousin had left without him. He went into the barn and untied Big Red and led him out.

Bishop Mose stood in a shadowy area just outside of the barn. The stern-faced old man spoke quietly and in a strong Dutch accent that Lenny could barely understand him. "Leonard, while you're visiting, stay away from the girls."

"Okay," Lenny nodded.

Noey met Lenny as he walked up leading Big Red, and they hitched their tall horse to the buggy and drove near the house so Aunt Ruth could join them. They rode home without talking much. Whenever Ruth or Noey did speak, it was always friendly and lighthearted.

In Junior's Home

Noey, Ruth, and Lenny came home and found Davy W. already stretched out on the sofa, taking a nap. Little Russell was curled up by the young man's feet. Aunt Ruth and Noey took a chair on either side of Davy W.'s couch and sat, quietly reading. Lenny felt out of place and bored. He decided to take a walk outside and wandered around the farm, looking things over. Davy W.'s fat cattle stood behind a fence, watching every move the visitor made, eyeing him suspiciously. It appeared that they wanted to run off in fear, but their curiosity held them captive. The cattle pasture rose up one side of a bluff on the edge of Noey's farm and back into the woods. He noticed the long dirt lane that he knew led down to the English River. It reminded him of the great memories he and his cousins had swimming in the river a few summers back. Ever since his return to the area, people were constantly talking about how swollen the English River was, that it was threatening to leave its banks. No one could even think of swimming in it under those conditions. Heavy foliage hung over the dirt road, casting dark shadows. Black crows fought up in the tops of trees, oblivious to the fact that it was the Sabbath. Sounds of rushing waters came up from the river, making Lenny shudder. He found himself near the path to Junior's place. He decided to cut through the woods and take a glance to see if anything was going on with Junior's sons.

When he walked past the chicken house, he took in a strong ammonia odor. He stopped by Herbie's beehive and watched them shoot out of their white box just over his head until he heard a commotion up by the house. Herbie and his brothers were on the porch laughing; their dogs were barking and chasing a girl on a pony. When he got closer, Lenny began to sort out what was going on. Herbie and his brothers were coaxing Fannie Ella to ride her pony up the porch steps.

Herbie called out, "Here comes Lenny! Just in time to see the show!"

Fannie Ella seemed to think that Lenny's presence made it worthwhile to take on her brothers' dare. She gave her pony the cue, and he clomped up all six steps, clattering around on wooden porch boards.

Howard opened the house door and said, "Come on in, Dusty!" The pony walked through the door with his little Amish girl on board. All the big boys followed her in, laughing, and Lenny hurried after them to see what would happen next. Junior's home was full of tall sons, little girls, and Fannie Ella riding a pony in the living room.

Junior was sitting in an easy chair, calmly reading a paper. He sat there with a slight smile, looking like the Lincoln Memorial statue. His daughter rode circles around him. Herbie popped the kitchen door open, and Fannie directed her mount through that doorway. Lenny feared the fun would end when Ruby saw a pony in her kitchen, but instead he heard Ruby's cackling laughter. Harvey, the youngest brother, popped open the kitchen door a crack to see what was happening. His eyes got big as saucers as he pulled the door wide open. Dusty came back through the doorway; Ruby was behind Fannie Ella, riding double. Everyone in the family let out a whoop, including Junior. Lenny leaned over, doubling with laughter, wiping tears from his eyes.

Ruby rode along until they got outside on the porch. She had dismounted before Lenny and the big boys could get through the door. When they all got outside, she was wiping her hands on her apron and scolded her sons. "You boys better get your chores started if you plan to go to the Singing tonight." The brothers all snapped to attention and jumped from the porch, heading toward the barn obediently. Ruby smiled at Lenny with her blue eyes twinkling and headed back inside. Lenny took her advice and headed home to get his own chores done. He couldn't wait to get to the Singing.

Rebecca

When it was time to go to the Singing, Davy W. made a statement: "I don't know if Lenny is planning on going, but if he is, he will need to take his own buggy. I'm gonna give a ride home to someone else."

Uncle Noey looked at his nephew. "Were you wanting to go?"

"I was kinda hoping to."

"Well, in that case, you could take Big Red."

"Hmmm, I'm not sure I can handle him." Noah looked Lenny in his eyes as though reading what the young man might have meant by that. "I'm a little nervous driving horses on the road," Lenny confessed.

Uncle Noey seemed surprised. After tugging on his beard in thought, he stated, "You could take my wife's old mare, Nelly. You could follow David to the Singing, so you would know your way back home."

"Dad," Davy W. whined, sounding more like a town kid than an Amish boy, "Nelly is so slow; I don't want to hold my horse back the whole way. Besides, it's not that complicated to get to Ruben's place; Lenny can do it."

Uncle Noey looked embarrassed that his son was carrying on. As if to end the shame, he didn't argue with him. Instead, he looked at his nephew. "I can explain how to get there. I think you should go and spend time with other young folks, and you can see your cousins; they will be there, too." Noey walked out with the boys as they got their horses ready. "You can take my two-wheeled cart." While he was explaining to Lenny how to get there, Davy W. called to his horse, Lightning, and it charged out of Noey's lane. With a rumbling sound, it disappeared down the road.

"See that dust cloud behind Davy? Turn that way." Lenny and Noey both laughed when he said it. Noey continued, "You will go straight on that road for three miles. You will come to a 'T' in the road, where you turn left. You can't miss your turn because of the T. After you turn left, you will go around a large curve. When the road straightens back out, you go about another mile. You'll find it; a crowd of young folks will be there."

"Thanks, Noey."

The younger man clucked, and old Nelly walked off at a fraction of the speed of Lightning. Nelly walked calmly on a flat road that followed a river bottom. A cool breeze came up from the water, bringing with it the scent of fresh spring vegetation. Lenny said out loud, "Nelly, you're a good horse for me! Most buggy horses are too high strung, but you're about my speed." The old mare picked up her pace ever so slightly when she heard her name. After passing through that 'T' intersection, the road curved, and other buggies came into view.

Lenny sat at the Singing, listening more than joining in. He couldn't quit thinking about Leah and wishing he was going to be driving her home. While four-part harmonies filled the long open building, he went over in his mind and thought about the reasons why he couldn't. He wasn't planning to be around for more than a month. He knew that Henry wanted to drive Leah home, and he had heard Herbie admit that he and Ruby wanted her to date Henry, too. On top of that, Davy W. had said that the only way he would stay Amish was if he could get Leah to marry him. Uncle Noey and Aunt Ruth clearly wanted Davy to remain Amish. Even though Lenny didn't like the idea of Leah dating Davy, for his aunt and uncle's sake, he almost hoped it could happen. Lenny also thought about the bishop telling him, "Stay away from the girls."

Long slow singing filled the air, but the visitor could hardly focus on the English words, much less German ones. He could only think of Leah. He reminded himself that the biggest factor of all was what Mose had said. It wasn't so much what the bishop thought, but he didn't want to get Uncle Noey and Aunt Ruth in trouble. He decided that he wouldn't date Leah or any Amish girl.

When the Singing was over, all the boys went outside. They stood in small groups, talking quietly about the weather or what they had been doing over the past week. Some whispered among themselves as plans were made for who would be driving whom home. Most of the girls remained inside; a few slipped out to help set things up for one of their friends. It seemed most boys didn't ask a girl directly—that was usually arranged through friends they had in common.

Ruthie came along among those who went to make arrangements. Lenny's heart skipped a beat as she walked past; he was inwardly hoping that Leah had sent her to talk to him. Instead, she went into the big barn where another large group of boys had gathered. The lone non-Amish boy stood hidden by darkness, listening to the cheerful banter of his Amish counterparts. One by one, most of them disappeared as a shadowy figure of an Amish female slipped out of the house to meet her suitor. Finally, after Ruby came out to meet up with Herbie, Lenny slipped off through the veil of darkness and found old Nelly waiting quietly where he had left her tied.

Lenny rode along, with only a few stars illuminating his way; most of the starry host were covered by clouds. Every so often, another horse and buggy caught up and passed Lenny's old mare at about twice her speed. It didn't bother him, though; he didn't have any reason to hurry. Lenny told his horse, "If it weren't for you, Nelly, I wouldn't have any girl in my life." Nelly's ears turned back intently listening. "I feel kinda lonely knowing that most of the other boys are riding home with a girl. Oh well, I will only be here for a few more weeks anyway. Besides, if the bishop got wind of me trying to date an Amish girl, he would make Uncle Noey's life miserable." Nelly let out a little snort and shook her mane. Lenny continued, "I will admit that the worst thing is thinking that Davy W. is driving Leah home." Nelly let out a long drawn-out snort, and then they rode on in silence. The young man took time to think about the variety of scents that met them along their way home. Hog farm odors, sweet hay, dairy cows, and soil of recently plowed fields. It stabbed like a knife if he thought about Davy W. visiting with Leah. He remembered his little chats with her in the past. How happy she always was and how cute her giggle sounded. His heart ached. He was so busy feeling sorry for himself that he didn't notice two shadowy figures in front of Nelly until his buggy wheels almost ran them over.

"Hello," a girl's voice broke through the silence.

"Hi, what's going on?" Lenny asked.

"Our horse went dead on us."

"What?"

"We were just about to go over the top of that next hill up there, and our horse stumbled. We thought he lost his footing and would recover—but he didn't. He just lay down and died." The two girls laughed at how silly their own story was.

Lenny asked, "Do you girls want me to give you a ride somewhere?"

"That would be nice," one answered. They both climbed onto Noey's cart beside Lenny.

The girl who sat right beside Lenny told him, "This is the second time you've rescued me!"

"What? I've never rescued you before."

"Don't you know who I am?"

"Uh, not really."

"I'm Rebecca; my sister is Salina."

Lenny was racking his brain. Those names seemed familiar, but he couldn't place them. The girl laughed and said, "Come on, Lenny.

Don't you remember when our horse Wilber ran off with us in the buggy, you know, on the way to church a couple of years ago? You and Perry took care of our horse, and I had to go to the hospital."

"Oh yeah, now I know who you are. I remember that! That isn't Salina beside you, though, is it?"

The girls giggled, and Rebecca told him, "No, she is married. This is my little sister Rosemary."

The younger girl said, "Don't you remember me? You came and helped us cut up that tree that fell on our chicken house a few days ago."

"Are you Nelson Hershberger's daughters?"

"Yes," they both said at the same time.

"Oh. Then, Rebecca, you're the one that sold me Bulltown bars at Beantown yesterday?"

"Yeah, one for you and one for your horse!"

They all three laughed. About that time, they came upon the deceased horse lying on the side of the road, and Lenny asked, "Do you think he will be all right there?

Rebecca laughed. "No. He won't be all right; he's dead!"

"I just meant, will it be okay to leave him there?"

"What else are we gonna do with him?"

"Let's get him off the road at least." Lenny climbed out of his buggy and took hold of the horse's hind hooves. It was way too heavy for him to move by himself. Both girls jumped down and helped. Together they rolled him over into the ditch. "There," Lenny said, "now at least a car or a buggy won't hit him until your dad can come and get him."

The girls nodded and giggled. They climbed back on Lenny's two-wheeled cart. Rebecca faced backward, holding on to the shaves of her cart, pulling it behind, and Lenny drove them home.

As Nelly trotted up to their house, Rebecca asked, "Are you going to come in for a bit?"

"No, I'd better not. Your dad and mom don't want me coming in, do they?"

"They are in bed. It's our tradition that we don't talk about who we are dating, not with our parents. So, they won't have any idea that you were here. If they did, they wouldn't say anything about it."

Lenny winced. "Well..."

"We have some apple pie!"

"Okay, I'll come in for a bit."

Rosemary disappeared. Apparently, she went off to bed, leaving Rebecca and Lenny alone. The Amish girl cut a huge slice of pie and got a glass of milk and set it in front of him.

"Aren't you going to eat any?" he asked as he took a big bite of delicious apple pie. She sat across from him, watching him eat in a dimly lit kitchen. He could taste a perfect touch of cinnamon sugar in it.

"I'll just share this piece with you," she said with a smile and took his fork and helped herself to a bite.

Lenny watched her eat and took a big swig from the glass of milk. She looked so pretty in the glow of a lantern turned low. Before he even set his glass down, she reached for it and took a drink, too. Rebecca looked Lenny in the eyes while she drank slowly. A smile on her face was visible behind the glass. The non-Amish boy didn't know what to think. He remembered what Bishop Mose had said about him staying away from Amish girls, and he wished he hadn't agreed to come in the house. When they finished off the big piece of scrumptious pie, he said, "Well, I guess I'd better get going.

"It will be morning by the time that old mare of yours makes it back to Noey's," she teased.

"She knows the way home if I fall asleep."

They both laughed quietly and he left.

Chapter 5

HORSE TROUBLES

Morning chores seemed quiet on Noey's farm. Davy W. slept in because, in his words, "Fat cattle are on full feed anyway. They have all they want to eat in front of them at all times; I just need to reload their feeders sometime during the day."

Noey told Lenny as they were walking out to do chores, "I used to see to it that Davy got up early every morning. After he moved away and then came back, I decided he was old enough to choose for himself how he wants to live."

Lenny called in his horse herd and began his summer job. Uncle Noey's barn seemed quite different than Uncle Alvin's. Alvin's barn had a stone foundation, but it was only a foot tall—everything seemed to be made of wood. Noey's barn had a stone foundation that was a story high, and his horse stalls were in what used to be a dairy parlor. A row of wooden dividers stood out from the stone wall, with feed bunks up against that wall. There wasn't a walkway at the head of these stalls, like at Alvin's. A person had to walk in from behind a horse to get up to their heads, which was intimidating for a guy with limited horse experience. First, Lenny had to scoop feed rations into each bunk, then let in his horses. And while they were eating, he had to step in with each horse to put on a halter.

He started with Tug and Train because he trusted them most. "Ho, easy Tug." Lenny slipped in beside the hulking black horse, dwarfed by its mass. Tug's halter was already attached to a chain hanging in the hay manger. All Lenny had to do was slip it on the horse's head and connect one strap that went under its jaws. Then he slipped under Tug's neck and did the same with Train. "Good morning, Train. You're looking fine this Monday morning." That done, he went to Stone and Jim's double stall. All of Noey's stalls were designed to accommodate two horses. Noey called them "tie stalls" because they are open at one end with no gate. Being tied kept the horses in place. Stone and Jim were also easy to halter up while they quietly ate their morning rations. After that, Lenny went to tie Noey's lightweight team; they were fidgety and almost done eating by the time Lenny got to them. He stepped in nervously beside Jack, Noey's oldest horse. He also let the young man halter him easily, but Mack was done eating when Lenny got to him. Mack backed out when he saw his halter, stepping into the wide-open area behind his stall.

There he was, joined by Mr. E and Misty, who also had finished eating.

Lenny immediately knew he made a mistake starting with the easiest horses. While trying to figure out how to get Mack and the colt and filly back into their stalls, he realized that all the buggy horses also finished eating and joined the herd in the large open area. Fortunately, the barn door was closed, or they all would have let themselves back out to pasture. An idea popped into Lenny's head. He went and got a bucket with more grain and thought that he could entice them into their stalls again with more feed. This would have worked if there had only been one loose horse, but it turned out that Mack and the buggy horses knew what a bucket of grain was. They all crowded around, fighting each other to get at the bucket. Lenny was in the middle of a swirling clump of horses that were biting at each other and letting out short squeals, a warning sound horses make before they kick. In only a moment, Lenny had dropped his bucket and rushed out of danger. He stood watching the group of horses fight over what grain remained on the cement floor.

Lenny tried to think what Grandpa might have done in the same situation. He spoke to himself, "Lenny, calm down. You can't get anywhere with horses if you're upset." He inhaled deeply and exhaled slowly until his heart quit pounding. Soon, the loose horses had cleaned up any grain and were standing in a clump. Another idea came to the city slicker. He went and got Mack's halter and calmly approached the crossbred, talking softly, "Easy, Mack, easy." Mack, a solid black horse, had enough draft horse blood in him that he was larger and calmer than a buggy horse. He stood while Lenny slipped his halter on and snapped it and tied him next to Jack.

"There, one down, five more to go," Lenny consoled himself. He knew old Nelly wouldn't be a problem, so he caught her next and tied her in her stall. Four horses remained, but they all shied away every time he came at them with a halter.

A door slid open and Noey came through it. Lenny felt his face get hot. "What happened?" Noey asked.

"Before I could get them all tied, they finished eating and, well…I can't catch the others."

Noey chuckled as he went and grabbed part of a hay bale. He tossed it into the hay mangers of the open stalls, and all the loose horses followed calmly and began to eat hay. "Hay isn't nearly as exciting as grain, so they won't get as worked up," Noey explained. When they finally got every horse tied, Noey told Lenny, "With so many horses, you may have to let them inside in two groups."

Lenny raised his eyebrows, having an aha moment. "Didn't think of that."

After breakfast, it was time to hitch horses and get plowing started on Noey's fields. Uncle Noey pulled his two bottom plow out of a corner of his machine shed. It was covered in a layer of thick dust.

"We haven't used this gangplow in years."

Lenny asked, "I thought a plow with a seat was called a sulky plow?"

"A sulky plow is a one-bottom plow with a seat; a two-bottom plow is called a gangplow even though it's a sulky style by the fact that it has a seat."

Noey and Lenny went in together to harness horses. Noey decided out loud, "I think we will use our crossbreds, Mack and Jack, in the morning while it's cool; those colts may be too frisky. In the afternoons, when it gets a little warmer, they will give us less trouble." Lenny felt his heart rate go up, and he wished he hadn't agreed to help do fieldwork.

"Until Aaron Burr finishes our new set of harness, we will have to use this older set on our crossbreds in the mornings and the colts in the afternoons."

Lenny looked over at the old harness Noey was pointing at; it was part leather, part nylon tied together in places with twine string. Even as a non-experienced horseman, Lenny knew that it was an accident waiting to happen. "Shouldn't we use that older harness on horses we trust? So if something breaks, they won't run off?"

Noey smiled, blue eyes twinkling. His beard was salt-and-pepper color, but Lenny thought that when it all turned gray, Noey would look exactly like Grandpa. Uncle Noey answered Lenny's question. "I'm thinking that we want our more dependable horses in good harness. That way, when something breaks, Tug, Train, Stone, and Jim will hold fast and keep everything from blowing up!" Lenny's heart sank. Uncle Noey had said "when" something breaks," not "if." The thought of everything "blowing up" sent a feeling of panic into the younger man's gut.

When all six horses were harnessed and driving lines snapped into place, Noey headed them to his gangplow. The two men

hooked all twelve heel chains to the long evener behind the row
of big horses, and Noey gave a cluck. It was beautiful to see six
draft horses step out together. A soft jingle of harness mixed
with a pleasant sound of hoofbeats and horse snorts. Lenny had
butterflies in his stomach, anticipating driving such a magnificent
team of horses, yet he was unsure of how things would go. Noey
sat on the plow seat while Lenny followed on foot, reminding the
young man of when he had followed Grandpa out to do fieldwork
at Alvin's place.

Once on the edge of a large field bordered by trees, they came to
a place where there was some plowed ground. Noey called, "Whoa!"
His horses all stopped, but they pranced eagerly, anxious to get to
work. "Do you feel comfortable enough to take over here?" Noey
asked, looking Lenny in the eyes.

"Oh … no, not really. Could you take a pass, so I can get a little
refresher course?"

Uncle Noey grinned and lowered the plowshares. He clucked
to his six-horse team, and they stepped off. Lenny followed on foot,
and he could hear sod ripping open and smell fresh soil, bringing
back good memories of when he first plowed at Grandpa's farm.
All six horses seemed perfectly behaved and well broke. By the time
they needed to stop for a rest, Lenny was not only comfortable about
taking over, he couldn't wait to get started. Uncle Noey climbed off
the seat again. This time he rose up slowly, trying to straighten out
his back with one hand pushing from behind. It made Lenny feel
bad that he had asked Noey to plow a row.

"Are you going to feel confident taking over now, or do you want me to go another round?" Noey questioned his nephew, looking at him as though reading his face.

"I'm ready. I just haven't driven a six-horse hitch for a couple of years."

"I think you'll do fine." Noey grinned again and passed the lines to his nephew. The older man knelt down slowly, keeping his back straight, and smoothed a spot on the ground. He took a small twig and drew a map, the way Grandpa always used to. "Here is the furrow I just plowed. Over yonder is the opposite furrow that you will come back down. When these two furrows meet, you will have to move further east." He pointed at that direction. "There you will have to start two new furrows: one next to the section already plowed and one about ten feet in from the fence. Understand?"

Lenny nodded that he did, but he felt a little worried he wouldn't quite remember when it was time. The younger man climbed up on the plow seat and clucked. All six horses stepped into action, their momentum plunging plowshares into the ground, which released a fresh earth smell. Blades of grass squeaked as plow blades sliced them in half and threw two long slabs of dirt over. Lenny looked back and saw his uncle walking away stiffly. Lenny's memories of plowing with six horses had been faint, but it all came flooding back. He loved the jingle of harness, random horse snorts, and quiet hoofbeats on soft soil. When he got near Noey's fence line, he realized that they had been heading up a steady incline onto a rise. He stopped his horses for a rest and

looked west. From that higher place, Yoder towers could be seen
way off in the distance, which reminded Lenny of the days when
he used to stare at those towers, dreaming of the modern world.
He realized that he didn't miss civilization at all; in fact, he had
been longing to get back out in Amish country. When he saw the
towers, he thought about how Alvin's farm was just beyond that
spot, and on past Alvin's, Leah's homeplace. He let out a sigh as
he thought of Leah and her sweet brown eyes. There was nothing
in the world he wanted more than to talk to her again and see her
face light up with a smile.

As his horses caught their breath, Lenny walked around front
and looked them all in the eyes. "Good job, boys. You're making this
fun and easy for me. I'm only here for a few weeks, but I won't ever
get tired of driving a big hitch like this!" He adjusted Train's collar
even though it didn't need it, smoothing a hand over the massive
horse's arched neck. He told Train, "I'd better stay away from these
Amish girls, or I'll get Noey and Ruth in trouble. I'm not gonna be
like that Davy W."

A horse whinnied off in the distance, inspiring Mack to call out
a loud response. His horses seemed rested, so he set them back to
plowing. Gray skies hung over the horses, with a few splotches of
blue peeking through. Crows cawed down by the English River.
A group of them came up flapping their long black wings, flying
aimlessly, and fighting among themselves. The big ruckus made
Lenny look down at the woods along the river bottom. He wished
Noah's farm wasn't close to a wild and untamed river. He knew

that it ran for hundreds of miles across the Iowan landscape, unchecked by fences, inhabited by wildlife. Like a railroad track, the river bottom stretched out in a long tunnel of cover in an otherwise open terrain. That cover provided a home for whitetail deer, rabbits, fox, wild turkeys, and pheasants. There were rumors of bobcats and even mountain lions being sighted in Iowa, no doubt in wooded areas with plenty of game, like river bottoms.

The young man decided not to think about those things but kept his focus on the six large black rumps before him. Their shiny coats began to glisten with sweat. From time to time, he caught a glimpse of Davy W. strolling around on Noey's farm with his shirttail hanging out. Lenny wondered if Davy had given Leah a ride home from the Singing last night. He couldn't tell by Davy W.'s body language; the guy was nonchalant no matter what.

A dinner bell rang up near the house. Ruth had told him, "I will ring the bell about a quarter to twelve. When you hear that, start your team in for a noon break and meal." Lenny let his horses finish the row they were plowing, and then pulled a lever hoisting his plowshares out of the dirt. Stone and Jim must have known what the dinner bell meant; they tried to break into a trot, though they were held back by Tug and Train, who obviously didn't recognize the sound.

Once his horses were unhitched from the plow and tied in a cool barn—away from flies and munching on a little hay—Lenny headed in for his own lunch. When he got cleaned up and slid his chair up to the table, he realized that an Amish girl in her early teens was helping Ruth in her kitchen. Lenny recognized her as Herbie's younger sister Fannie Ella. She was a dark-haired girl like the rest of Junior's family. She also had kind features and honest eyes like her siblings.

After they prayed a silent prayer, everyone dug in and ate a substantial meal of roast beef and mashed potatoes. Uncle Noey teased Herbie's sister about her plate having large helpings of food. Surprisingly, she teased right back, "Looks like you have as much food in your beard as I have on my plate!"

Even Davy W. got a chuckle out of that. Ruth only said, "Well." Lenny noticed Noey running his fingers through his beard to see if the little girl was right. He smiled at Fannie Ella when they saw his uncle check his beard.

Colts

After a nice break, everyone headed back to work. Uncle Noey said, "It's warmer out now—a little better time to work with colts."

Lenny didn't disagree, but he dreaded it, anticipating troubles with younger horses. Mr. E was big-framed, strong, and seemed easygoing. He accepted the harness and stood calmly while Lenny snapped everything in place. He only sidestepped a little when a currycomb dropped off a ledge nearby. Misty, on the other hand, was nervous and fidgety. Noey had to help getting her harnessed. She was a pretty black horse, but she shook her mane often while stomping her feet. She sniffed everything, even Lenny, trying to mouth whatever was close. Her soft black mussel nibbled Lenny's shirt gently like a set of fingers, but he feared that she could bite. When the older man and his nephew led their horses outside to hitch, five of them walked calmly up to the plow. Misty sidestepped all the way. Her eyes were wide and seemed to be looking for something scary, as if she wanted the thrill of fear.

Once all six horses were ready, Lenny asked his uncle, "Would you mind driving them out to the field? This young mare is making me nervous."

The older man hadn't seemed to notice her antics, but when Lenny said that, his uncle smiled and nodded. He climbed carefully on the steel seat because of his back troubles. Everything seemed okay as they headed out to where they had plowed their last row earlier. Noey climbed off the seat and commented, "The colts seem fine. I think you'll be okay with them."

"Thanks for driving them out," Lenny answered, "Misty was making me nervous up in the barn, but she looks relaxed now."

Noey nodded and headed back to his barn. Tug and Train were Lenny's lead team in the middle, with Jim to the right of Train and Mr. E to his far right. Stone was placed to Tug's left, and beyond Stone was Misty. So there were black horses in the middle and on the ends and dapple grays sandwiched in between, reminding Lenny of Oreo cookies. After their driver clucked, they all set off plowing calmly. While he watched the horses plowing, there was plenty of time to think. Most of the afternoon, Lenny kept an eye on the colt and filly on either end of his hitch. He couldn't help but notice how similar they seemed. At first, he told himself that all black Percheron colts would seem alike, but he had learned that horses can vary a whole lot, even within the same breed. Mr. E and Misty moved with an unusual stride that the other horses didn't have—lifting their front hooves higher than usual. Lenny's mind poured over the idea of the colt and filly being related, wondering if being young and energetic were the only traits that made them alike.

Lenny thought he was alone out in the middle of nowhere, but while the horses were resting under a large shade tree, their heads bobbed up, giving a signal that they saw or heard something. Lenny turned around and Herbie was right beside him. Lenny jumped a little, "Oh, Herbie, you scared me!"

Herbie chuckled. "If you had been one of my brothers, I would have snapped your suspenders and scared the vinegar out of ya!" Lenny laughed, but he was glad it didn't happen. Herbie asked, "How is it going out here?"

"Pretty good, really. Misty is fidgety but manageable."

Lenny took a chance at asking Herbie a question. "Do you know if Davy W. took Leah Yoder home from the Singing last night?"

"Just so happens that my brother Henry took her home."

Lenny gave a quick look at Herbie to see if he was serious, and then replied, "That's funny, Davy let on like he gave her a ride home."

"Really? Ruby told me that Leah likes Davy. That's why she wanted Henry to take her home."

Lenny looked Herbie in the eyes to make sure he heard it right, then asked, "What sense does that make?"

"Well, I never quite understand girls, but she told Ruby that even though she likes Davy, she doesn't think he will stay Amish. And she doesn't want to get her heart broke. Leah asked Ruby to set it up for her and Henry, just to be sure Davy couldn't ask her."

Lenny tried not to show any disappointment on his face, but he was struggling. He figured he'd better let Davy W. know about this; it may be an answer to Aunt Ruth's prayers.

Herbie told Lenny, "Why don't you walk over after chores, and we will go see about getting parts to fix your car?"

"Seriously? That would be great!"

Herbie gave Lenny a funny look but grinned and said, "All right, in the meantime, keep that Misty under control."

Lenny laughed, but right after Herbie walked away, he looked over at Misty and realized she was cockeyed and had stepped over her heel chains. "Oh man, Misty, I should have seen this before Herbie left. He could have held your halter while I fixed your tugs." Misty was tied onto Stone, who was like a rock, which made Lenny feel a little better as he reached back behind the young horse to fix her heel chains. "Easy, Misty... easy, girl, easy." As he was adjusting things, he looked at her old harness; it was almost ready to fall apart.

He kissed to his team, and they set off plowing again. For a while, everything seemed to be okay. Both colt and filly looked calm. All at once, Lenny's horses all got fidgety, ears twitching. The colt and filly shook their manes. He called, "Whoa," stopping his team to see what was bothering them, and heard a roar coming from the river-bottom lowlands. Lenny began talking to his horses, "Easy...ho there. Easy." The growl grew louder as a red four-wheel-drive truck came barreling up a dirt road just beyond the fence row. Stone and Jim must have had experience with the truck before because they stood calmly. Tug and Train held up their regal heads and snorted, unafraid but inquisitive. Mr. E got upset, but he was farthest away and had Train between him and the truck, giving him confidence. Even so, he sidestepped over his traces. Misty was nearest to the big red monster, and she seemed stunned at first, and then decided it would suit her best to take off running at full speed. She had a little problem, though: she was securely tied to ten thousand pounds of draft horses that weren't going to run with her. Misty's legs were trying to go but got caught up in her heel chains. The old harness tore off her like cobwebs as she started kicking at the chains grabbing her ankles. What made Lenny the most upset was that the guy driving the big red truck revved his engine as he went by.

"Easy, boys...easy, Tug...whoa, Train. Easy, Stone, whoa, easy." Lenny tried to keep the big horses calm while Misty continued kicking until she was so tangled she fell to the ground. The city boy wanted to panic and run, but he knew he had to stay calm and face the situation. The big red truck was gone, but all the ruckus Misty was causing started to upset Mr. E. He was prancing at the other end, pulling back on his bit, and shaking his mane. "Mr. E...Mr. E...easy, boy, easy," Lenny said in as soothing a voice as he could produce at that moment. He tied his driving lines onto his plow and walked around to Mr. E first, taking a hold of his bridle. "Good boy, Mr. E, good boy," he said as he smoothed his hand against the big colt's warm neck. All the while, Misty was lying there thrashing. Just when he thought that everything would turn into a full-fledged disaster, he heard another voice talking calmly, a girl's voice.

"Whoa, Misty Girl. Whoa, Misty. I got you, girl." Herbie's sister took a hold of Misty's bridle even as the young horse thrashed. Lenny circled around and came up by Misty's back, talking, to let her know he was there. Stone moved a little in place, not liking that Misty was bumping his legs while she moved about. Stone held fast, and Lenny somehow found a way to unhook her torn harness from the evener.

"Well, that ends plowing for this afternoon!" Lenny directed his statement toward the young Amish girl standing there.

She looked up and said, "Sorry."

"It's not your fault; that's for sure. How did you happen to come up just when I needed help anyway?"

She stood there barefoot in the plowed dirt and shrugged her shoulders. Her little dark green Amish dress had a rip on one sleeve.

Lenny asked, "Did you tear your dress helping Misty?" Fannie Ella nodded that she did. Lenny told her, "Oh, I'm sorry about that."

"It's not your fault; that's for sure!" She smiled coyly.

Lenny instantly liked this girl. "Well, thank you for helping me out. I was in real trouble!"

She smiled at Lenny again and ran off toward her home. Lenny gathered the torn harness and hung it on Stone's hame. He unhitched the other five horses from his plow and left it setting idle in the partially plowed field. When the six huge horses clomped into the cool insides of the barn, Noey and Davy W. showed up to see what was going on.

"I had a little mishap," Lenny stated.

"Oh no, did they run off?" Noey asked, looking pale.

"No, but Misty tried to run off by herself and couldn't get the others to go along. Some neighbor kid with a huge, red four-wheel-drive truck scared her. She got all upset and tore her harness. Lucky for me, Junior's daughter, Fannie Ella, happened to come by and help me, or I might have had a disaster."

Noey looked relieved and told Lenny, "It turned out pretty good then, didn't it?"

"Yeah, but we tore up Misty's harness."

Davy W. hadn't said anything, but as his dad and Lenny looked over Misty's harness, he sneered, "That's what I hate about farming with horses. You don't have to worry about a tractor getting spooked and running off!"

Noey was nice and agreed, "I guess your right about that." Noey ran his fingers through his graying beard and looked at Lenny. "Since we can't plow anymore today, I guess you might as well haul this torn harness up to Aaron Burr's harness shop and get it patched up." Lenny nodded and Noey added, "Let's leave these work horses rest up for tomorrow. You can take Nelly on the cart."

It took a while to get his other five horses un-harnessed, brushed, then turned out. He had to catch Nelly, then harness and hitch her. He said aloud to Nelly, "I guess this is all part of being Amish."

Aaron Burr

Lenny walked into Aaron Burr's shop. Before he could say a word, the old, blind, Amish man spoke cheerfully, "Hello, Leonard, how's the horseman doing?"

"Not so good. I had a little mishap this afternoon and got my harness torn up a little."

Aaron Burr walked along his counter, running a hand along its edge until he came to the place Lenny had laid the broken harness. Lenny moved the harness a little to let Aaron know where it was. The old blind man ran his hands carefully along the harness, feeling it. "We can fix this up, I believe." He started taking some buckles off and laying pieces out neatly into sections. While he worked, he asked the younger man questions.

"What caused your horses to get upset?"

Lenny looked at Aaron, surprised the old man knew they were upset, and tried to explain what happened. "Some English guy in a big four-wheel-drive truck raced past our place, and I had colts in my hitch. One of them, named Misty, got all upset and tried to run off. Good thing all my other horses are trustworthy."

Aaron Burr didn't speak but continued mending the harness. After some time had passed, Aaron said, "The smartest colts are the hardest to break, but if you stay patient, they make the very best horses in the end. My brothers and I used to have trouble with our colts when Model Ts sputtered past." Lenny sat and quietly watched Aaron Burr work. He started thinking about Misty, wondering what kind of horse she would be. The old, blind harness maker stopped sewing abruptly and announced with a smile, "You know what would be really good right now? A Bulltown bar!"

Lenny grinned. "That does sound pretty good."

Aaron went to his cash register and, with a ding, took out a few bills. "I'll pay for it if you and Nelly will go get us a couple of 'em!"

"It's a deal!" Lenny said, taking the money and hurrying out the door. Nelly faithfully trotted off in the right direction. An elderly Amish woman in a top buggy zoomed past, her horse twice as fast as Nelly. That didn't bother Lenny. There was no hurry. Nothing else better to do than enjoy a quiet ride on a dirt road. He watched cows, just beyond a fence, grazing peacefully, grass squeaking as they pulled out juicy mouthfuls. Lenny told Nelly, "I guess I'm gonna see both Leah and Rebecca today." Nelly turned her ears back as though interested in what he was saying. "Nelly, you probably agree with Bishop Mose. He says that I'd better stay away from Amish girls." Nelly shook her mane vigorously. Maybe a fly was bothering her.

When Lenny got to Beantown, the dry goods store, he saw the horse and buggy that passed him on the road. That elderly woman had already tied up her horse and was inside shopping. A bell attached to the door rang as Lenny walked in. Skylights in Beantown's ceiling illuminated the non-electric Amish store with a soft glow. Shelves were stacked with plastic bags of flour, spices, dried banana chips, nuts, candies, and a million other things all colorful and enticing. The temporarily Amish young man took his time looking everything over.

"Lenny!" Rebecca spotted him first, calling out his name. He glanced at the old Amish woman who was standing nearby; she returned a disgusted glare. Rebecca hurried over. She kept her voice quiet, "What are you shopping for today?"

"Just stopped in to get a few Bulltown bars."

"One for you and one for that old mare, Nelly." She giggled. He liked her laugh; it reminded him of a horse nicker. She continued with her teasing, "I bet you really came to see me, didn't you?" Lenny smiled but out of the corner of his eye noticed an Amish woman looking at them. He looked over and realized it was Leah, her glare sharper than the old woman's. His face got hot and his shirt itchy.

"What is wrong with Leah?" he asked.

"Oh, she has been in a bad mood ever since I told her about my horse dying. Apparently, she cared more about that old horse than I did."

"Hmm ... that does sound like Leah. I guess I'd better not keep Nelly waiting for her Bulltown bar," he told Rebecca, which brought on another horsy nicker. He hurried to make his purchase and headed out to untie Nelly.

Nelly headed off slowly, trotting parallel to a woven wire fence. He drew in a deep breath of fresh country air spiced with dairy cow smells and a hint of hog lot. "Nelly, I don't know what to do. I'm supposed to stay away from Amish girls, but I really want to see Leah. And that Rebecca is cute, too." Nelly, a good listener, turned her ears back quietly waiting for more. "Nope, I just can't talk to either of them; I don't want to get Noey in trouble. It makes me mad that Davy gets Noey in trouble. Why would I do the same thing?" Nelly snorted as she made her way up the slope of Aaron Burr's shady lane. She seemed happy to stand tied under a tree while Lenny went inside with his ice cream bars.

Aaron Burr stopped working on Misty's harness when Lenny handed him a Bulltown bar. While he ate, the old man told Lenny, "I lost my eyesight when I was about your age." The younger man was quiet, not knowing what to say about a tragic thing like that. Aaron Burr smiled. "You know the good part of it is that I remember everyone just as they looked back then ... nobody has aged."

Lenny replied, "I guess that would happen. I never thought of that."

"My wife and I were not married yet, but we had been dating. I got sick and had a high fever. When I learned that I would never see again, I told Suzanna that she ought to move on and find a man who could see. But that didn't set too well with her. A lot of water has gone over the dam since, but, in my mind, she hasn't changed looks. I can still see her, just as she looked at that last Singing before I went blind." Lenny continued eating his ice cream bar, listening.

"My brothers and sisters are all old or deceased, but I can only remember them, just as they were over fifty years ago." The old man laughed. "I can still see my brothers, chasing each other around, teasing, and having fun, just like Junior's boys do now. We used to plow with horses and break colts, down where you are working on Noey's farm. That was where I grew up."

"Are you serious?"

"Yep! Enjoy your time plowing with those horses. And don't give up on that Misty; she will surprise you if you don't lose patience with her." The old man stood up, and, in only a short time, finished mending Misty's harness. "There," he announced, "now I can get back to work on that new team harness you ordered."

"Thanks. And thank you for the ice cream bar, too!"

Aaron Burr didn't reply.

Hershey's garage

After supper, Lenny told Noey, "I guess Herbie is going to try to help me fix my car. We are going to go get parts to fix it, if that is okay with you."

"Sure, that sounds like a good idea," Noey answered in a friendly way, but Lenny still felt awkward as though owning a car was an evil thing and to be ashamed of. He hurried through the wooded area between farms and found Herbie working on an old hay baler.

"There's my buddy Lenny," Herbie announced, though nobody was there to hear it.

"If you're too busy, we could do this car thing some other time," Lenny offered.

"Are you kidding? I've been looking forward to this all day!"

Herbie climbed out from under his hay baler and trotted over to his waiting horse and buggy, with Lenny trying to catch up. Herbie and Lenny rode off together behind Smoky.

Herbie explained, "We should be able to get everything we need to fix your car at Hershey's."

"Where is this Hershey place?"

"Right across the road from Yoder Feeds."

Lenny looked at his friend with surprise. "Oh, you have to be kidding me? Yeah, I know where that is, but I never thought of going there."

"It's not really a car parts store, but the Hershberger guys who own it are super nice. They will get us the parts we need and give me advice about how to fix it."

They rode along for a bit listening to Smoky's hoof beats. All at once, Lenny piped up, "Won't Hershey's be closed at this time of the evening?"

"Ha, ha, you would think so, but I know those guys; they work late every evening."

Yoder Towers rose up before them, and they turned in at Hershey's and tied Smoky to a telephone pole. Things looked just like they had two summers ago when Perry and Lenny snuck away on horses to the same place late one night. The boys found Jerry working on a little S-10 pickup. Herbie did the talking.

"Hi, Jerry, could you give us a little help with something?"

Jerry slid out from under the pickup, and Lenny noticed his Yankee hat. "Hello, Herbie, I can help you as long as it's not about a horse."

The boys laughed and Herbie told him, "No, it's an Impala. My friend here took his Impala in the ditch, and his rear wheel is bent out of whack."

Jerry looked at Lenny's clothes. Lenny pulled on his suspenders and said, "Oh, I'm not really Amish. I'm just staying at my uncle's place this summer."

Jerry didn't comment on that; instead, he led them into the office part of his shop and looked it up in a book. "I'm thinking that what you need is called a trailing arm. Impalas don't have a rear end like cars used to have. Here we go. I'll order one for ya; it should be here in a couple of days. They're not bad to replace, just a few bolts." Jerry grinned at Lenny and said, "In the meantime, you might have to keep driving a horse." Lenny laughed and snapped his own suspenders on the way out.

Lenny asked Herbie, "Do you want a pop to drink on the way home?"

Herbie looked around to see if there were any Amish nearby. "I'll take a root beer if they have that?"

Lenny fed a couple of bills into the machine, and it spat out two cold cans of root beer. They rode back home sipping on their pops and talking. Herbie told him, "There are a lot of new houses going up in our area."

"Really? Are they Amish homes?"

"No, that's the bad thing. The English keep putting up new housing developments further out of town, and they're kind of flooding us out of our farmland. They pay so much for the land us Amish can't compete. We used to be alone in the quiet countryside, farming. Now, we have big fancy houses just over our woven wire fence." Just as Herbie was saying those words, they passed a development of huge, modern homes on a lush hill. The faces of those fancy houses seemed to be looking down on a small Amish farmstead in the valley below. Lenny didn't know what to say. He felt guilty about it because he was part of the infringing English population.

When they got near Junior's lane, Herbie told his friend, "I need to check on our chicken house." He turned Smoky in his drive.

Lenny said, "I thought we were going to your chicken house?"

"We are. Watch this!"

He wheeled his horse around in a short circle. Lenny almost fell out of the little cart.

"What are you doing?"

"I'm faking out my dogs!"

Blue and Tick were out in an open field nearby, snooping around. When the hound dogs saw Herbie turn in, they took off at a full run. By that time, Smoky had spun into the chicken house lane, trotting off quickly. Herbie watched closely for his dogs, laughing. "My dogs try to outrun me. They try to guess which lane I'm going up and beat me there, so I like to trick 'em."

Smoky sped up to the chicken house and stopped. Blue and Tick were bay-oo-ing up by the house, fully expecting Smoky to appear there. Herbie broke out in a belly laugh. "I got 'em!"

The Amish guy headed off to check on his chickens, and the other guy walked through the woods toward home.

Chapter 6

DOG AND PONY

Little Russell followed his master, Noey, into the barn and trotted in among thick-boned draft-horse legs, weaving around and sniffing, as if on a hunting trail. Russell, a mostly white dog, had black patches covering each ear and brown patches that seemed to be hiding under the black ones. Uncle Noey chuckled. "Our little Russell isn't very useful on a farm. He gets into more mischief than he does good, but my wife is awful fond of him." Russell heard Noey say his name and hurried over to the older man. Noey cradled his arms, and the small dog jumped up into them. He set the dog onto a stone ledge and scratched his little buddy vigorously behind the ears.

Lenny asked, "Where did he get the name Russell?"

"He came to us with that name." Uncle Noey grinned and looked affectionately at his tri-colored dog. Russell looked back up at Noey with shiny black eyes, his little dog face so sweet anyone would love him.

"Where did you get him?" Lenny asked his uncle, hoping for a good story.

"I was at the horse sale in Bulltown one day watching equipment being sold. Some English people had a cage with a sign on it: "Puppies for Sale." I didn't think much about them until this little guy"—Noey nodded at Russell—got out of his cage somehow and chased a kitty into a big pile of horse harness that was being auctioned off. The kitten slipped into that mess of harness and on out the other side, but Russell here, got stuck in a tangle of leather. I had to dig him out. He was such a cute little helpless pup; I had to buy him for my wife. He wasn't cheap, but I thought he may pay his way by being a good farm dog. That hasn't happened yet." Noey laughed and continued his story, "The English children I bought him from told me that his name was Jack Russell. Since we already had a horse named Jack, we decided he could just go by Russell."

Lenny knew that Jack Russell terrier was the name of a breed, but he concluded it wouldn't be necessary to mention that to his kind, old uncle.

While they talked, a rat scampered through the barn, and Russell jumped off the ledge he had been sitting on. He chased the rat, leaping over a board into the oat's bin. Noey hurried over and Lenny followed. The little closet-type room that held oats was dark, making it hard to see what was happening inside. Lenny was barely able to see Russell's hind legs as the dog sank down into oats like a person would get sucked into quicksand. Uncle Noey grabbed a hold of one foot and hoisted his dog out. Russell held a dead rat in his teeth.

"You ornery little dog," Noey scolded. "If I hadn't been here to rescue you, you might have died in those oats." He brushed oat dust off his little dog's white coat and said, "If anything happened to you, I don't think Ruth could take it.

They all headed in for breakfast, Russell leading the way. Ruth asked, "Is that dog staying out of trouble?" Noey just laughed. Ruth had a pile of fried mush waiting to be devoured when the men came in.

Uncle Noey called up the steps, "Davy, we're eating down here!"

Davy W. lumbered downstairs and joined them. His dark hair stood straight up, making him look more like Elvis Pressley than usual. He never bothered to speak but helped eat his share of the mush.

Noey told Lenny, "I guess we can use the same combination of horses this morning and switch out again in the afternoon?"

Lenny finished eating a mouthful of mush, and then told Noey, "I have an idea. We can switch out Stone and Jim as the lead team, which will give Train a break from walking in the plow furrow."

"Good idea!" Noey exclaimed. "If we switch them up right, we won't wear them down as much."

Davy W. seemed annoyed that Noey and Lenny got along so well, but Ruth was smiling.

After breakfast, morning plowing went as well as could be hoped for. Noey's crossbred horses were pretty calm for being part buggy horse and looked like lightweights next to the four full-blooded Percherons. While plowing, Lenny took time to notice how picturesque Noey's home and buildings were. Everything was crisp, clean, and painted white, accented by those four huge oaks at each corner of the square farmhouse. The enormous barn had a beautiful stone foundation, giving Lenny an idea of just how old it must be. It looked like a massive wooden ship that had run ashore and been mired in black river bottom soil. The corncrib that held Lenny's Impala wasn't far off, and it captivated the young man's attention and got him worrying about how he was going to get it fixed. He could see Aunt Ruth scratching in her lush garden, which was producing way more than a three-person family could ever use.

All six huge horses leaned heavily into their collars as they plowed a trench uphill, and Lenny rewarded them with a break at the top, letting them stand on the highest part of Noey's field. From there, Yoder Towers could be seen rising in the distance, reminding Lenny of his summer at Uncle Alvin's. He remembered how Leah used to stop out for short visits, adorably happy and talkative. He missed those days. When Aunt Ruth rang the dinner bell, it seemed they had only been plowing for an hour. Lenny wished that he could use the same six horses in the afternoon, instead of working with a frisky colt and filly.

Aunt Ruth

As Lenny neared the house, he noticed Aunt Ruth hanging clean laundry on a clothesline. She nimbly clicked clothespins on each item. He stopped and watched. He had always liked Aunt Ruth and Uncle Noey. They were kind, gentle people, who never seemed to complain, unfailingly thinking of others more than themselves. Aunt Ruth was not necessarily attractive, but her sweet nature made her seem pretty. Whenever anyone made a comment, her first response was to say, "Well." That was it, just "well." She said it with so many different inflections that it seemed to mean a number of things. Lenny remembered her using that word for everything, even when he was a small boy. Especially when someone gave her a compliment, she would smile softly and reply, "Well."

After a few moments, she realized Lenny had been standing there watching her, and she laughed. "Oh, Leonard, how long have you been there?"

"Just a few moments. I wanted to thank you for making these clothes for me."

She smiled and said, "Well." After a bit, she added, "Thank you for encouraging Davy."

She shook out a pair of pants. With a click and snap, she had them hanging in the breeze and was on to the next clothing item. She slid her wash basket with her foot. Lenny marveled at how she could work so quickly without missing a beat, yet talk slowly and sweetly at the same time in a completely separate rhythm. He sensed she had something to say, so he stood quietly waiting. About four pairs of pants later, she said, "Noey was so happy when Davy W. came back to the farm." She paused with a catch in her throat and continued, "It broke his heart when Davy went away a few years ago. He is the only son we ever had. It's very lonely for an Amish man to work on a farm without a son. Family is such a big part of our lifestyle." She looked Lenny in his eyes to see if he understood what she was saying. He nodded.

She started hanging socks in rapid succession but continued talking slowly. "We have this grandpa house here," she said, tilting her head toward the smaller, vacant house next to their large white farmhouse. "We hope that someday, Davy will move in there when he gets married ... and when they have little ones, we will trade houses." She looked at Lenny again, her eyes sparkling with anticipation. Lenny's heart felt heavy in his chest, fearing that Davy W. would let them down. This was the first he had thought about how sad it was that Noey and Ruth had not been blessed with children. He stood watching Ruth hang socks and felt like crying for her. He remembered that Ruth's adopted daughter had left the Amish the day she turned eighteen. Lenny couldn't imagine why. He was sure that Noey and Ruth had always been very kind parents; their home and farm were such a welcoming place.

Lenny knew, as well as anyone, that the outside world held an alluring power, with all the pleasure and comfort provided by electricity. And it had always seemed reasonable to him when anyone left the Amish. That is until he lived at Uncle Alvin's two summers ago. After working with Grandpa and his horses, Lenny had concluded that there was something rich and fulfilling about life on an Amish farm. He quietly walked away while Aunt Ruth continued hanging her clean wash on the line. As he headed in, he determined in his heart that he should have a talk with Davy W. to try to convince him to stay Amish.

Queen

After lunch, Lenny resigned himself to the reality of working with Mr. E and Misty, remembering that after all, it had been his own idea. They got off to a good start plowing. Lenny felt relieved to see Train walking on solid ground instead of in the plow furrow again. It didn't bother him at all to see Misty walking in plowed ground. He chuckled to himself and told her, "Stomping over those dirt clods ought to take some of the sap outta you, Misty." The filly was manageable while plowing, but when the others were resting, she whinnied loudly and stomped nervously. Mr. E was calm even though he and Misty both had about the same amount of experience; she was more of a nervous type. Every time they got to the field's edge, Lenny had to fix Misty's traces; she stepped over them constantly.

"Misty … what is going on with you? Lenny stood beside her and smoothed his hand on her soft neck. "Why can't you calm down like Mr. E?" She snorted and let out a deep belly nicker, not a friendly reply to Lenny but an unsettled sound. "Easy, missy, easy."

Lenny looked over at Mr. E and told Misty, "You and Alvin's colt look and move so much alike; you must be related."

He would have rested them longer, but Misty was unsettled, making him nervous. He clucked them back to work, and the world seemed peaceful again. A red-tailed hawk circled high over them, casting a shadow on Lenny. He looked up, squinting into the blinding sunlight, watching the bird of prey soaring above. He knew that from the hawk's point of view, fields below resembled a vast Amish quilt. Most of the neighboring fields were various shades of green, but Noey's wet, lowland farm was still black unplanted soil. He imagined that the hawk could see the serpentine river bordering Noey's farm and threatening to leave its banks. Lenny thought of the swirling muddy waters coursing through woods on his left and shuddered. He made an effort to focus on his horses instead.

Soft jingles came from their harnesses, and a gentle breeze passed over the horses toward Lenny, carrying a horse aroma. He drew in a long, slow breath and enjoyed it until he was interrupted from that simple pleasure by a rumble. A deep, low growl rose up through the woods. Lenny instantly knew that the English kid was coming with his huge red truck. He tried hard to get Misty facing away from the road, hoping it would help. As the roar grew, she tried to run, pulling all of his horses into a semi circle. When the horses all were facing the road, the truck had sped off and could be heard growling on the highway beyond Aaron Burr's place. "Misty, you almost made this plow flip with me on it! Grrr."

After a full round, he stopped his horses at the opposite fence under their shade tree. Lenny fixed Misty's traces again. She seemed to be tired enough to stand still, so the young man took his chance to lie back beneath the big oak and look up into its branches. A bird sang out the most incredible string of notes Lenny had ever heard— spastic sounds up and down the scale, yet beautiful. The bird wasn't visible until the young man walked around in circles under his tree, finally locating it. He watched the tiny gray bird hidden among leaves, chirping wildly, until it noticed him and flew away.

"That must be a catbird," he said out loud. His six-horse hitch looked rested, so he clucked and harness jangled as they set off plowing. He thought about how Leah had said, "Catbirds are my favorite birds." He remembered her explaining that catbirds have two modes, singing in the spring and meowing in mid-summer's heat. She told him that he should come back earlier in the spring when the catbirds are singing. He could see why—its warbling was amazing. While his horses calmly plowed, his mind drifted, remembering his picnic with Leah a few years back. How she had laughed at him for thinking he heard a cat up in the tree.

He caught himself smiling while the horses worked peacefully until it occurred to him that his team was behaving perfectly. He looked over at Misty. She was walking along better than he had ever seen her go, but a strange feeling came over him. She looked like she didn't have any harness on. His heart began to race, thinking that her harness must have torn and fell off. He called, "Whoa!" All of his horses stopped and stood still while Lenny sat staring at them, trying to figure out what was wrong. He was afraid to move, thinking everything may be ready to blow up. Suddenly, he realized there were seven horses in front of him. His heart skipped a beat, and he stood up on his plow looking at the far horse, which should have been Misty. It wasn't a two-year-old filly, but an older horse with no harness. He jumped off his seat, running around the front to see what was up.

"You ornery old cuss! What are you doing here, Queen?" He tried to shoo her off, but when he did, the other horses got upset, especially Misty. The old mare resumed her place beside Misty, ready to get to work. Lenny stood looking at her, frustrated. "You're probably the reason I've had troubles with Misty all along, aren't you?" Queen stood peacefully, looking back at the young man. He scolded her again, "I thought I heard you whinnying to Misty. No wonder she was always upset." She bowed her head and looked away, making Lenny feel bad that he was being so hard on her. "Okay … you can walk along, as long as you don't cause any trouble." He went back and got on his plow seat and clucked, and they all returned to work in a business like fashion. From that moment on, Misty was perfect, never stepping over her traces again all afternoon. The old mare walked in time with the herd of draft horses even though not in harness. When it was quitting time, they all headed in toward the barn together.

Uncle Noey stood watching as they came walking up. He called out to Lenny, "Since when did you start driving a seven-horse hitch?"

"How do you like that? I'm a pretty good horseman, eh? And one of my horses doesn't even wear a bridle!"

Noey and Lenny both laughed. When Noey heard the whole story, he told his nephew, "We should ask Junior if we can keep Queen here and use her in our hitch."

"I gotta say as soon as she showed up, Misty calmed down." Lenny looked at her affectionately and added, "Maybe because Queen is so old, we could hook her loose. Then she wouldn't have to work as hard as the others."

"You should talk to Junior and see if we can use her. I'm guessing he won't mind."

As soon as Lenny got his horses unhitched, he headed over to Junior's farm, Russell at his heels. "You'll have to stay out on the porch with Blue and Tick," he told his little sidekick as he knocked on the door. Fannie Ella came and invited him inside. Lenny sat and waited for Junior to come into the room, so he could talk to him about Queen. Little Elma, one of the twins, teetered up in her plain-colored dress, looking so cute; it was hard not to stare at her. Her tiny blue head scarf matched her dress with a teeny white apron. Jabbering in Dutch, she held out her hand to pass something to Lenny. He reached and took it. Herbie and Howard walked in the room at that moment and immediately broke into laughter and couldn't quit.

"What? Tell me what she said." Lenny was still holding what she had handed him.

The brothers couldn't get themselves together enough to talk. Fannie Ella took it upon herself to help Leonard. "Elma said, 'It came out of my nose.'" At that the big boys roared with laughter. At first, Lenny didn't know what to do with what he had in his fingers. He took out his hankie, and, after cleaning off his own finger, he asked Elma, "Do you need to blow?" She came right up and blew her nose heartily into his hankie and grinned.

Junior came into the room, and Lenny asked, "Junior, did you notice that Queen was missing?"

"Not yet, I guess?"

"She joined my hitch today." Everyone looked confused at Lenny while he explained, "Misty has been owly in the harness, but this afternoon, all at once, she calmed down and was behaving perfectly. That's when I realized, I had a seven-horse-hitch. Your mare, Queen, was walking along beside Misty as though she was part of my team."

Junior stood with his arms folded, scratching his beard while he listened. He broke into a big grin. "Queen loves to get out there and work!" All Junior's boys were nodding in agreement.

Lenny asked, "We were wondering if we could use her for a few days. I know she's retired, and so we won't hitch her tight. We'll take it easy on her."

"Sure, go ahead. She'll be happy to help," Junior told him, but the others laughed.

Henry muttered, "Good luck with that." Lenny didn't know what was funny.

Herbie asked, "Hey, Lenny, you're going up to Alvin's for the volleyball game tonight, aren't you?"

"Sure am!"

Herbie smiled, "Why don't we all ride together on a hay rack. You could drive some of those big horses you're plowing with."

"Okay, I guess we could," Lenny mumbled.

" All right, I'll come over with ya and help get a team hitched up."

Holes

Lenny followed Herbie back through the wooded area between Junior's place and Noey's. Some type of creature scurried through tall grass up ahead, sending Russell into a frenzy. The small black-and-white dog scrambled past Lenny's leg, causing a shiver to race up his spine. Herbie sprang into action following Russell, enthusiastic about the chase. Lenny tried to keep up with his barefooted friend as he sped over sticks and shrubs. A thick-bodied, brown-coated creature ahead of all of them found its hole and disappeared into it. Lenny was thinking the ordeal had ended when Russell vanished down into the tunnel after it.

Barefoot Herbie stood over the mouth of a burrow, coaxing Russell on. "Get him Russell! Good dog, sic 'em, boy... sic 'em!"

Half out of breath, Lenny reached the spot and joined Herbie looking down into a dark hole. Muffled, growling sounds came out of the ground. "Oh no, is Russell going to be killed down there?" Lenny asked Herbie.

His buddy didn't seem alarmed and continued urging Russell on, "Good dog, Russell, good dog!" After a while, there was no change in the action. Herbie stood up from his crouching over the burrow and announced to Lenny, "I'd better go get a shovel."

"Is Russell going to get killed down there?"

Herbie laughed. "No, I'm betting on the dog. That groundhog doesn't stand a chance against Russell. Anyway, I'd better go get a shovel; that critter is in a hole, and Russell won't come out without him."

Herbie hustled back home to get his shovel, leaving Lenny standing alone in the woods. Growling sounds rose up from the burrow, and Lenny backed away, fearing the dog and groundhog may come snarling out at any moment. He looked around nervously, not liking the idea of standing in the woods alone. A dark canopy of leaves hung over him. A crow sat on a limb not far away, watching intently, as though hoping to get a free meal from the creatures fighting below. The crow produced a clicking sound. Lenny had heard those sounds coming from the woods while plowing, but didn't know that it came from a crow. He eyed the big black bird suspiciously while waiting for Herbie.

Finally, Herbie came trotting back with a shovel on his shoulder. He got busy digging just behind where the snarling sounds seemed to be coming from. Lenny bit his lip while watching, "Careful. Don't hurt Russell with that shovel."

The Amish young man seemed to have experience with this type of thing and slowed down just as Russell's tail appeared in the soft dirt. Herbie fearlessly reached into the hole and pulled Russell out by his tail and handed him to Lenny. The little, mostly white dog looked like he needed a bath. It was all he could do to hold onto the pooch trying to escape his clutches. Russell's little legs were going hard against Lenny's chest, tangling in his suspenders.

Herbie continued digging. "I'm kinda curious about how this groundhog could keep Russell held off; he must have a hole he was backed into. If he comes up out of here, let Russell go." Lenny watched close, ready to release the dog. Herbie was beginning to work up a sweat, digging a trench before he unearthed the varmint. It came scampering out of the hole, almost climbing over Herbie. Before Lenny even had time to decide to release Russell, the dog was already leaping out of his arms in hot pursuit. In a matter of seconds, the pair of them disappeared into another hole. Herbie started laughing and handed the shovel to Lenny. "Your turn." Lenny could hear growls and snarls coming up out of the earth as he dug. All at once, everything below them got quiet. Lenny feared Uncle Noey's dog may have met his match. He started imagining himself having to tell Aunt Ruth that her little dog had died.

After considerable digging, Lenny spotted Russell's milky tail and pointed it out to Herbie. The Amish guy took hold of Russell's tail again and pulled, dragging out a dirty white dog. As Russell emerged, they realized he had a dead groundhog clutched in his teeth. The groundhog was only slightly smaller than the dog.

Herbie scratched Russell behind his ears and said, "You are one tough little guy."

Grand Entry

Lenny and Herbie pulled into Junior's lane with Tug and Train on the hayrack. Blue and Tick came romping out to meet them, howling like they were treeing a coon. Lenny's horses pranced past the hounds, as if to show that they weren't intimidated by dogs. Lenny tied up his team, looking around for Herbie's brothers. Fannie Ella appeared riding her pony. "Hi, Lenny, whatcha doing?"

"Hello, Fannie Ella. I'm here to pick up your brothers. We're going to a volleyball game and taking a hayrack, so we can all ride together."

Fannie Ella rode up close to where Lenny sat. "That sounds like fun; I can't wait until I can go to young folk's gatherings."

"How old are you?"

"Thirteen. I can go as soon as I turn sixteen."

Lenny smiled. "That will be sooner than you think."

"No, it will be in two and a half years."

Lenny chuckled because Fannie Ella misunderstood him, but he didn't try to explain it. Herbie and his brothers came out of their house all cleaned up, looking ready to go visit girls. The boys, all tall and lean, might have been a starting lineup for a basketball team if they hadn't been Amish. Herbie told Lenny as he walked up, "We like to take Dusty along on hayrack rides sometimes."

"What? How do you get him on a hayrack?"

Herbie laughed. "He is such a great little pony he will jump right on board!"

"I gotta see that sometime." Lenny shook his head.

Herbie turned to Fannie Ella. "Let's show Lenny what you and Dusty can do. Fannie Ella clucked to her pony and took him in a wide circle.

Herbie told Lenny, "You better drive your team down in that low place along our lane, so that Dusty doesn't have to jump quite as high." Lenny kissed to Tug and Train, driving them where Herbie pointed. When they came to a stop, Lenny looked back in time to see Fannie Ella coaxing her pony into a lope, her brothers all cheering her on.

Just as Dusty got near the hayrack, Lenny spoke to his horses, "Easy, boys, easy." He worried that they may spook when they heard a big clunk. There was a loud, CLUNK, CLUNK, CLUNK! Tug and Train both got startled and jumped in place, harness jingling. Lenny held to the driving lines and spoke softly as he had learned from Grandpa, "Easy, boys, easy." They held firm and Lenny looked back at Fannie Ella; she sat smiling, mounted on her pony, onboard the hayrack. All the boys broke out laughing even though they had all seen it before. They carried on as if they hadn't. Lenny laughed at their laughter almost as much as what he had seen and at Fannie Ella's cute smile. She looked pleased that she and her pony pulled off a great feat again.

When everyone finally calmed down, they realized Junior and Ruby had come out on the porch. Lenny glanced in their direction, wondering if they would approve of what had just happened. Both parents were grinning. Lenny drove his team toward the house.

Junior spoke up, "Why don't you boys take that pony along to the volleyball game? I kinda think Dusty would enjoy going along for a ride!"

The boys all looked at each other, nodding with a grin on each face. Fannie Ella was the only one who seemed disappointed as she climbed down off her pony, and then off the hayrack.

Lenny felt bad for her. "Sorry, Fannie Ella. We'll take good care of Dusty. Someday soon, you will be able to come along." She smiled and stood quietly, playing with the strings of her white head covering, her dark eyes looking at Lenny. As they pulled away, Lenny wondered if little Amish girls got crushes on older boys like English girls do.

Tug and Train clip-clopped merrily along a gravel road, toting a load of boys, a medium-sized pony, and a row of hay bales that doubled as chairs. Herbie said, "Milkman Tom saw Dusty's tricks and offered Dad a thousand-dollars for him."

"Will your Dad sell him?" Herbie gave a clear, "No."

Lenny got an idea. "Hey, guys, why don't we make a big entry when we get to Alvin's?"

"What do you have in mind?" Herbie asked, grinning as though whatever Lenny thought up would be fun.

"I think one of us ought to sit on Dusty. Just as we pull in Alvin's lane, we should have Dusty jump off the moving wagon and gallop into the yard."

Henry laughed out loud. "That would be great if you did that, Lenny!"

"Oh no ... I have to drive this team. I think Herbie should do it. I know just the right place where I can line up the horses. There's a low spot in Alvin's lane that I can pull into. I will tell ya when to take off, and the back of the wagon will only be about a foot off the ground."

They all looked at Lenny with a new respect because he had come up with such a good idea and had thought out the details. "Okay, Lenny, I'll do it." Herbie laughed. Henry, Howard, and Harvey whooped again. They all moved the hay bales aside, so that Herbie would have a little runway off the hayrack.

In only a short time, they got to the place where a road split two hills. They came barreling down Alvin's lane, Tug and Train trotting at a good clip, obviously happy to be pulling into their home farm. A volleyball game was going already in the orchard area, but everyone stopped playing and stood staring when they heard the thunder of draft-horse hooves and steel wagon wheels. Just as planned, Lenny turned his team short into a low area near the barn and gave Herbie the queue, "Go!" The front of the hayrack was heading slightly uphill, making the back end close to the ground. Dusty obeyed Herbie's cluck and took off, leaping onto the ground and galloped in a short circle. Herbie somehow stepped off Dusty and calmly walked toward the large group of Amish young people, as if he had just got up off a couch. Lenny wasn't sure about what kind of reaction Amish young people would give to such a scene.

At first, they all seemed unimpressed. Their faces showed no expression, but Lenny soon discovered it was the look of shock. All evening, he heard comments like, "I was so surprised to see the pony on the hayrack and even more surprised when he jumped off!" Everyone seemed to get a big kick out of discussing the moment. Even Uncle Alvin witnessed the event with a smile on his face. Lenny couldn't quite guess what things the Amish would approve of. He thought that his idea might be considered to showy, but for some reason, nobody took it that way. They all seemed to know that Junior's boys were always involved in some adventure, not being show-offs. Lenny was sure that if he had been the one on Dusty, it would have seemed different, and he was glad he hadn't tried it.

Leah was there but made a clear effort to not even look in Lenny's direction. Rebecca, on the other hand, was right beside him all evening. She made sure to be next to him while playing volley ball, even bumping into him when they both went to hit it at once. Rebecca laughed her horse-sounding nicker every time Lenny said anything funny. Leah was on the other side of the net most of the time. At one point, Lenny ran after a ball that was hit a distance from the game. Just as he came around a bush, he bumped into a girl. She let out a, "yeow!" Lenny looked up, and there stood Leah, hands on hips, glaring at him. It was shadowy, away from the lanterns, and far enough that the others couldn't hear. As he picked up the ball, he said under his breath, "Catbird!"

"What did you call me?"

Lenny threw the ball back in. "You remind me of a catbird."

"What is that supposed to mean?"

"Well, when I first met you, you were always happy and energetic, like a catbird singing in the spring. But now you just yowl like a summer catbird."

Leah looked at Lenny for a moment, as if surprised. He saw an angry look appear, and then a tear formed in the corner of her eye. Her lower lip began to tremble, and she walked toward Alvin's house. The young man felt terrible; he wanted to follow her in, wrap his arms around her, and hold her close. None of that was possible. He wished he had never called her catbird, but now that it was said, there was nothing he could do about it. It was done.

Uncle Alvin and Aunt Lydia sat on their porch swing throughout the evening, watching the teenagers play volleyball. Lenny passed close by, and Aunt Lydia spoke to him. "It looks like you're having fun here with the young folks?"

"I am. I really did want to come back to the Bulltown area. I'm glad it worked out."

Aunt Lydia smiled. Uncle Alvin cleared his throat, and Lenny knew he had something to say.

"I've been thinking … maybe we should send Perry, our mares, and crossbreds over to help you finish working up those fields of Noey's?" He stopped talking and looked at Lenny for a bit, but Lenny didn't know how to respond. Alvin cleared his voice again and added, "It's getting awfully late for him to plant. If I sent Perry to help out, would you be willing to come back with him to help make hay later this week?"

"That would be great!" Lenny tried to hide just how excited he was about it.

Alvin seemed pleased and told him, "You could bring Tug and Train with you. We will be helping Harold make hay, most likely on Thursday, and then they would help us on Friday."

Lenny couldn't believe his luck. He tried to make it sound as though he was mostly happy about Perry coming to help. "Noey will really appreciate this! If we could get everything disced and harrowed by Thursday, Davy and Noey could probably plant with a tractor while we're making hay."

That's what I was thinking!" Alvin was grinning about his good plan. Aunt Lydia was nodding her head in approval. As Lenny walked away Alvin called, "I will send Perry over in the morning!"

"Thanks!" Lenny called back and hurried to join the young people.

Everyone seemed to be having a grand time, except Davy W. He had shown up late without a straw hat. As an outsider, Lenny wanted to fit in and couldn't imagine why Davy W. didn't care if he did. All the boys seemed content to wear suspenders. The girls all looked happy to have long Amish dresses with aprons and crisp white prayer coverings. Everyone seemed willing to comply with the rules. Lenny eyed Davy W. resentfully; he wanted to scold him. Then he remembered what Herbie had said about how Leah liked Davy W. and felt a wave of guilt sweep over him. Maybe if he had done the right thing and told Davy W. and Leah what he knew, they would both be happy.

Lenny and Herbie put on a show with Dusty again when it was time to leave. The whole group of young people watched as Lenny drove Tug and Train, maneuvering them perfectly into that low spot. Just as they passed through the dip, Herbie rode Dusty, galloping toward the hayrack. The little pony barely needed to jump as the back end of Lenny's hayrack dipped low and Dusty clomped aboard. Everyone there was laughing as Tug and Train pranced out of the lane, Dusty standing contentedly like a dog going for a ride in a pickup bed.

Davy W.

Davy W. was already home when Lenny got back. He put his horses away and quietly slipped upstairs, trying not to wake Noey and Ruth. He had seen Davy in the kitchen reading a paper when he passed through, but they didn't speak to each other.

Lenny sat in his room alone; he looked over at his Bible laying on a nightstand. Before getting to know Grandpa, he thought of the Bible in the same way he thought of the Amish—harsh and strict. Both seemed to be a plain, black-and-white, unfriendly world. After everything that happened two summers back, the Bible and the Amish world both seemed vividly full of life and color. Fields had seemed bare when he first went out to farm with horses. After a summer of it, he found that those fields were teeming with life. In much the same way, a once dull and boring Bible seemed to be alive. During the past year of college, reading the Bible had been overlooked. He wanted to read it, but it was hard to get started again, especially since he hadn't kept up his end of the relationship with God. Lenny looked back at his nightstand. The Bible lay there, patiently waiting to be opened. He decided to start reading its pages again tomorrow.

All at once, there was a loud clumping sound, it almost scared Lenny, but then he realized it was Davy W. running up the steps. When Davy W. came in the room, they didn't speak to each other right away. Lenny had been planning to turn down the lantern, but he left it burning, so Davy W. could see. Lenny wanted to talk to his cousin about staying Amish but wasn't sure how to get that conversation started. He lay back staring at one spot on the ceiling as though if he looked close enough, he could read the perfect words to tell Davy W. Finally, his cousin got in bed and said, "Turn that lantern off, will ya?"

It got completely dark in their room. In some way, that gave Lenny a little more courage to say what he wanted. He started by asking a question. "Davy, why don't you just wear suspenders?"

"What?"

"Well, I'm only saying that because, you know, Mose came by and got after Noey about you breaking the rules. I'm thinking it wouldn't be that hard to just do it." It became as quiet as it was dark. Lenny began to wish he hadn't said anything.

After a long agonizing silence, Davy spoke again. "I don't have Amish in my blood like you do."

His answer sent Lenny's mind into a tailspin. A young man who grew up Amish telling a guy who didn't even know Dutch that he had more Amish in him seemed strange. Davy W.'s words dismantled everything Lenny had planned to say. If he pushed Davy W. to follow the rules, he would sound like an Amish preacher. Lenny decided to try another angle. "I understand what it's like not knowing who your real father is. For years, I didn't know who my dad was."

"I know who my real dad is, and he's a jerk!"

"You do?"

"Yeah, he's a no-good alcoholic and refused to marry my mom, so she gave me up for adoption."

Lenny winced in the darkness, knowing Davy W. couldn't see his face. He was stumped again by Davy W.'s response. Instead of giving him the lecture he had planned, Lenny only said, "Huh, I didn't know that."

Chapter 7

BEST FRIENDS

Acool morning mist hung over Lenny's field. Tug, Train, Jim, Stone, and Noey's crossbreds stood quietly, waiting for a signal, as the non-Amish horseman knelt under an oak tree, adjusting heel chains. Clattering of steel wheels combined with thundering hooves brought a smile to Lenny's face while he watched Perry pull in Noey's lane with a four-horse hitch. Lenny could see Uncle Noey meeting Perry at the hitching rack and pointing toward his disc near the machine shed, sending Perry off with his four horses. Lenny was glad that he was going to finish plowing himself; he had been hoping to be able to have that sense of accomplishment. However, he was glad to have some help discing.

Lenny's team finished a row of plowing before Perry met him in the field. "I guess I'll start discing at this end while you finish up over there," Perry called.

Lenny told his horses, "Whoa," and headed over to talk to his cousin. He knelt down and drew a map in the soil. "I have to finish this end over here." He drew a line on one side of his map. "If you angle back and forth like this"—Lenny made angled lines at the other end—"I think I can finish plowing this field this afternoon. Junior's son, Barefoot Herbie, is coming over with his disc this afternoon. He can start in the middle and finish my end." Perry nodded in agreement. Lenny concluded, "I will start harrowing if I'm done before you guys."

"And if I finish my end first, I'll go to harrowing." Perry's eyes were smiling as usual.

Lenny started to head back to his horses but stopped short and said, "By the way, there's a guy who drives a huge, red pickup truck by here every day. It's super loud and scares the colts all the time, so I'm just warning you. It may scare Bell or the crossbreds." Perry waived his hand, showing that he understood.

After a solid hour of plowing, Lenny's team was making good progress. Perry and his horses seemed to be making good time at the other end with their disc. Friendly sounds came out of the top of an oak tree. Lenny listened for a while. He squinted, searching the limbs, until he saw a small gray bird singing out a happy tune. "There's that catbird again," Lenny told his horses. "Now, whenever I hear a catbird singing, I think of Leah." And then he looked around nervously to see if perhaps Fannie Ella was close by.

Time seemed to go by faster with so much activity in one field. Perry's team of four horses was moving along smoothly, and everything looked peaceful. Birds sang in big trees on the bluffs bordering Noey's farm. Rabbits hopped along field edges, nibbling on grasses. Weeds that smelled like sweet onions released a final dose of their aroma as they got plowed under. And then it started—a rumbling sound came up from the timber. Lenny knew it was that big red truck and felt sure his draft-horse hitch was going to be fine, but he worried about how it would go for Perry. Calling his horses to a stop, Lenny tied them to a fence in case he needed to help his cousin. As he hurried over plowed ground, he kept an eye out for a flash of red. The rumbling got louder, turning into a roar. Bell's head was held high; her nostrils flared. Lenny tried running, hopping over dirt clods, but as he got near to Perry, he realized that the big red truck wasn't getting any closer. "I think that guy is stuck," Perry said as Bell stomped and the crossbreds pranced in place. Perry tied his team to the fence, and the boys headed toward the growling sound.

A few steps later, they could see the big, red truck stuck in a low area off to one side of the gravel road, wheels spinning. Perry whispered, as if the guy may hear them, "What is he doing over there off the road?"

"I think he does that on purpose. He loves to see how far he can push it without getting stuck."

Perry's eyes were twinkling at the sight. "I think he just crossed that line!" Both boys laughed heartily.

Lenny suggested, "Why don't we take Tug, Train, Stone, and Jim down there and pull him out?"

"Let's watch for a while first and see if he can get himself out," Perry quipped, and they both laughed again.

Lenny headed off anyway; he wanted a chance to see his four heavy horses really pull something. Lenny un-hitched his crossbreds because he didn't trust them around the big truck. He unhooked his evener from his plow and drove his horses to where there was a gate, and then headed up the gravel road, his steel evener rattling. The big, red truck growled and sputtered, throwing mud thirty-feet into the air, trying to free itself. Lenny eyed the scene as he got closer, hoping the guy couldn't get himself out. Perry jumped the fence and joined Lenny, walking behind their huge team of four. All four horses held their heads high, not too fond of all the racket, but they obediently walked directly toward the terrible growls.

When they were beside it, the driver noticed them and wound down his window. He had a frustrated sound in his voice as he called to them, "I think I'm stuck good! I'm gonna have to call someone with a big tractor!"

Lenny called back over the deep rumbling of the truck's idling engine, "Won't need a big tractor; we're gonna get you out with these horses!"

The guy shut down his engine so they could talk, but he didn't get out, maybe because he was surrounded by mud. "Thanks, boys, but I don't want you to hurt your horses. Ain't no way those plow horses are gonna budge this truck!"

Perry looked at Lenny and said quietly, "Maybe they can't?"

Lenny answered them both. "These guys can do it. How about a bet?"

The young man in the pickup seemed interested in a bet. "How much?"

"Not money," Lenny said. "If we can pull it out, you've gotta do me a big favor."

"What?"

"You gotta promise you won't rev up your engine when you drive by my field."

The guy laughed. "Okay, what if you can't do it?"

"Then we go get my uncle's tractor and pull you out ... and my cousin and I wash your truck!"

"Ha, ha, well, quit wasting my time, hurry up and give those ponies a try. And then you can go get that tractor!"

Lenny felt his fist clinch behind his back, and then he asked the guy, "Do you have a chain?"

"In the bed of my truck!" Perry hustled up to the back bumper and found a heavy log chain and waded out in the mud at the front end of the massive vehicle. In a moment, he had it hooked on. "Do you want me to start my truck and try to help these ponies, or will that be too scary?"

"I don't think they need any help."

The guy in the truck said, "If they don't get it right away, I'll start it up, and they will pull it out trying to run off!"

Perry surprised Lenny by agreeing. "Yeah, that may work!"

Lenny shook his head. "NO, if they can't do it, I'll go get my uncle's tractor, and you win! But put that thing in neutral."

The guy looked offended and snarled, "I'm not that dumb!"

Tug and Train were the lead team in the middle; Stone and Jim were on either side. Lenny watched them as they backed to the truck. He felt sure they could pull out an army tank if they tried. Before he let them pull, Lenny looked over everything carefully, making sure he had a good angle. He clucked and his horses stepped forward. The chain wasn't quite tight before they moved, and when his horses felt it come against, they stopped pulling.

The guy in the truck called down, laughing, "Go get Uncle's tractor! I told you, boy; there ain't no way they can touch this thing!"

Lenny's feelings were getting hurt, and he snapped back, "You need to hold your horses; we haven't even tried it yet!"

"Oh, tough guy! Okay, but hurry up. I don't have all day."

On the second attempt, Lenny asked the guy, "Would you mind turning your wheels a little...out toward the road? Then when we get it moving, turn 'em back and straighten them."

"Don't you mean if we get it moving?"

Lenny didn't respond but backed his team again. This time he angled them across the road where they were almost heading down hill and had better footing. He made sure to draw the log chain tight and that all four horses' heel chains were snug. Lenny called loud, "GET, BOYS...GET...GET...GET!" All four heavy horses heaved at once. Out of the corner of his eye, Lenny saw the big red truck lurch forward. Without pulling his driving lines, Lenny turned his team by calling, "Step, Train … Step, Train!" That turned his team in Train's direction and gave his horses a little slack as they turned, but immediately they came against again. Just as they did, Lenny called, "GET, BOYS … GET!" They all leaned again, arching their necks, muscles rippling in their hind quarters. The truck's driver actually cooperated by turning with the team, which helped pull the wheels out of holes they had dug. All at once, everything jerked forward and moved easily, as if the horses were pulling a wagon down the road. Lenny didn't stop them right away but let his horses trot a little just to show off.

When they came to a stop, the guy jumped down out of his huge red truck. Lenny almost laughed when he saw how small the guy was; he had looked so big up in his monster truck. The little guy hurried over to the Amish boys. "Man, those horses are the bomb!" Perry and Lenny grinned, but didn't say anything. "No, I'm serious. Those horses really are the bomb. I gotta get me some of those big horses some day!"

Lenny smiled. "Thanks … we like 'em!"

"Could you, guys, give my friends a horse-drawn wagon ride sometime?"

Perry piped up, "Sure, when?" Lenny tried to give Perry a look that meant, "Don't offer that," but it was too late.

The little guy said, "This Friday, we are having a party up by Yoder Towers. Maybe you could swing by there and give us a little hayride or something?"

Perry spoke up again. "Perfect. I live up near there, and Lenny is going right past Yoder Towers on Friday anyway!"

Lenny wanted to tell Perry to keep quiet, but instead he said, "Yeah, that should work out great."

The little guy shook Lenny's hand and told him, "Thanks, and I won't rev my engine anymore when I drive by your horses."

Lenny gave a big smile and a thanks.

Nicknames

After dinner, they switched out horses on Lenny's hitch. Misty, Mr. E, and Queen took over for Noey's crossbreds and Train. Lenny also switched things up, making Stone and Jim his lead team. Because of Queen being in the hitch, Train got a break, having walked in the plow furrow all morning. Stone took his turn in the furrow; Tug, who had been to the left of Train on solid ground, took his turn walking in dirt clods with Mr. E on his right, also on plowed ground. Jim, on the left of Stone, got a turn on sod. Queen, to Jim's left, and Misty, on the outside, made up the third horse walking on the grass. Lenny wanted to make Misty walk in dirt clods to give her a workout, but he didn't want to make Queen work that hard, and she needed to be beside Misty.

The horses had barely gotten into a rhythm when Lenny looked across his plowed field and saw that Herbie was pulling up near

Perry with his team of Percherons, Prince and Duke. He could see his cousin explaining their plan of action to Herbie. On one pass— Herbie was close enough—Lenny called to him, "Thanks for giving us a hand!" Herbie gave a thumbs-up and continued with his work.

Lenny couldn't help but smile as he looked across his field adorned with three teams of Percherons. His own six horses were plowing perfectly. Even Misty and Mr. E acted like they enjoyed being part of such a big field day. In an effort to go easy on his oldest horse, Queen, Lenny hooked her heel chains loose. He knew that if he hitched his colt and filly in the third link of their heel chains— as Grandpa always called "drop two," meaning two links were dangling—then they would have to pull most of the load. Queen, on the other hand, would be hooked on her last link. If she walked even with the other horses, she would be barely pulling. At first, it seemed to be working. The colt and filly were working hard and starting to sweat, while Queen looked fresh. As time went by, Queen kept leaning forward, taking on more of the load.

After a while, Lenny noticed that Queen was way up ahead of the colt and filly.

"Queen, why can't you just relax? I'm gonna have to hitch you more even with the others because you are walking so far ahead." Lenny re-hooked her heel chains one link closer and set his horses back to motion with a cluck. Queen wasn't up ahead as much as before but still leaning forward. "Queen, you're not happy unless you are pulling a big share of the load, are ya?" Her ears twitched back and forth when he said her name. "Now I know why Junior's boys laughed at me when I said I wasn't going to work you as hard as the others."

Finally, Lenny felt that all his horses were working perfectly together. He began to notice how similar Misty and Mr. E looked as they stepped high on either end of his big hitch. They were about the same age, size, and same shade of black. He told them, "Mr. E and Misty, I'm almost sure you two are related."

The horseman stopped his six-horse hitch under the big oak tree for a shady break. He walked around the front of the line of horses and looked them over. They all puffed, catching their wind. Even though all six horses were tired, the colts continued to hold their heads high. Lenny talked to Misty. "You sure seem happier now that Mama is here with ya." He checked her harness and smoothed a hand over her neck. "I still don't know how you'll act when that big red truck comes by?" Lenny looked over at Mr. E and said, "Someday, I want to see you two colts hitched together as a team. I think you two are going to match perfectly!"

His horses stood under their shade tree enjoying a break. Perry and Herbie stopped their horses under a tree at the opposite end of the field. Lenny laughed when he thought about how everyone called Herbie, Barefoot Herbie, because he never wore shoes. Glancing up toward the house, Lenny saw Davy W. strolling across the yard, shirttail hanging out with no suspenders. Lenny looked at his resting horses and told them, "I don't know why that Davy doesn't want to wear his suspenders. You all wear harness without complaining. Suspenders don't bother me. What's the difference between a belt or suspenders? We need to come up with a nickname for him … something like 'Loose Pants Davy.'" Lenny laughed at his own joke, and then said, "I wonder if they got a nickname for me." He turned, heading back to his plow seat and almost tripped over Fannie Ella. "Would you quit sneaking up on me, little girl!"

She smiled and said, "Horse Pull Lenny."

"What was that?"

"You said, 'I wonder if they have a nickname for me.' They do. All the young folks call you Horse Pull Lenny."

Lenny was stunned. "Most of them don't even know who I am, do they?"

"Everyone knows who you are. They all know about the horse pull and about you dragging that burning shed off Harold's Johnny with Tug and Train."

"Huh, I didn't know that." Fannie Ella seemed pleased that she knew something important. He told her, "I was just noticing how much these colts look and act alike. Can you see that? These colts on either end of my hitch look like they would make a perfect team."

Fannie Ella answered matter-of-factly, "Well, they are half brother and sister."

"What? Why do you think that?"

"I don't think that, I know that."

Lenny shook his head and told her, "We named the colt Mr. E—from the word 'mystery'—because we didn't know who his daddy was." Lenny stared at the young Amish girl waiting for some kind of explanation.

She smiled, looking smug that she knew something else he didn't. "Last summer, we figured it out! Alvin's boys were at our place and saw Misty. They told us about Mr. E, and my dad told them that both colts had San Hosea for a daddy." I guess your grandpa knew it, but he never told anyone else before he died."

"Why didn't you tell me sooner?" Lenny asked almost mad.

The little girl had an ornery grin. "You didn't ask!"

Lenny gathered his driving lines. His horses all stirred; they seemed to know that he was ready to get back to work. Fannie Ella stood and watched while Lenny clucked and set off plowing again. She followed, walking behind his plow seat. She didn't say anything until he got to the end of the field closest to her home. "Herbie wanted me to come tell you something."

"What's that?"

"He said to tell you that he went to fetch your car parts this morning. He can fix your car when you're done with this field."

"Oh, okay, thanks for telling me." She headed off and Lenny called to her, "Thanks for telling me about the colts, too!"

She climbed the fence and disappeared into the timber between her place and his.

Three Teams

The remainder of the day played out like a majestic scene from a movie. Lenny watched twelve horses working in three teams. They walked peacefully against a backdrop of forested bluffs on one side, a wooded river bottom on the other, and Noey's beautiful homestead at the far end. All made even better because he was working with two of his favorite guys in the whole world, and they were helping him prepare Noey's field for planting. As soon as Lenny's horses finished the last furrow, he un-hooked his team from the plow and hurried them over to a waiting harrow. After plowing, it was clearly easy work for six horses to pull the much lighter harrow. Perry finished his discing and hooked on a second harrow that Uncle Noey brought out with a tractor. Herbie continued on with a small disc and his team of two, while Perry's four horses and Lenny's six harrowed swiftly. They all seemed to finish at about the same time and pulled all the horses up under Lenny's huge shade tree, smiling.

"Thanks, guys!" Lenny said with a big grin. "I'm so happy we finished this field. Tomorrow, Perry and I are going to help Harold Yoder's make hay, and then on Friday, we make hay at Alvin's. This way Noey and Davy W. can get this field planted with a tractor while I'm gone."

The other two didn't say anything but nodded, looking pleased. Herbie asked, "Did Fannie Ella tell ya about me getting the car parts?"

"Yeah, she did!"

Herbie looked excited. "Come over when you're done with your chores and help me finish mine. I'll come back here with you guys, and we can fix your Impala this evening." Perry nodded, his eyes smiling, always ready to be part of whatever was going on.

It didn't take long for Perry and Lenny to do their small amount of chores, which mostly entailed brushing and un-harnessing draft horses. Russell trotted among the big horses' legs, hot on the trail of some imaginary prey, or maybe the real scent of a rat. As the young men passed the house, Aunt Ruth came out and asked, "Where are you both off to now?"

"We promised Herbie that we would help him with his chores, since he helped us in our field," Lenny answered.

"Well, here are some cookies to tide you over until supper." Ruth smiled, obviously pleased that they were all working together. Perry, Lenny, and Russell almost ran through the woods toward Junior's place, eating deliciously sweet cookies as they went. They stopped for a moment by Herbie's bees to watch them shoot out of their hive just above head height. They were spellbound until Blue and Tick noticed them and came romping up howling, sending Russell into a barking frenzy of his own. The barking dogs snapped them out of their trance, and they hurried into Junior's barn. Milking was in full swing. Perry and Lenny jumped right in helping wherever they could. When they were finished milking the last black-and-white cow, Herbie took a glass off the ledge over the bulk tank milk cooler. They took turns drinking ice-cold milk dipped out with a ladle.

While Perry and Lenny waited on the house porch for Herbie, little Elma teetered up to Lenny with a mason jar. She was trying to open it but couldn't. She lifted it up with pleading eyes toward Lenny. He took it from her small hands and had to work hard to twist the cap off. When he finally succeeded, he spun it open and pulled the lid off. A terrible stench rose out of the jar, filling the air around Lenny and Elma. Elma wrinkled her little nose and said, "Fatza!"

The sound of big boys trying to keep from laughing came from just inside the screen door. At first, there were a few snorts, then snickers, and finally all-out belly laughs. Lenny looked at little Elma, baffled. "What just happened?"

Fannie Ella came up to see what was going on and fanned her hand in front of her face. Elma repeated, "Fatza." This inspired a whole new round of laughter from inside.

Fannie Ella looked at Lenny with pity and interpreted, "My brothers tricked you. They tooted in that jar, and then got Elma to bring it to you. The smell stays in there until someone opens it."

Lenny, Perry, and Fannie Ella couldn't help but laugh, and even little Elma giggled.

All three—Herbie, Perry, and Lenny—ran back to Noey's place with little Russell at their heels. They snuck into the corncrib and got to work on the car. While Herbie worked on the Impala, Perry asked Lenny questions. "Do you miss driving a car?"

"Not really. I mean it is fun to drive a car … but I'd rather drive a team of horses."

Both Perry and Herbie looked at Lenny with a surprised expression. Perry asked, "I guess you miss having electricity and watching TV and all that, though, huh?"

Lenny pulled on his suspenders while he thought about how to answer. "Yeah, I guess sometimes I do." Nobody said anything for a few moments, then Lenny added, "I've been having a lot of fun here, though. I guess I forgot about all of that."

Perry questioned him again. "It seems like once a guy got used to having a car and a TV, he wouldn't want to give that all up?"

"You're not thinking about jumping the fence, are you?" Lenny teased his cousin.

Perry smiled and said, "No, just wondering."

Herbie had been making grunting noises as he worked under Lenny's Impala, but then things got quiet, and he slid out from under it. He stood up and wiped his hands on a rag.

Lenny bit his lip and then asked, "Can't you fix it?"

Herbie laughed. "No, it's fixed."

"You fixed it already?"

"Yep!"

The Ride

The boys stood looking at the car, and then at each other, until Perry said what the others were thinking. "Let's take it for a ride!"

Lenny stepped out of the corn crib and looked up toward the house. He came back in and said, "I don't want Noey and Ruth to see us drive out of here in my car." The others nodded that they understood. Lenny whispered, "Hey, guys, I just got a great idea, though. Why don't we pull this car out through the field with Tug and Train?"

Perry got a huge grin and nodded his approval. Herbie stepped out of the crib and looked around. He came back with a straight face, and Lenny assumed his friend didn't like the idea. He said with a sober tone, "Get a log-chain." Instantly, Lenny wished he hadn't suggested it, but his friends seemed determined at this point.

A few moments later, they had Tug and Train harnessed and hooked to the Impala. Lenny got in his car, steering, while Herbie drove the team. Perry followed along on foot, making sure everything was going all right. The big horses quietly pulled the Impala across the edge of Lenny's field, behind the cover of some trees. When they got to where there was a gate leading out to the road, Perry unhooked the chain, and Herbie tied the team to the fence. Both Amish boys climbed in the car beside Lenny. Perry sat the middle and Herbie by the other window.

Lenny started up his car and drove out onto the gravel road. "Good job, Herbie, I think it's running perfectly!" The Amish boys both had big smiles as they wound down the windows and Lenny sped off.

There was a buggy coming opposite them, and Lenny thought quick enough to say, "Guys, take your hats off. I don't want anyone to notice it's us!" They all tossed their straw hats in the back seat.

Perry laughed. "Good thing we took our hats off; I think that was Bishop Mose in that buggy!"

Herbie said calmly, "Yep, it sure was."

Lenny got a sick feeling in his stomach, afraid they were going to be found out, and he didn't want to disappoint Noey. He thought

about what Junior, Herbie's dad, would think, and then of what
Uncle Alvin would say.

Herbie asked Lenny, "Could you take us over to McDonald's?"

"Sure!" Lenny heard himself say as he turned onto the pavement
and headed toward the interstate, driving to the hamburger place,
where he had stopped before the big storm.

Perry asked Lenny, "Can you turn on some country music?"

"Okay," Lenny turned on his radio, and country music came
pouring out of the speakers. It sounded clear and smooth. A nice
rhythm mixed with harmonies filled the car, both Amish boys
obviously enjoying it more than Lenny, who couldn't wait to get back
to Noey's safe and sound. They pulled up at McDonald's and saw a
huge red pickup parked there.

Perry exclaimed, "Hey, that Justin guy we pulled out today
is in here!"

Herbie looked surprised. "What happened?"

Perry told him, "The guy that owns this big truck got it stuck
down near Noey's field today. Lenny pulled him out with Tug, Train,
Stone, and Jim. You should have seen it, Herbie! I didn't think they
could do it, but Lenny did some great driving and pulled that monster
truck out." Herbie looked at Lenny to see if it was true. Lenny felt
his face flush; he didn't know what to say. Herbie laughed. "Nice!"

The Amish boys instinctively grabbed their hats and put them
back on. Lenny left his on the back seat, not having the same
background. They headed in and Herbie stepped up to the counter

and placed an order without any hesitation. Perry hung back. Lenny asked, "What do you want, Perry?"

"I don't need anything ... I don't have any money anyway."

"I'll buy you something, Perry. What do you want?" Lenny insisted. The boy shrugged his shoulders and wouldn't say. Lenny told the girl at the counter, "I'm buying for all of us. Give me a couple of number one meals."

They got their food and went to sit down, and Justin spotted them. "HEY, here's my buddies!" he called out. Lenny winced, having hoped not to attract any attention. Justin was with a group of teenagers. He told them, "These Amish guys pulled out my truck with horses today!"

When he said it, Lenny noticed that Justin had cauliflower ears, and he remembered that Justin was the guy he saw on his first day in the area. It flashed into his mind that he had overheard a girl telling him that she was going to have a baby. Lenny looked at the group of teenagers, and that same girl was with them. She eyed Lenny when he looked at her.

Justin said, "Hey, sit here with us!"

The three Amish boys sat near the group of teenagers, and the English kids weren't shy at all. "So, did you guys drive a buggy here?"

"No, we took Lenny's car." Perry nodded at Lenny, and the young people all looked at him and started laughing.

One of them said, "Oh, we got a wild Amish guy here, huh?"

"No, he's not Amish. He's my cousin, and he's just visiting for the summer."

Perry's words stunned the group of English young people, and they all looked at Lenny, as if trying to figure out how that could be.

Justin changed the subject to Lenny's relief. He told his friends, "This guy promised he would give us all a hayride with his horses this Friday up by Yoder Feeds."

The group of English young people all got excited about it, but Lenny started worrying. He ate his food while Herbie asked Justin questions about his big truck. Justin and Herbie hit it off right away, both being interested in engines. The English kids were continually cussing and talking about getting drunk.

Lenny realized he was biting his lip and told Herbie and Perry, "We gotta get back before anyone notices we're gone."

All the English kids laughed out loud, and Lenny wished he hadn't said that. He knew he embarrassed his Amish friends and himself. They got up to leave and one of the girls said, "See you guys on Friday!" The Amish boys nodded sheepishly and headed out.

Lenny sped out of the parking lot, not stopping until he heard a loud screeching sound. He slammed on his brakes, just barely missing a car on the highway. Herbie and Perry laughed but Lenny felt sick.

Perry asked, "This has to make you miss driving a car, doesn't it, Lenny?"

"Sometimes. But to tell you the truth, I was really missing driving a team of horses before I came back to stay here."

Perry and Herbie looked surprised again. Perry questioned him further. "What about air-conditioning or phones? You probably really miss all of that, too?"

"Hum, I guess, but I've been so busy at Noey's, I haven't had a chance to think about it."

Herbie had been listening quietly but added a question of his own. "How about your English friends? I bet you miss your best friend."

"I've never really had a best friend. My two buddies, Brad and Nathan, are each other's best friends, and they let me hang out with them if I want."

Herbie and Perry got really quiet. They didn't seem to be able to grasp what kind of world their English friend came from.

Herbie told them, "I don't think I'll ever leave the Amish . . . but if I did, I would want a car like this one."

"Well, I'd be happy to trade with you, for your horse Smoky!" Lenny teased, and all three of them laughed.

Lenny's mind was set on getting his Amish friends back home safe and sound without anyone finding out about him taking them for a ride in a car. As they crossed the river bridge, they looked over into dark swirling waters.

Perry told the others, "I sure wish we could go swimming in the river again."

Herbie laughed. "The river is too full right now; it would be dangerous."

And Lenny agreed. "You couldn't pay me enough to swim in that water!"

The Impala raced toward Noey's and coasted in through the gate beside the waiting team of horses. Perry helped hook the log chain on again. They quietly pulled the car back to its hiding place in the corn crib. As Herbie got ready to leave, Lenny told him, "I will pay you for fixing my car, Herbie."

"You already bought me a meal at McDonald's!"

Lenny said, "Well, let me know what I owe Hershey for the parts."

Herbie laughed as he trotted off. "It's no big deal. I already paid for it, the least I could do for my good friend."

Shunned

Perry and Lenny headed up toward the house and realized there was a buggy at the hitching rack. Perry told Lenny soberly, "That's Bishop Mose's buggy. He's been here the whole time we were gone."

Lenny's heart sank. He didn't want to go in, but he knew they couldn't stay outside any longer. The boys took their hats and shoes off in the wash room, cleaned up, and walked in. Russell rushed past the young men and somehow found Bishop Mose's pant leg. The dog took it in his teeth, growling ferociously. Lenny quickly grabbed his little friend and apologized. "I'm so sorry about that. I forgot that Russell followed us in."

Bishop Mose straightened out his pant leg but didn't respond to Lenny's apology. Ruth and Noey looked appalled that Russell had attacked Mose again. Ruth said stiffly, "Please, Leonard, take that dog out of here."

However, Lenny was sure he saw a twinkle in his aunt's eye even as she said it. He got the feeling she almost enjoyed Russell's outburst. There were two other men with Mose, and they all looked at Lenny with hard faces as he headed upstairs, with Perry following.

They found Davy W. in his room, lying on the floor, listening to the men talking through the floor vent.

Lenny whispered, "What's going on?"

Davy W. got up and sat on his bed. "Well, they're just about to shun Noey."

"Because of me?" Lenny asked, not trying to hide his concern.

Davy W. laughed. "No, because of me."

"Oh, good!" Lenny said with relief, then caught himself, "I mean, really ... bummer."

"Yeah, I'm being shunned. And if I don't leave, Noey and Ruth will get shunned, too."

For the first time, Lenny saw Davy W. look upset. Perry was as white as a ghost; his face gave away just how serious this all was. Davy W. started gathering an armful of his things into a pile on his bed while Perry and Lenny watched without talking. Finally, Lenny asked, "Where will you go?"

Davy W. tried to sound tough. "I got friends up in River City."

Perry and Lenny sat on the other bed, stunned, not sure what to say. When they heard the men leaving and the door close, Davy W. got up, took his things, and left. The set of cousins sat for a long time without saying anything. Perry coughed and Lenny looked to see if everything was okay. Perry coughed harder, covering his face with his pillow.

"Perry, are you okay?" The young man was holding his stomach and writhing. Lenny started to panic. "Perry, Perry, what's the matter?" The younger cousin pulled back his pillow, and the older cousin realized that he was witnessing a laughing fit.

"Did you see Bishop Mose's face when Russell grabbed his pant leg?" Perry sputtered out, trying to keep quiet so Noey and Ruth wouldn't hear him laughing.

Lenny felt a wave of relief sweep over him, happy that his young cousin was okay. He told Perry, "That is the third time Mose has come over here and Russell has done that same thing every time!"

The younger boy motioned for his older cousin to keep his voice down by holding one finger to his mouth even while he laughed uncontrollably, holding his belly and rolling on the bed. Russell sat watching Perry laugh. The little dog cocked his head to one side as though trying to figure out what was so funny. That made Lenny laugh, which in turn made Russell bark.

Aunt Ruth called up the stairs. "Is everything okay up there?"

Lenny quickly gathered himself and opened his bedroom door, calling down as soberly as he could, "Sorry, Ruth, Russell got a little wound up with Perry being here and all. We will get to sleep now."

"Do you and Perry need some supper?"

"Oh, no, we already ate with Herbie."

Lenny said, "Good night," and went back into his room. He looked at Perry and said, "I feel bad for Noey and Ruth. Davy has caused them so much heartache."

Perry nodded and added, "I wish there could have been something good happen for Davy; something that would have given him a reason to stay Amish."

Perry's words came down on Lenny like a sword, cutting him to the core of his being, knowing that he could have helped Davy W. He didn't dare to even look at Perry, feeling that if their eyes met, everything would be known. Finally, Lenny said, "We'd better get to sleep. We got to get going early to make hay at Harold's."

Perry nodded and they blew out the lantern and went to sleep.

Chapter 8

HAROLD'S GIRLS

As soon as Lenny heard Freddie the rooster crow, he jumped out of bed. His heart instantly began racing as he thought about going to Harold's place to help make hay. It reminded him of how he felt when his family got up to go on vacation when he was a kid. Perry heard Lenny and stood right up, gathering his things. Lenny pulled on his broad fall pants and looped his suspenders over his shoulders. He tried pulling on socks as he walked toward the steps and stumbled. Russell barked at him as though he could tell something fun was going to happen.

Aunt Ruth was already working in her kitchen when Lenny walked through. "You better eat something before you go!"

"Oh, I'll be fine."

"You go hitch up your horses; I will bring you and Perry fried egg sandwiches to eat on your way."

"Mmmm, that actually sounds really good!"

He glanced at his aunt. She was smiling and said quietly, "Well." Ruth followed the dog and boys out the door. "Leonard, maybe you should take that dog with you to Alvin's. He's used to sleeping with Davy; he may be lonely if he is upstairs by himself."

Lenny nodded. "Okay that will be fun!"

In short order, Lenny had all of his horses fed, brushed, and turned back out to pasture. Moments later, he had Tug and Train all harnessed and hitched to the fore cart. He helped Perry hitch his four horses to Alvin's fore cart. As they clattered past the house, Aunt Ruth came hurrying out with a little sack and a thermos jug for each of the boys. "I put two fried egg sandwiches in there, and here is some garden tea."

Lenny said, "Thanks, but you are too good to me."

Ruth looked surprised to hear him say that and replied, "Well, I hope you have fun."

The young man felt guilty as his horses trotted out of Noey and Ruth's lane. His aunt and uncle were both very kind, and he had let them down by not getting Davy W. and Leah together. Russell stood on the footboard while Tug and Train trotted merrily along the road toward Yoder Towers.

Lenny told his dog, "Poor Noey and Ruth are going to be so lonely now that Davy's gone." Russell cocked his head sideways and looked up, eyebrows twitching. "And now you and I are going to be at

Alvin's for a couple of days. Ruth's house is going to seem so empty." Russell's dark eyes glistened, fixed on Lenny while he spoke. Perry was only a short distance ahead with Babe, Bell, and his crossbreds. The temporarily Amish fellow couldn't help but enjoy watching his big horses trot along steadily, his view even more scenic with a four-horse hitch ahead of them.

Lenny took out an egg sandwich. It was so good on perfectly toasted homemade bread, but he felt more guilty with every bite. He washed it down with Ruth's wonderfully sweet garden tea, yet it was hard to swallow because of her kindness and his failure to help Davy W. He determined within himself to make it right when he saw Leah.

Yoder Towers cast shadows on the horses and boys when they trotted by. Tug and Train headed past Hershey's, and Lenny saw Jerry outside loading pop in the machine. Lenny slowed his horses to a walk and called, "Jerry, we got my car put back together!"

Jerry looked up and grinned. "You should drive it up here sometime, so I can see it!"

Lenny gave him a thumbs-up and continued on his way. Soon, Uncle Alvin's place was in view. The young man felt his usual twinge of excitement when he saw that place. It was such a pretty farm and held good memories.

Tug and Train tried to head to their home, but Lenny held their bits, turning them toward Harold's instead. "Don't worry, boys, I'll take you home tonight when we are done making hay at Harold's." Both horses turned their black ears listening, quietly submitting to Lenny's wishes. Perry stopped in at his home for some reason, but Lenny went on by. He could see Bob the dog barking in their direction as they passed. Russell let out a low vibrating growl that lasted until Bob was out of sight.

Tug and Train's hoof beats rang out a hollow sound as they trotted across the Old Man's Creek Bridge. The creek swirled, dark and swollen below, threatening to come out of its banks at the next rainfall.

Just beyond Old Man's Creek was Web's haunted-looking place, with a few turkey vultures circling overhead. Web happened to be near the road and stood waiting for the big horses to come close. "There's my boy, Will!" He laughed as Lenny pulled up his team. "Hi, Web, how have you been?"

"Not bad. Not bad at all. I hear you've been hanging out with my brother's boy?"

"What?"

"Yeah, that little ruffian Justin is my brother's son."

Lenny couldn't believe his ears. "Justin is your nephew?"

"Yep! He was telling me about this non-Amish kid that pulled his truck out with Amish horses. And I asked if the guy happened to be named Lenny?"

Lenny shook his head. "It's a small world!"

"I told him to call ya 'Will.' I told him you 'will' probably stay Amish if you can get that Leah to kiss ya."

They both laughed, but Lenny felt his face heat up. "I gotta get going, but it was good to see you again."

"Are you headed up to Harold's?"

"Yep, we are helping them make hay."

Web sneered, "You better hurry then; Sam and David came by a half hour ago with some hayracks!" Lenny clucked, and his horses took off. Web called after. "Hurry up, or they will buggy whip you, boy!" His cackling laughter could be heard over horse hoof beats as Tug and Train trotted uphill toward Harold's.

Lenny told Russell, "We are going to see Leah today." The little white dog looked up at his friend, brown eyebrows twitching as he searched Lenny's face, trying to understand his words. Lenny continued, "Leah used to be such a happy girl every time I looked at her. She used to glow, but these days she won't even smile. I'm worried, Russell, that I'll never see her face light up again." Russell licked Lenny's hand as he reached down to pat him.

Sisters

Tug and Train seemed to be almost as familiar with Harold's lane as with Noey's. They had obviously been to both places often on work projects. Their hoofbeats and Lenny's steel-wheeled cart thundered as they rolled up near the house. Lenny was met by a group of Harold's daughters as he arrived.

"Well, if it isn't Horse Pull Lenny," Ruby teased.

Lenny asked Ruby, "Do you have a nickname?"

"Nope, everyone calls me Harold's Ruby. An Amish girl is called by her dad's name until she gets married. When a girl gets married, she is known by her husband, like, for example, Herbie Ruby."

She giggled at the sound of her own words. Leah walked up while they were talking and listened, her dark brown eyes contrasting her light-brown hair. Her face was so sweet, Lenny forgot what he and Ruby had been talking about. He looked down at his feet until he remembered what Ruby had said.

"Herbie's Ruby?" Lenny asked to make sure he understood.

"No, a daughter is Herbie's Ruby; a wife is Herbie Ruby, without the s!"

"Oh, I get it." Lenny looked back down at his feet and took a moment to think of how it would sound to say Lenny Leah. He looked up and met eyes with Leah; her cheeks flushed, and he felt his own get hot. He hoped she had just run the same words through her pretty little head, which he had in his.

"Hi, Leah." Lenny looked at her, waiting for a response. She gave a slight nod but nothing more.

Harold, who also was walking up to the group, must have noticed her response. He told Lenny under his breath, "She hasn't been quite herself ever since that buggy wreck." He looked Lenny in the eyes with a serious face.

Lenny asked cautiously, "Maybe she should have seen a doctor?"

A moment later, little Russell jumped off Lenny's fore cart and ran toward Leah. She opened her arms just as he jumped up into them. He immediately started licking her face, making her giggle, her dimple sinking deep in one cheek as her whole face lit up with a smile.

Harold said, "Well, I'll be ... haven't heard that giggle lately."

Harold's eyes wrinkled with a smile. "Good to see you again, Leonard. This will be just like old times. You remind me so much of your dad, Jake." Lenny grinned. Harold told him, "Unhook your team from that cart and put them on my hayrack. It has a long tongue, so you don't need a cart. We can use that wagon to pick up bales that we already dropped on the ground."

"Why did you drop bales on the ground?" Lenny asked, and then wondered if it was a rude question.

"We baled some of our hay yesterday but didn't have enough wagons or help. We are running out of time with rainstorms coming; we thought it best to get them baled. Alvin told me we would have lots of help today, so we'll get everything picked up and in the barn before nightfall."

Sam and David were already in the hayfield baling. Lenny took Harold's hayrack down to the field loaded with girls sent to pick up those bales dropped on the ground earlier. Harold's daughters were all laughing, finding a way to make a game out of every job. Their dark, solid-colored Amish dresses floated over the hayfield; their barefoot frolic looked like fun, yet they accomplished a lot. Lenny marveled that such thin young women could hoist hay bales up on the hayrack with ease. Heavy clouds hung in the sky; nevertheless, they didn't seem to make any shade. A haze of humidity lay over farmlands around them.

Harold told Lenny, "It's not a good haymaking day, but we can't wait. The hay is ready, and Milkman Tom told me the radio is calling for big storms this weekend."

A red-tailed hawk flew in circles overhead. Lenny imagined the bird could see lush green hayfields mowed in long strips over rolling hills. Heavy-bodied horses pulled loaded wagons of neatly stacked hay bales toward a white barn. The barn seemed to open its dark mouth, greedily swallowing bales as fast as the Amish girls could feed them in. Leah's sisters all had such carefree faces. Lenny wished he could see Leah smile more, but she had returned to her somber ways.

At one point, Leah was nearby and alone. Lenny had a feeling she wanted to talk, so he paused his team and looked at her. Finally, she spoke, "Did Davy W. really leave?"

"Yeah, I guess he did." Lenny shrugged his shoulders and looked to see Leah's response.

She looked sad and told Lenny, "I figured he would go away again. I knew it somehow." Her countenance turned sad, and she looked ready to cry.

Ruby came near and said in a cheerful way, "What are you two fighting about now?"

Neither of them answered, and Ruby looked embarrassed that she had asked.

Leah

Tug and Train pulled a full load of bales near Harold's barn. Lenny helped Perry unload his wagon, then they both went up into the mow and helped Leah and her sisters finish stacking bales. Rachel drove Sally and Lucy—Harold's blond team of Belgian mares— on the hay rope, hoisting loads up into the air through the power of a pulley system. Perry worked tirelessly, stacking hay in the dark haymow while Lenny handed bales up to him. Suddenly, there was a thick buzzing noise, and Lenny stopped to listen, thinking someone had started up a generator. As he looked around the dimly lit hayloft to see what could possibly make that sound, he caught a glimpse of some big flies buzzing around Perry. Huge flies.

Perry shouted, "Ouch!" He swatted as they encircled him, buzzing.

Lenny instinctively backed away; he wanted to help but didn't know what he could do. Thick, yellow-jacket bees hovered like helicopters, as his poor cousin made his way to the ladder, climbing down with one hand, while the other swatted at bees. Lenny winced as he heard Perry say, "Ouch!" again, and then there was a thump. He hung back in the shadows of Harold's dark haymow, wondering if Perry was okay, but he didn't want to go anywhere near the ladder until he was sure the bees were gone.

When Lenny finally had the courage to venture near the ladder, he could see the others were all gathered around Perry. Once down the ladder, he joined the group, who all stood looking at massive welts on Perry's back. Mildred bought out a paste of secret ingredients she had put together that removed stingers. Perry began to smile with his eyes again, and everyone headed back to work.

As they unloaded wagons, Mildred, Leah's mom, came by with a large pitcher. They all stopped just long enough to drink gulps of garden tea, which tasted like summer in a glass. Mildred kept telling the young people, "Drink plenty. You need lots of fluid in this heat!"

They all hurried back out to get another load of hay. Sam and David kept ahead of them with their tractor and baler. It produced a constant purr and clunking sound as it spat out bales. At one point, they had to wait while Sam and David reloaded bailing twine in their machine. Leah stood next to Train, smoothing her hand on the big horse's neck. Lenny watched until he realized that Harold was coming toward them, happy as usual.

"Leonard, I think we can get the rest of this hay on that empty wagon you just brought out. Go ahead and get this full one unloaded. By the time you do, we will be bringing the last one up with our tractor, and we'll unload that and be done." Lenny nodded and headed to his horses, but Harold called after him. "Wait, take Leah up with you; she can help unload!"

Lenny hesitated, waiting for Leah. She didn't move. Lenny heard Harold saying to her, "Go ahead. There is no point in walking up to the barn. Ride up there with Leonard."

"I like to walk," she started to say, then stopped and looked up at Lenny. He reached down and offered her a hand to help climb up the hay bales. She seemed determined not to make eye contact but took his hand and climbed up, and then sat on the opposite edge of bales. Lenny's heart pounded. He couldn't help enjoying the chance to have her hand in his, even if for only a moment. He had been waiting a long time to get a chance to talk to her alone; he had to tell her about Davy W. once and for all. He clucked to his horses, and they lurched forward impressively. For a few moments, he had to focus on Tug and Train until he got them turned and heading up that long lane lined with trees. A cool breeze passed over both passengers who were wet with sweat. That same breeze moved through tree branches, and the limbs seemed to swirl in a circular motion. This, in turn, caused a strange phenomenon of swirling shadows upon Tug, Train, hay bales, and the young man and woman. Little circles of light danced on Leah's face and dress, accenting first her eyes, her lips, and then those few strands of hair that couldn't be kept under her white scarf. Those stray wisps of hair weren't playing in the breeze the way they usually did; instead, they were curled and held tiny droplets of sweat.

He had waited for so long to talk to her, but when he had the perfect opportunity, he found himself speechless. She rode along looking ahead as though she were the one driving. Lenny didn't look at Tug and Train; he trusted them completely to stay within the worn tracks of the lane. Instead, he was mesmerized by those swirling, circular shadows and contrasting rays of light that played on a Leah's face, making a beautiful girl appear even more breathtaking. Finally, it seemed she could not pretend any longer that she didn't know she was being stared at. She turned and looked Lenny in the eyes. He had no idea, at all, of what she saw; he was too focused on what was in his sight to think of that. When her eyes met his, something seemed to tether their gaze to each other. They said no words; there wasn't any change in expressions. Lenny thought about giving her a kiss. Then he remembered that she was Amish. And that she was dating his friend and liked his cousin. Tug and Train pulled their load of hay up by the barn, and Lenny had to turn his eyes away from her.

Talking with Harold

When Sam and David finished bailing hay, they waved and headed back home with their tractor and bailer. Perry took his four-horse hitch soon after. He gave a two-finger wave as his horses and wagon rumbled out of Harold's lane. Lenny stood near Tug and Train, not in a hurry to leave the Yoder farm. Harold came and stood nearby and spoke quietly, "Thank you, Leonard, for coming along to help." The younger man nodded but didn't know what to say. Harold took off his hat and held it in his hands as though reshaping it for a moment, then put it back on and said, "I'm so glad you are spending some time with Noey and Ruth; they need company right now."

"Did you hear about Davy W. getting shunned?" Lenny asked.

Harold didn't look up but nodded that he had. Russell sat in between the men, looking up, as though listening to what they were saying. Harold continued, "It would be nice if you could stay on with them for the rest of the summer. With Davy gone, Noey could really use some help around there."

Lenny pulled on his suspenders and finally said, "I think I might." He climbed on his fore cart to leave. Harold followed him over and stood near and watched Russell jump up, taking a seat by Lenny. It was obvious that Harold wanted to say something more, so Lenny waited.

"I believe you saved Leah's life that day of the big storm."

"Well, I didn't do much; I just took her up to Aaron Burr's place."

"If you hadn't come along at that time, she may have been in that ditch for a while. Cold and confused, she wasn't able to help herself. God must have brought you here."

Lenny nodded. "I'm just glad she is okay." He clucked and his team stepped off, trotting out toward the road. It was starting to get dark as Tug and Train trotted past Web's house. A blue glow gleamed out of Web's kitchen window, indicating that a TV was on. Lenny remembered driving Tug and Train home from Web's place after they had been at the horse pull. That was the night he found out that he was Grandpa's real grandson. Lenny's heart ached, missing Grandpa.

Russell Trouble

Perry was brushing Babe and Bell when Lenny came in, leading Tug and Train. Lenny felt at home in Alvin's barn. He spent so many hours brushing horses in that barn a few years back. Tug and Train seemed happy to be in their own stalls. They munched contentedly on sweet-smelling grain that Perry had poured into their feed bunk while Lenny un-harnessed them.

"Where is Russell going to sleep tonight?" Perry asked.

"Well, he usually sleeps with me ... but ... your mom won't want him in the house, will she?"

"No," Perry clearly stated, "but she wouldn't have to know that he came in. I have an idea." Perry's face was lit up. "You go on in and talk to my folks. If they ask where I am, tell them that I ran down to shut a gate and that I'll be along shortly. I will bring Russell in with me and sneak him upstairs while you visit with them.

"Okay."

Aunt Lydia was wiping off her counter, and Uncle Alvin was reading his Amish newspaper, *The Budget*, when Lenny came in. "How did things go at Harold's?" Alvin asked.

"Pretty good. Harold was worried that the hay was kind of tough, but he thought it would be all right."

Alvin nodded with a concerned brow. After a moment, he spoke again. "This has been a really wet summer. There just aren't many good haymaking days; it's too cloudy, and you need sunshine to dry hay properly."

Alvin's words reminded Lenny of Noey's troubles getting corn planted. He told his uncle, "Thanks for sending Perry to help us get Noey's fields ready. We got it all worked up, and he was going to plant today."

Alvin's brow continued to be furrowed with concern as he spoke again. "We heard about Davy W.; that's the last thing Noey needed right now, with the weather already making life difficult."

Aunt Lydia stopped her aggressive counter wiping and looked Lenny in the eyes. "I'm glad you are here, Leonard; they would be terrible lonely otherwise."

Alvin added, "Stay as long as you can, Leonard. Noey really could use your help." He looked at Lenny until the young man nodded, then went back to reading from his paper. Lydia continued scouring her long countertop.

Lenny stood in the kitchen awkwardly for a moment and noticed Perry sneaking through the other room with Russell in his arms. "Well, hopefully, we have a better hay day tomorrow," Lenny said and followed Perry upstairs.

Perry sat on his bed and took his socks off. He shook one in front of Russell, and a short tug-of-war contest ensued. When the boys got started laughing, Russell barked. Aunt Lydia called upstairs, "Perry, come here." They looked at each other for a moment, realizing they were caught.

Perry went to the top of the steps, "Yes, Mom?"

"Come down and take your asthma medicine. Your cough is getting pretty bad."

Perry said, "Okay," and tromped downstairs.

Chapter 9

HAYRIDE

66 "Time for chores," Aunt Lydia called up the stairway, just as she had when Lenny spent a summer in her home. Everyone stood up without words and pulled on their work clothes quickly, heading out into the soft morning air. Russell kept quiet inside Lenny's shirt until it was unbuttoned, freeing the small white dog. As soon as he was released, Russell sprinted after a loose chicken. It ran off clucking and flapping its wings, leaving behind a few floating feathers. The little white dog plucked one of the feathers from the air and shook it, flapping his black ears. Lenny offered to go down and fetch the milk cows for old time's sake. He enjoyed listening to songbirds rejoicing at sunrise. He walked along the creek bank, listening to trickling water's gurgling sound. A slow-moving cow stopped to bellow a long drawn-out moo, interrupting a catbird that was warbling spastically. When the cow started walking

again, the catbird resumed its wild string of notes, reminding Lenny of his moment with Leah the day before. He thought about how he had looked into her sweet eyes.

Horse chores felt very familiar to Lenny, having stayed at Alvin's farm before. The smells of sweet grains mixed with those of horses and hay brought back good memories. He thoroughly enjoyed brushing all of Alvin's horses, even Bell, who was always cantankerous. He helped Perry harness up horses as Russell watched. They hurried inside for breakfast, excited that it was another haymaking day.

"We're having Breckle soup this morning. It's fast and easy on a busy day," Aunt Lydia announced when everyone came into the kitchen. No one seemed to mind. After all, it was haymaking day and too exciting for anyone to be hungry. Lenny didn't remember what Breckle soup was until Viola showed Lenny how they broke bread into small pieces in a bowl, covered it with strawberries, and poured fresh, creamy milk over it all.

Perry said with smiling eyes, "Sprinkle sugar on it and it's even better!" They ate bologna slices on the side, which seemed odd for breakfast, but it was delicious. They all bowed for their after -meal prayer, and then raced outside.

Rosie drove a tractor while Sam and David loaded hay, just like the last time Lenny made hay on Alvin's farm. Alvin thought they ought to let Lenny drive horses because he was a guest, and that Perry, Ruby, Rachel, and Della should stack hay in the barn. Leah drove her team of blond Belgians, bringing in loads of hay as well.

Little E rode along with Leah but also did her part to help by kicking off hay bales to those who were stacking.

On his way by, Lenny noticed Aunt Lydia's lilac bush radiating a beautiful sweet smell. He didn't know why, but he had an urge to share that beautiful scent with Leah. He could imagine watching her sweet face while smelling it and smiling. He pulled off a handful and put it beside him on his cart seat until the right moment came along. After bringing in the next load, Lenny went to tie his team.

Leah was standing next to Train, shoulder to shoulder, and put her arm under his jaw, cradling his head. She stroked his forehead gently and talked to him, "How have you been, Train? I haven't seen you for such a long time."

It made Lenny jealous. She didn't say anything nice like that to him when he came back. Leah stepped over to Tug and gently cleaned sleepy out of his eye and began rubbing him on his nose as only she could do. The young man watched, wishing she would be half as nice to him as she was to his horses.

Lenny walked over and spoke to her. "How has your summer been going?"

Leah looked up, startled that he was beside her. She turned her face away, averting her eyes from him again. Instead of acknowledging him, she gave Tug a share of her affection. He began to wonder if she heard him at all, or if he should repeat himself. Just before he asked again, she spoke, "Tug and Train, would you boys please explain to your friend here how dating works?"

"What are you talking about, Leah?"

"Tug and Train, would you please let Lenny in on this one little thing? When a boy is dating a girl, he shouldn't try talking to that girl's best friend, especially if she is dating one of his good friends!"

Lenny felt his face get hot. He turned away, tipping his head so that his hat covered his red face. Dropping his handful of lilacs that were hidden behind his back, he put one foot over them to cover them. Lenny bit hard on his lower lip, frustrated, and not sure how to answer her. He wanted to tell her that he was just trying to be a friend, but he knew that wasn't true. He quietly started tying his horses. Train nodded his large head, bumping it against Leah's backside, which in turn caused her to stumble into Lenny.

"Oops, sorry about that," Leah said with a giggle.

Train let out a deep nicker. Lenny's foot came off the lilacs as they collided, and Leah saw them.

"Lenny, why are you stomping on those lilacs; they are my favorite flowers." Scowling at him, she walked away.

Lenny said quietly, "Thanks, Train, I owe you one."

Rain

Later in the afternoon, Lenny had one more chance to talk to Leah. They were both driving teams of horses. Leah was bringing in a load with her golden Belgians, and Lenny was heading out with an empty wagon behind his black Percherons. They met at a tight corner where four horses couldn't pass through, so one of them needed to back up. They were facing each other, but it was hard to see because each of them had a team of huge horses in front of them. Lenny couldn't help but remember two years ago when they met at the same spot. Leah had given him a sweet smile then, but this time she called, "Better back up that empty wagon, so I can get through with my full load!"

Lenny didn't answer. He started backing Tug and Train, struggling to get his empty wagon to turn the right way.

"What's taking so long?" Leah called.

"Hang on. It's tough backing a wagon in the lane without getting into a fence!" Lenny felt his face getting hotter by the moment. He finally got his wagon backed, and, as Leah came past, he asked her, "Don't you think you should have gone to a doctor after your accident?"

"What?"

"I'm worried about you, Leah. You're not acting like yourself." She glared at him. "Leah, do you really like Henry?"

"Why?" She looked at him as though really annoyed.

"Well, he's a nice guy, and you shouldn't be leading him on ... if you like someone else."

"Like who would you be talking about?"

Gnats were orbiting around Lenny's head like planets in a solar system. He opened his mouth to tell Leah about Davy W., and a gnat flew in and got stuck in the back of his throat. It tickled, making him cough but couldn't get it out. It felt as though its tiny wings were stuck to the wet part of his throat.

As Leah drove her horses away, she asked, "You gonna be okay?"

He nodded but continued coughing.

The young people picked up the last few bales, and a dark cloud rose up over Alvin's hay field. A sudden cloudburst shot down thick raindrops on the little group of haymakers. They scurried about, gathering the remaining bales and flinging them on Lenny's hayrack. The raindrops each seemed huge, landing in a spread-out pattern, about a foot apart from each other at first. Those droplets smacked the ground with an audible thud, and stung the young people who laughed it off. The distance between raindrops began to fill in, with more but smaller rain turning into an all-out downpour. A cool mist blew over them in waves, causing Lenny to shiver as a trickle ran down his back. When the last bale was picked up, they all jumped aboard. Tug and Train trotted quickly toward the barn. Leah and her sisters were laughing and looking pretty with wet faces and drenched head scarves and dresses. Lenny noticed little ringlets peeking out from under Leah's head scarf.

"Where's Russell?" Lenny suddenly thought of his little friend.

Leah answered, calling over the sound of pounding rain, "He's right over here, curled up between a couple of hay bales, snug and dry."

Alvin was standing in front of his machine shed with the doors slid open wide. He motioned for Lenny to drive Tug and Train into that building in an obvious effort to get his hay out of the rain. Lenny's big horses pulled their load of wet hay and young people inside, coming to a stop with barely enough room to get the whole wagon under roof. Raindrops were singing a melodious tune on the tin roof of Alvin's shed, making such a racket they could hardly hear each other talk. Alvin called over the music, "Set the wet bales over here," pointing to an open area off to one side. "We will let those dry out before putting them in the mow." Everyone worked together getting the top layer off Lenny's hayrack. When everything damp was off the haystack, Alvin said, "Leonard, take the rest of these bales home for Noey as payment for your labor."

"Okay, thanks."

The sound of rain singing on the tin roof mellowed into a light tune overhead. Lenny's female cousins and the Yoder girls all stood in a circle, quietly chatting about gardening and canning fruit and vegetables. Lenny stood near Alvin and took the opportunity to ask, "Are you really going to sell Mr. E?"

"Yeah, you want to buy him?"

"Well, I found out that he is a brother to Junior's filly, Misty. I think those two really ought to be kept together; they match so well and everything."

Alvin nodded and pulled on his beard in thought. He looked at Lenny and said, "Tell Junior that I will sell you Mr. E for eight hundred dollars if he will sell you Misty for the same."

Lenny laughed. He didn't mean that he wanted to buy them, but he didn't know how to explain that to his uncle, so he said, "Okay, I'll ask him."

At last, it quit raining and everything became quiet. The Yoder girls were all looking drenched and pretty as they excused themselves to head home.

English Party

After Leah and her sisters left, Lenny told Alvin, "I guess I should be heading back to Noey's."

Alvin nodded, "You let me know what you decide about buying Mr. E."

Lenny laughed again and clucked to Tug and Train. Russell ran and jumped on the footrest of the fore cart, his usual riding spot. Bob the dog ran along behind, barking, until Lenny scolded him, "Go home, Bob."

Perry came up from the barn, riding on his pony, Patches. Lenny could hear him tell his dad, "I'm gonna follow Lenny as far as Yoder Towers to keep him company." It was impossible to hear if Alvin said anything, but Perry kept following, so Lenny assumed Alvin didn't say no.

Patches caught up, trotting furiously, with Perry almost bouncing off. Finally, Perry got close enough to ask, "Are you going to meet up with that Justin and his friends?"

"I guess so. If they're there by Hershey's garage, like they told me they would be."

Tug and Train had worked all day, but they still pranced under the street lights as they came into the little hamlet. They were so impressive, with their sleek, black coats, arched necks, and huge hooves ringing out on the concrete. Lenny couldn't wait for the English kids to see them, sure that there wasn't any way they could fail to impress. He drove Tug and Train behind the repair shop, just as his buddy Justin had instructed, stopping long enough to grab a couple of cold root beers from the pop machine, tossing one to Perry.

"They told us they would meet up at that gray house ahead, didn't they?" Perry nodded.

As they rounded the bend, a glow could be seen from a campfire. Justin's huge truck was parked close with windows down. Rap music was thumping out. Train's head was held high, ears forward, examining everything as they drew near. Tug tried to turn off on a side road, but Lenny reined him in.

"You should probably just go on back home; this looks like trouble," Lenny called to his cousin.

Perry turned his pony and called back, "Be careful, Lenny!"

The music, blasting out of Justin's truck, was so loud it drowned out the wonderful sound of massive horse hooves clapping on the road. The teenagers were singing along with their rap music and didn't notice Tug and Train until Justin hollered at them between songs. "Hey, guys, our hayride is here." The loud group of young people ran up toward the horses, but instead of looking at them, they pushed and shoved each other.

Lenny tried to control the crowd, "Guys, guys, take it easy around the horses!" They all crowded around anyway, and one of them fell back into Tug's side. The big horse sidestepped a little but held firm.

Lenny told them, "Hey, guys, if these weren't such good horses, they might have kicked you!"

Justin's little brother piped up, "Yeah, like that pony of yours kicked me off my bike that time!"

One of the other boys teased him, "What? His pony kicked you off your bicycle?"

"Yeah, I was just riding past it and boom! It kicked so hard I hit the ground. I had a black-and-blue hoof print on my behind the next day, too!" Everyone there laughed at that.

Lenny told them, "If we're going to have a hayride, we'd better do it now."

One of the guys called over to a group of young people who were still around the campfire, "Hey, everyone, c'mon, let's go on a hayride!"

As the group got closer, Lenny realized there was an Amish girl with them. It was dark enough that her face wasn't visible. He didn't recognize her until she said loudly, "Hey, this is my boyfriend!"

"Rebecca, what are you doing here?"

"I was at my friend Dorothy's house this afternoon, and Perry's sister stopped in and told me you were coming here for a hayride and that I could catch a ride home with you." She leaned against Lenny, something an Amish girl would never do in public, making it clear that she had been drinking. "You are my boyfriend, so you better give me a ride home." She laughed. Her black hair and dark eyes accented her pretty face in the glow of the street lights, but Lenny didn't know how to deal with her condition.

"Yes, I'll give you a ride, but you better sit here before you fall down." Lenny lifted her up on the hayrack and sat her on a bale of hay.

"Okay, boyfriend, whatever you say."

Once everyone was on board, Lenny spoke to his horses, "Get up, boys!"

Tug and Train trotted off obediently with a full load of young people sitting on hay bales. They were all talking and laughing as they headed down a gravel road. Lenny purposefully took a road that didn't have any Amish homes that he knew of. The wild group seemed out of control, and Lenny was worried that someone was going to fall off, but he didn't know what else to do but keep his promise. Justin offered Rebecca another cup of whatever it was that they were drinking.

Lenny said, "NO, she has had enough of that crap!" Rebecca sat back and giggled.

Justin told Lenny, "I'm just trying to help you out. Don't you want your girlfriend nice and drunk?"

"No, thanks, I have to take her home soon; she needs to sober up first."

"What do you care, man? You're not Amish. Let her worry about that."

There wasn't any way Lenny could explain to Justin about how nice his uncle Noey was and that he didn't want to cause trouble for him.

The English kids didn't seem to notice the horses until Tug lifted his tail and broke wind. The girls let out a chorus of "ugh" and "ick," and the guys all laughed. Russell hunkered down, almost hiding from the loud group. After what seemed like an eternity to Lenny, they finally got back to the campfire. Everyone jumped off talking loudly. They all went directly to a table with their alcohol punch and began to fill their glasses again. Justin's girlfriend came back with a couple of cups in her hand and asked Lenny, "Here, do you and your girlfriend want something to drink?"

"No, thank you, we really got to get going."

"Okay," she said and started drinking out of one of the cups.

Lenny leaned over and said quietly to Justin, "You shouldn't let your girlfriend drink."

"Why not, Amish boy? Are you too righteous for that?"

Lenny whispered, "No, because she's going to have a baby."

Lenny had no more than got those words out when he felt himself hit the ground. Justin, though much smaller, quickly had Lenny in a headlock and through clinched teeth snarled, "How do you know that she is pregnant? I haven't told anyone that."

Lenny couldn't answer because Justin's arm was around his throat, cutting off his air. All at once, Justin shouted, "OUCH!" He let go of Lenny and jumped up. "That dang little dog of yours just bit my butt!" Lenny slowly got to his feet, rubbing his throat. Justin was rubbing his behind and looked Lenny in the eyes and asked through clinched teeth again, "How did you know that?"

"When I first came into town, I sat near you guys at McDonald's by the interstate. I overheard her telling you."

Justin started coming at Lenny again, but Russell grabbed the little guy's pant leg, snarling. Lenny heard laughter and realized that Rebecca and Justin's girlfriend were standing together, watching Russell torment Justin and giggling. Justin tried shaking the dog off his leg and said, "Just take this dumb dog and your girlfriend and get out of here, would you?"

Lenny picked up his straw hat, put it back on, and grabbed Russell. "Come on, Rebecca, let's go!"

Rebecca stumbled over to Lenny's hayrack, and he helped her climb on. As they drove off, all the other teenagers, oblivious to all of what had just happened, called, "Good-bye!"

Some called, "Thanks for the hayride!"

Rebecca waved happily as Lenny shook his lines at Tug and Train. He and his horses wanted to get out of there as quickly as possible.

Lenny and Rebecca

Lenny was so happy when they finally pulled away from the group of wild kids; however, he still had to get Rebecca home. She seemed a little better, but not sober enough to be dropped off at her house yet. He was happy that it was several miles to her place. Stars hung brightly above them as Tug and Train walked along slowly; the young man didn't push them. Instead, he tried talking to Rebecca to be sure she was ready to walk into her own house without getting into trouble.

"So, Rebecca, did you have fun this evening?"

She giggled and leaned back against the stack of hay bales piled behind her and answered, "I had the best time." She laughed at her own words.

Lenny looked at her, concerned about what he was going to do. He noticed that she was taking straight pins out of her covering and carefully placing them in the front of her cape dress. "Rebecca, what are you doing?"

She laughed and took her white prayer covering off, setting it neatly behind her on a hay bale. Looking up at Lenny in the starlight, she told him, "Lean back against these hay bales by me. Are you scared of me or what?"

There were just enough stars in the sky to make her face glow. When the young man leaned beside her, he could see that her black hair was tied up in a bun on top of her head. She was staring at him, and he asked her, "Rebecca, why don't you put your covering back on? Why did you take that off?"

"Some of us Amish girls think it's respectful to take our coverings off before we kiss a boy."

Lenny looked in her dark eyes. "Rebecca, put your covering back on."

"I will in a bit"—she giggled—"but first you have to give me a kiss."

Lenny didn't know what to say, he looked up at his horses as they calmly walked down a quiet country road, wide-open fields around them all glowing under the stars. He looked back at her, and she was staring at him as pretty as could be, waiting for a kiss. He was planning to give her a short peck, but she held on to him for a better one. Just then Tug and Train sidestepped and took their hayrack through some potholes; Rebecca fell back onto a hay bale, and Russell yelped. Lenny caught his balance and said, "Rebecca, you're not yourself. Why did you drink what those boys gave you?"

"I didn't know it was anything! I had been working all day, and I was thirsty, so I drank a couple of glasses of it right off. I didn't know it had anything in it. You're not mad at me, are you, Lenny?"

"No, I'm mad at those boys. They knew you were innocent; that's why they gave it to you. Please, Rebecca, stay away from those guys, will you?" He could barely see her nodding, so he pushed his point. "I'm serious. Please promise me that you won't hang around those guys!"

"You really do like me, don't you, Lenny?"

"I think you're a really nice girl, and I don't trust those guys at all. What would have happened if I hadn't showed up? You would have been stuck there, and one of them would have tried to take advantage of you."

She just looked at him, listening, as though finally coming to her senses. She pointed up the road and whispered, "Here comes a buggy."

Lenny looked up ahead and, sure enough, a horse was coming toward them. It occurred to him, in an instant, that she may say something silly.

"Rebecca, hide down here between these bales. I don't want anyone to see that I have a girl with me." She laughed and took her white prayer covering and hid between two bales. He told her, "Shhhh now. Please keep quiet." She giggled a little, then kept still.

The open buggy got closer, and Lenny could see that the horse had one white sock like Bishop Mose's horse. Russell began to let out a low growl. Mose slowed his horse and called over, "Is that you, Leonard?"

"Yes, I'm on my way home from Alvin's. We were making hay this afternoon. Noey has been borrowing Alvin's team, so we can do fieldwork with them. We had a deal that we could use them as long as we brought them back when it was time to make hay."

"That's good. You keep busy and stay out of trouble. Your uncle doesn't need any more of that." Mose shook his driving lines, and his horse stepped up its pace, then they passed each other. Rebecca sat up and started laughing again. Mose called to Lenny, "Who was that laughing?"

Lenny hollered, "It sounded like a horse's whinny to me!"

Mose let his horse step into a trot, disappearing into the darkness.

Lenny scolded Rebecca, "Do you know who that was?"

"Yeah, that's my grandpa," she giggled.

"No, that was Bishop Mose."

"I know; he's my grandpa!"

"Are you kidding me? You are Mose's granddaughter?"

"Didn't you know that?"

"No, I didn't know that! I'm trying to stay out of trouble for my uncle Noey's sake. What would have happened if he saw you here with me? If he ever finds out that you were with me, I will get sent away for good!"

"Sorry, Lenny, I was good. I didn't laugh until he was gone." She sat up looking cute and put her prayer covering back on.

"Oh man, he would have killed me if he knew you were hiding there and without your covering on!"

"No, he wouldn't have," she sputtered. "He's Amish; he doesn't believe in killing people."

"Well, he might have made an exception in this case," Lenny said, and they both laughed out loud. They arrived at the lane to Rebecca's house shortly, and he told her, "I'd better just drop you off here. Can you walk up to your house okay?"

"Of course I can," she stepped off the hayrack and stumbled.

"Oh no, what am I going to do with you?"

She giggled but recovered. "Really, Lenny, I'm fine. I just stumbled a little, but seriously, I'm fine now, really!" She set off walking and seemed to be okay. Lenny sat under the stars and watched her make her way up the lane. When she was almost to the house, he couldn't see her anymore because of darkness. He clucked to his big team, and they trotted off into the night.

Hollow Tree

When Tug and Train rumbled in Noey's lane, it was getting late. Lenny hurried as he un-harnessed and brushed his horses; little Russell watched. As they headed toward the house, a shadow crossed in front of them, slinking into the timber between Noey's and Junior's farms. Russell took off after the shadow as fast as his little legs could carry him, and Lenny went hard after him. By the time Lenny caught up, the dog was trying to jump onto a very low hanging limb of a tree.

"Come on, Russell, whatever it was, it got away!" Russell ignored Lenny's words and continued growling and trying to jump onto that low limb. Lenny finally decided to appease his little friend and hoisted him up onto the limb. Russell took off, running up the limb toward the trunk. The young man fully expected that the dog would come to a dead end when he reached the tree trunk, but instead, Russell disappeared into a hole in a crook of the tree. Lenny rushed up, only to hear a terrible ruckus of growls and snarls coming out of a hollow in the trunk. He stood there, helplessly listening to a vicious fight. It sounded horrible. Making matters worse, Lenny looked around at his dark, wooded surroundings. He called, "Russell, come up out of there! Russell!" The young man climbed up to try to see down into the hole, but just as he did, something came snarling out of it and ran off through the woods. After half falling, half climbing down, Lenny told himself, "That was an old raccoon." He climbed back up, desperate to check on his little friend.

"Russell! Are you okay in there, Russell?" The little dog let out a muffled bark from within the tree trunk. Lenny climbed higher and tried reaching down into the hole, but he couldn't feel his dog at all. "All right, Russell, I won't leave you in there. You helped me tonight! I'm not gonna let you down!" He stood and looked at the tree. Another muffled bark came from within. "I'll be right back. I'm gonna go get a saw!" Lenny ran through the dark woods, making plans as he went. He knew where to find a lantern, some saws, and an axe in Noey's machine shed. Lighting the lantern first, he could then see clearly to gather what he needed. When he went to get a handsaw, Noey's chainsaw caught his eye. Quickly checking it for gas and oil, he rushed back out with his lantern swinging.

It took a bit to find Russell's tree, but when he did, there were still muffled barks within its trunk. Lenny knocked on its trunk and hollered, "I'm back, Russell! I'm gonna cut this tree down!" Lenny listened carefully to Russell's barking and tried to determine how low he needed to cut. With his lantern glowing in a very dark woods, the young man sized up his project, remembering what Grandpa had taught him about felling trees. Grandpa warned him that if a person isn't careful, they may drop a tree into another tree, getting it lodged halfway down. As he swung his lantern around, the trees seemed to move, too, shadows changing, making everything look creepy. At last, he made a decision about where to cut and set down his lantern. Russell urged him on with his subdued barks. Lenny felt less afraid once he heard the roar of his chainsaw, knowing that growling sound would scare away anything wild.

Russell's tree wasn't really huge. It didn't seem to take long to cut out a wedge in the direction he wanted the tree to fall. A short time later, Lenny was making a clean cut from the opposite side and feeling good about his work. He looked up to see if the tree was swaying, then turned around to see where it would fall. His eyes fell on a circle of Amish men standing just at the edge of his lantern's glow. The sight startled him significantly, and he quickly shut down his chainsaw. He couldn't recognize any faces, but he saw broadfall pants, suspenders, and straw hats.

One of them spoke. "Leonard, what on earth are you doing, cutting down a tree in the middle of the night?" Immediately, Lenny recognized Noey's voice, and then his eyes adjusted and identified the other men as Junior and his sons. They all stood looking at him as though he had gone off the deep end.

Lenny asked, "What brought all of you out here?"

"Just the sound of a chainsaw in the middle of the night," Junior answered for the rest of them.

"Oh yeah, I guess I was in such a hurry I didn't think of that."

"A hurry? For what?" Noey looked at Lenny as though he was quite concerned for his nephew's welfare.

Lenny answered, "I'm trying to get Russell out of this tree!" The others looked even more worried after his answer than before he gave it.

Junior asked, "Did Russell climb this tree?"

Lenny began to laugh, realizing how silly his answer sounded. The others weren't laughing; they were still giving him confused expressions. While Lenny tried to think of how to explain his situation, Russell helped by starting up his muffled barking again. All at once, Junior's boys started laughing, and Herbie asked, "How in the world did Russell get into the trunk of that tree?"

Lenny explained as quickly as he could. "I was heading up to the house when something ran into these trees. Russell took off after it and I followed. When I got here, Russell was trying to jump on this low-hanging limb." He pointed to the limb. "I didn't see what it could hurt to hoist Russell up on it, not knowing that it led to the crook in that tree and down a hole into its trunk."

Herbie asked, "Is the coon still in there?"

"No, it came up out of there right away, but Russell couldn't climb out."

Junior told Lenny, "Well, I think you should finish cutting that poor dog out of there, then."

Everyone laughed and Lenny started up his chainsaw, feeling self-conscious with a group of Amish men watching a novice cut down a tree by lantern light. In a few moments, the tree began to sway; Lenny shut off his saw and backed away.

Herbie called, "Timber!"

A few limbs snapped as his tree brushed against other nearby trees on its way to the ground. Then a heavy thump sounded, and Russell scampered out, running up to Noey and leaping into his cradled arms, licking the older man's face. The whole group of men laughed heartily. Noey scolded Russell, yet he did it with a smile on his face, "You ornery little dog."

He looked at Lenny and said, "You could have waited until morning to get him out of there."

"I couldn't leave my friend stuck out here in a tree all night."

Junior laughed. "Well, you're a pretty good friend, I'd say!"

They all had one last laugh before everyone headed back home for the night.

Chapter 10

SUMMER SNOW

N oey and Lenny finished their morning chores, and then stood in the barn looking at their horses. The horses all lifted their heads at once, letting them know that someone was coming. Junior walked in, lanky and kind-looking, and asked, "How's this Misty working for you, Leonard?"

"Really good. Ever since Queen came along, that is." The two older men laughed. The younger man thought it would be a good time to bring up keeping the colt and filly together. "You know, Junior, these colts match great. My uncle Alvin is thinking of selling Mr. E, and I've been thinking he and Misty ought to be kept together."

Junior took off his tall black hat and slicked his dark hair down, then put his hat back on. "I would be willing to sell Misty to you if you wanted to make a team out of 'em."

"I didn't mean 'me' necessarily."

"Well, I don't really need a filly-colt around, but I don't think we would sell her to just anyone. We would sell her to you if you wanted to put her together with Mr. E...how much is Alvin asking for his horse-colt?"

"Eight hundred dollars."

Junior looked at Misty for a moment. "Okay, that sounds fair."

Lenny began biting his own lower lip; he didn't know what to say. There was no doubt that it would be fun to own Mr. and Misty, but he was planning to go back to town in a few weeks. While he was thinking it all through, Noey told Junior, "I owe Leonard for his work here. I'll pay for the colts with that money. When he's done working with them, they'll be worth something. And if he wants to sell them, someone in our community will be interested."

Junior nodded and eyed Lenny with a slight smile, then asked, "It's too wet to get into your fields this morning, isn't it?"

Noey answered for him, "I believe so, but by this afternoon, we are hoping to have Lenny disc up our north field up by the road. We can still get soybeans planted in there before it's too late." Lenny and Noey stared at Junior, who studied the ground near his feet, obviously planning to ask them something more.

"Is there any chance Leonard could come help catch chickens this forenoon. We have a truck coming for a load and could sure use an extra hand."

Noey answered quickly, "I don't see why not!" He then looked at Lenny, who was biting his lip. Noey added, "That is, if it works for you, Leonard?"

"Uh, oh sure ... I think?"

Junior gave a mischievous grin. "I'll take your wages off the price of Misty."

Chickens and Catbirds

Catching chickens wasn't complicated work, although it took some getting used to for a guy who hadn't done it before. Lenny watched Herbie's smooth motion as he reached in a cage, snagging a couple of chickens at a time by the legs, and pulling them out upside down. Junior's boys—Harvey, Howard, and Henry—were all quickly catching cackling birds and loading them in portable cages on a set of wheels. What needed to be done was obvious; accomplishing it was not as simple. After several attempts, Lenny finally snatched a rubbery, yellow chicken leg, scratching his arm on the cage door while pulling the bird out. His captive chicken flapped its wings furiously and hoisted itself up, possibly in an effort to peck Lenny's arm. He quickly gave the bird a shake and placed her in the battery of portable cages. Herbie's sisters, Frieda, Elaine, and Eleanor, were helping. They were all younger than Fannie Ella but looked something like her. All three were barefoot even though walking in the chicken building with debris on the floor. They smiled often, and when they weren't working, they stood in a clump giggling and whispering. It was obvious enough that all of them had fun personalities like the rest of Junior's family. All three girls wore a light yellow apron, though their dresses were one green, another blue, and the smallest girl in plum.

Ruby called, "Let's eat!" When they had washed up and walked into the kitchen, they were surprised to see a few extra girls helping Ruby set the table. "Fannie Ella and I stopped at Beantown, and we saw Rebecca and Leah there. Fannie Ella suggested that we have them join us for lunch."

Henry seemed happy enough that Leah was there, but Lenny's mind was in a blur. Rebecca kept looking his way, flashing her dark eyes. He couldn't help but grin when she did. He wanted to watch Leah, who was busy helping Fannie Ella get lunch on the table. She went about her business as though she didn't notice Lenny at all.

When they all were seated, Junior said, "Leonard, would you pray?"

Everyone turned and looked at Lenny, whose heart began pounding and his mind raced. All at once, he remembered that when an Amish man invites someone to lead a prayer, he is only asking for a sigh, to signal the end of a silent prayer. Lenny looked at Junior and nodded. He knew that it was still expected that he would say a prayer in his heart, and the others would be agreeing with him.

Lenny bowed his head and prayed silently, "Dear Lord, please give me wisdom to know how to handle this situation with these girls. This whole love triangle has got to end." He opened one eye and snuck a glance at everyone; they were all bowing their heads politely, except the twins. They both gave Lenny a big smile when they saw him look at them. In the silence, a kitten could be heard mewing just beyond the window. He took the opportunity to glance at Leah's pretty face, her eyes closed in prayer. When sufficient time had passed that it would look like his prayer was long enough, Lenny let out a slow sigh. Everyone raised their head. No one said an amen out loud, but he was sure they all had said it in their own hearts. It felt good to know that everyone, including Leah, Rebecca, and Henry, had joined with him in praying for this love triangle to be solved.

Ruby made a feast. Although he knew it was great, Lenny had no idea what he ate; he was too nervous about the girls. Junior's boys focused on their plates because they took eating seriously. Lenny looked at his plate to keep himself from staring at Leah. He didn't want Leah to see him looking at Rebecca, and he didn't want any of them to see him staring at Leah, especially Henry.

After they ate, the boys all went directly into the living room and stretched out on the floor for a quick nap before going back out to work. Lenny headed in with them and found a place on the floor, but there was no way he could sleep, with both of those girls in the other room. In a few moments, there was a single snore, and a short time later, there was a chorus of heavy breathing. Lenny lay there listening and wondering what the girls were doing. That kitten continued meowing outside.

The little girls came teetering in, looking for toys. Edna found a baby doll and began singing to it; Elma tried to take it, and they began to squabble. Rebecca came in and whispered sharply, "Girls, can't you see the men are sleeping?"

Lenny pretended to be asleep, he kept his eyes shut and listened, pleased that Rebecca called them men. Both little girls tried to get the dolly from each other quietly, but their voices began to get loud again. Lenny heard footsteps enter the room; he listened carefully to see what Rebecca would say this time. Instead, he heard Leah's voice softly saying, "Oh dear, baby, where is your little sister? Oh, I see your sister in the toy box." Her whisper was gentle and cute. The twins drew silent while Leah dug down in among other toys and pulled out another faceless doll. In a moment, she had both little girls sitting side by side in their little rocking chairs, each rocking a baby.

Lenny's mind went back to what Aaron Burr had told him about not looking at a girl's face, but instead listening to hear what her heart is like.

After a ten-minute nap, everyone began to stir, heading out into the great outdoors and back to work. Edna and Elma teetered around near the garden among some white dandelions that had gone to seed. Lenny stopped to talk to his little friends even though they didn't know English and spoke Dutch in their own toddler dialect. "Are you girls picking flowers?" They each held up a handful of ugly white-headed dandelions and chattered about them.

Elma backed up and sat on her behind and said seriously, "Oh, oh!"

Edna broke into a giggle and said, "Bum, bum." She mixed in a row of cute mumble-jumble Dutch words and a few more. "Bum, bums." Elma didn't seem to mind and joined in singing a little song that included the words "Bum, bum." Lenny laughed knowing they were making a song out of Elma falling on her behind.

Leah came along and spoke to the twins, but Lenny couldn't understand her Pennsylvania-Dutch words. He was trying to figure it out when she took one of Edna's seedy white dandelions, lifted it up to her mouth, and gave a soft blow. Lenny was mesmerized watching Leah's pretty mouth as she seemed to be blowing a kiss. A few moments ago the white dandelions were hideous, but Leah turned them into something wonderful. Tiny, colorless parasols drifted away through the sunlight that beamed through tree branches above. She took another from little Edna's hand as the twins chattered with delight. Lenny was enjoying watching her as much as the toddlers. She puckered her lips and gently blew. Tiny seedlings rushed away from her pretty mouth, billowing out into an orb of sparkling, magical flying objects, which slowly floated off.

Leah's dimple was sinking in her soft cheek while the little girls giggled until she saw Lenny gawking at her. "Don't tell me you've never blown on dandelions before?" Her dimple disappeared, and she looked annoyed.

Lenny shot back at her, "No, we don't have dandelions in town."

The twins burst into laughter when he spoke. He was sure they didn't understand him and concluded that his words must have sounded like something else in Dutch, but it made him feel better when they laughed.

Lenny headed out to where the big boys were gathered in the drive. The kitten that they had been hearing through the meal meowed again. Henry looked around at everyone else and said, "I'm gonna shoot that barn cat that's making a fuss in that tree." Just as Henry said 'cat in the tree,' it hit Lenny; he knew what was happening.

"That's not a cat, Henry; it's a bird."

"Well, then, am I the only one that is sick of hearing that bird?" Nobody answered, so Henry directed a question toward Howard. "Where is your .22 rifle?"

Howard didn't answer but hurried into the machine shed and came out grinning, gun in his hands. Lenny looked at Leah; she ignored his gaze.

Henry asked, "Howard, is this thing loaded?"

"Six shells in the clip. I hope you don't need that many shots!"

"I think I'll only need one." Henry laughed, his personality was infectious.

Everyone else laughed, too—that is, everyone but Lenny, who said loudly, "Don't shoot that catbird, Henry!" The handsome young Amish man had the riffle up to his shoulder, but he put it down when Lenny spoke. He looked at Lenny with a confused brow, "What? You don't like that yowl, do you?"

"I like catbirds a lot!" He glanced at Leah; her dimple flashed. "I like how they sing in the spring, so even when they meow, I'm thinking about how nice they can be. Come on, Henry, don't hurt that little catbird." Lenny looked into Leah's eyes; she didn't look away. He turned his head first, not wanting Henry to notice.

Henry told Lenny, "Okay, Lenny, you don't usually say much, but if you feel that strong about a little catbird, it's yours."

Leah's face flushed, and Lenny felt his cheeks get hot, too. Rebecca and Leah left in a buggy, and Lenny returned to Noey's to do some fieldwork.

Boom

Noey told Lenny, "Stone has been a little lame in one foot. Maybe we could use Lightning in our hitch."

"Lightning, a buggy horse hitched with our drafts?"

"Sure"—Noey grinned—"we used to do that all the time when I was a boy. A buggy horse like Lightning can have a lot of gumption and can hold up their end of the work. He's thin but strong; those wiry horses will surprise you." Adding Lightning to his hitch was the last thing Lenny wanted. It was enough to have colts to deal with without adding an uncontrollable buggy horse. Noey reasoned, "I don't think we have any choice right now."

"Can you help me get him started then? Once we get him going and a little tired, he won't give me as much trouble."

The older man nodded with a grin on his face and wrinkles in the corners of his eyes. "Oh, by the way, Leonard, would you take this concrete block back to that old shed beyond the barn? Slide the door open, and put it on the stack of blocks in there."

Lenny nodded that he would, but as he rounded the barn, he heard a sneezing sound come from that direction. He stopped and stared into the dark shadowy area around the shed and thought he heard a man blowing his nose. He hid the concrete block in some tall grass near the corner of the barn, thinking he could put it in the shed sometime later, and headed back inside to harness horses.

Lenny chuckled as he watched Lightning struggle to keep up with the heavy horses. A thin horse looked out of place with drafts; however, it was impressive how much stamina and determination Lightning had. He obviously was determined not to be outdone by any other horse.

On the second pass, they stopped under their massive oak tree to rest. Lenny happened to notice that right under his feet, an ant colony was constructing a series of tunnels. He watched carefully as they carried out grains of sand like huge boulders, dragging them into a pile. A small group of them were heading to their home with a bug ten times bigger than any of them. They all worked together cooperating without any words.

Even though it was cloudy, it got warm during the afternoon. Lenny got drowsy watching his big team of six horses walking on and on. He had to shake his head and slap his own cheeks to keep from falling asleep. At one point, he was almost dreaming even though his eyes were open, though glazed. In this dreamlike state, an idea came to him. He decided that in the evening, he would try driving Lighting over to Aaron's harness shop.

While his horses were working faithfully down in a low area of the field, a strange phenomenon began to take place. A huge cottonwood tree up on a nearby bluff was shedding its cotton seedlings. The old wind blew at the tree, exactly like Leah had the dandelion, and in a similar way, a million puffballs came floating down like snow. It reminded Lenny of being inside of a snow globe, like the one his mother displayed at Christmas time. Cottonwood seedlings landed on horse manes and tails like a midsummer snowfall. The whole world seemed surreal watching a line of beautiful horses pushing through a warm blizzard. Cotton sailed about like snowflakes and accumulated in drifts on the ground.

A growling sound came up the road from the direction of Aaron Burr's place and jolted Lenny out of his momentary bliss. He roused himself and peered through trees to see what was barreling downhill on the road. He caught a glimpse of a blue pickup truck, but, as it came around the curve near Junior's farm, there was a loud BANG. After that, everything went quiet. Lenny quickly tied Train to a fence post, knowing the other horses could go nowhere because their driving lines were connected to Train. The young man took off running across his tilled field, struggling to look up the road as he went. He could see that the blue pickup truck was partly in the ditch, and his mind raced as he went, wondering what he would find when he got there. As he got closer, he saw that its front end was smashed. By the time he arrived, Howard was standing on the road, looking into a ditch.

"What happened?" Lenny panted out as he came up.

Howard pointed down into the ditch. "It's Dusty," he said quietly.

An older non-Amish man was standing there, too, obviously the pickup driver. "I was just coming up the road, and that little horse ran right in front of me."

"Does your truck still run?" Lenny asked the heavy-set older man who had a feed cap tilted off to one side of his head. The guy hiked up his pants that were sagging and said gruffly, "Nope, we'd better get it off the road before someone comes along and hits me."

Howard told the man, "I got a team tied right up the lane. I'll go get them and pull you out of the way."

While Howard was getting his team, Lenny went and knelt down beside Dusty's lifeless body. He was surprised that the pony looked fine, except that he had blood trickling from his nostrils. He reached out and brushed Dusty's mane gently aside.

"It's his own fault," the older man said. Lenny didn't respond.

A loud rattle of steel wheels sounded as Howard drove Prince and Duke next to the damaged pickup. Lenny helped Howard hook a chain to its frame while the older fellow climbed into his cab behind the steering wheel. Henry had come out on foot by that time and stood by Lenny, watching soberly. Prince and Duke heaved forward obediently when Howard gave a cluck, easily dragging that big truck off into Junior's field until other arrangements could be made.

Bill climbed back out of his truck and told Howard, "You ought to pull that little horse out of there, too." Howard drove his team in Dusty's direction, not questioning an older man's instruction. Prince and Duke snorted heavily, taking in Dusty's scent. The boys hooked a chain to the pony's leg, and Howard clucked again. This time Junior's horses shook their manes and stepped in place but didn't pull forward. Bill ordered Howard, "Hand me that whip off your cart; I'll get those horses going." A buggy whip was clipped to Junior's fore cart, and Howard took hold of it, but before he could hand it over, another voice surprised everyone.

"Give that whip to me, Howard." Junior's voice boomed, his eyes full of fire. Howard surrendered the whip to his dad, and Junior said, "Dusty was their friend. Horses often refuse to drag another horse. Go up and get our stone boat. If we lay Dusty on there, it will be different."

In a short time, Howard returned with his flat wooden sled pulled by Prince and Duke. Lenny and Henry carefully rolled Dusty onto the sled. Howard made a point of letting his horses watch, and it seemed they understood this was different. When they were asked to get up, they complied willingly, pulling their friend up into Junior's farm lane. The gruff old man began retelling his story of hitting Dusty, but Lenny didn't want to hear it again, so he slowly walked back to his horses and resumed discing. All he could think about was Fannie Ella. He kept imagining what her reaction would be when she heard about Dusty. When he stopped to rest his horses, Lenny walked around in front of them to check their harness. He looked at Queen and Misty; they both returned his gaze with their big, dark, shiny eyes. The young man took off his straw hat and wiped the sweat off his brow with his shirt sleeve. He left his hat off and said, "I know Dusty was a good friend to you, Queen and Misty."

Lenny felt weak and sick. He didn't feel like discing, but he knew it needed to be done. Before he went back to disc, Lenny leaned his forehead against Queen's thick neck and prayed, "Dear Lord, please help Fannie Ella when she gets the news about Dusty. Please, Lord, comfort her somehow."

Fannie Ella

When he finished discing, Lenny headed over to see Junior's family. He dreaded seeing Fannie Ella but hoped to talk to her just the same. When he passed Junior's chicken building, he saw Blue and Tick sitting at the base of a big tree. They didn't come up bawling as usual, which surprised Lenny enough to make him look back at them. All at once, it occurred to him that they were sitting under that tree for a reason. On further investigation, it became clear that Fannie Ella was up in that tree. Lenny climbed up against scratchy bark until he came to where the girl sat. She was on a smaller horizontal limb that seemed too thin for the two of them. He opted to sit on a much larger limb just below hers. He could easily lean forward onto her limb and put his arms over it. He looked up at Fannie Ella, but she didn't look back. She gazed off into the distance. At first, Lenny tried to think of something nice to say, but giving up on that idea, he chose to gaze at the view she was watching. Her tree was the type that had very few leaves around its trunk, yet there was a dome of leaves on the outer edge, making a room of sorts. This made her tree a perfect hiding place—that is, if a pair of hound dogs wouldn't have been sitting below. There was an opening in the leaves, creating a window with a view of Junior's dairy pasture below. The two of them sat, watching black-and-white cows meander aimlessly, tails swishing. Occasionally, a cow would thrust her head back to her side and try to lick the flies off her backbone, slinging saliva that in turn, drew more flies. A long, sad bellow came from one of Junior's cows, answered by a far-off cow somewhere the distance.

Fannie Ella mourned the loss of her pony without tears. Lenny felt like crying merely witnessing her sadness. She looked so sweet sitting in a tree, wearing her little Amish dress and head scarf. Her brown hair, visible under her scarf, matched her dark eyebrows. He was planning to say something as soon as he could get past how tight his throat was. She looked him in his tear-filled eyes and said, "You loved Dusty, too … didn't you?"

Since he couldn't speak right then, Lenny gave a nod. After he regained his composure, he told her, "Dusty was the best pony I ever knew." After a few deep breaths, he let out his next sentence. "But what really makes me sad is that I know how badly you'll miss him."

Fannie Ella didn't respond but sat staring through her little window in the leaves for a long time. Way off in the south, a soft rumble of thunder rolled, gently warning that more rain would be heading their way. They didn't see any flashes of light, but faint murmurings of thunder continued, sending vibrations that could be felt through the branches of the tree. When Lenny finally started to climb down, Fannie Ella said to him, "That was the nicest thing anyone ever told me, in Dutch or English."

On his way back home, Lenny stopped at Herbie's bee hive and stood a safe distance from it. He watched in amazement, as usual, while the bees shot out of the white box, as if they had been shot from a gun. How they could fly out of a box at that speed remained a mystery, zooming out only inches above his head. Lenny had left Russell in the house because he didn't want him causing trouble at a time like this. However, as he walked through the woods, he wished his little buddy was with him.

Aunt Ruth quietly stirred something in a large pan that hissed on her stovetop, and it filled her kitchen with a warm delectable scent of chicken. Noey and Lenny washed up and sat without words, both watching Russell, who stared back at them. Ruth dropped something and Russell slowly walked over and ate it. Ruth set a large bowl of chicken soup on the table and took her normal seat across from Noey. They bowed their heads and prayed a silent prayer. During the prayer, Lenny looked at the table, wondering why Davy W.'s place was set even though he wasn't around anymore. Ruth hardly touched her meal, and Noey commented, "Don't you feel well, Ruth?"

"I can't quit thinking about Fanny Ella. She is such a sweet girl ... and she loved that pony so much."

Noey nodded and said, "Junior's whole family is sad. They are all such good people. Leonard, did you know Barefoot Herbie came over while you were at Alvin's and helped me plant my cornfield?"

"He did?"

"That was the day after Davy got … sent away. As soon as Junior and Ruby heard about it, they sent over Fannie Ella and Herbie with cinnamon rolls. Fannie Ella helped Ruth in her garden all day while Barefoot Herbie and I planted corn."

They bowed their heads and prayed their after-meal prayer. Lenny prayed for Junior's family and especially for Fannie Ella. He glanced at Ruth, and then prayed for her, too. As soon as they finished praying, Ruth stepped out of the room. Lenny looked at Noey to see his reaction, having never seen Ruth walk out of the kitchen with dishes on the table. Noey stood up slowly, holding onto his lower back, and quietly began to clear the table. Russell watched, cocking his head to one side.

Lenny's chair groaned as he slid it back and helped Noey with the dishes. They worked in silence until everything was about done, and then Noey said in a very low whisper, "Leonard, if you could stay on a little longer … it would really help Ruth to not be so lonely."

Lenny nodded. "I will."

Faster Horse

After supper, Noey reminded Lenny that he wanted him to go to Aaron Burr's harness shop and see about how his work harness was coming. Lightning was still sweated from all the hard work he had done that afternoon. It seemed like the perfect time for Lenny to try driving him. He put buggy harness on the horse that had been wearing work harness all day. Lightning actually stood calmly without chewing his lead rope. Even when being led out to Davy

W.'s cart, he walked slowly behind Lenny. "Good boy, Lightning. That is the way a good buggy horse should act."

Lenny climbed on the cart and gave a cluck. Lightning took off trotting but not ridiculously fast as he usually did. At Aaron Burr's harness shop, Lenny tied Lightning to the hitching post and smiled as he headed in, feeling good about driving a faster horse.

Dark as usual, Aaron Burr's shop felt cool almost like walking into a storm cellar. Harness oils filled the air with a pleasant scent, along with a whirring, repetitive click of the old man's sewing machine. Lenny assumed that Aaron didn't know he was there. After all, how would a blind man notice someone enter a room? Especially when the sound of a treadle sewing machine was clicking in rhythm to the old man's foot tapping that powered it. The younger man stood and watched his elder. He admired the way Aaron felt his way through his work, sewing perfect seams in leather and nylon harnesses. At long last, Aaron's foot ceased its tapping. He held up his work and examined it with his fingers, running his hand along the length of the piece while he turned his head in Lenny's direction.

"How are those colts coming along?" he asked, causing Lenny to jump.

"Not too bad. The filly finally settled down, after her mama joined up with my hitch."

Aaron laughed, "I heard about that. Junior also told me that you were planning to buy Misty and make a team out of her and Alvin's colt."

"Yeah, I think so."

The old man sat as though looking out the window and spoke as if to someone way off in the distance. "My brothers and I used to break colts in those same fields." He sat for a moment in silence, and then chuckled. "One day my younger brother and I were sent down to cut weeds along the edge of the field near that huge old oak tree." He turned to Lenny and asked, "Is that old tree still there on the west edge of that lower field?"

"Yeah, it is."

"Well, there were some horse weeds along that west edge of the field. We were sent down there with hand scythes to clear them out. We had been cutting for an hour or so when I got into a nest of bumble bees. They came up out of their nest, rumbling like thunder, and I dropped my scythe and took off running. Those bees would have caught up to me if I hadn't been older and faster than Jesse. My poor younger brother came running up behind me, yowling every time a bee hit him."

Lenny laughed until he noticed Aaron's face had gone sober. When Lenny was quiet again, he heard Aaron saying, "I always felt bad about outrunning my brother that day. I wish I could go back and do that over; I'd be happy to take the sting for him."

"You didn't commit a sin; you just tried getting away like anyone would." Lenny tried to justify Aaron's actions with his own story of Perry and bees in mind. Aaron grasped his long gray beard quietly for a moment.

"Leonard, there are two types of sins: sins of commission and of omission." He sat as though waiting for Lenny to ask for an explanation.

Lenny only said, "Huh?"

"Commissions are sins that you commit. Omissions are the good things you should have done but omitted."

Lenny sat monumentally still. Silence in the harness shop felt heavy, and the small room seemed to be closing in on him.

Aaron broke the painful silence with a happier voice. "Did Noey send you to check on your team harness?"

"Yes, he did."

"Well, you tell him that it will, Lord willing, be done the first day of next week." Aaron followed Lenny outside and stood looking off into the distance while the younger man untied Lightning. The old man quietly rehearsed a saying that he had told Lenny the first day they met. "When storms come, remember Him who spoke and calmed the storm and sea. When troubles rise around you like a flood, keep your head above the waters and look for your deliverer." His words seemed to sink deep into Lenny's heart, though not quite making sense in his mind.

Aaron Burr stepped closer and took hold of Lightning's halter and said, "I wasn't sure who came up the lane at first. I thought it sounded like Davy's horse, but I had heard that Davy W. went away. Then I thought to myself, 'That Leonard must be trying Lightning out.'" The old man laughed and so did Lenny.

"Yep, I used Lightning in the field today. He's tired enough I can almost handle him." They both laughed again. Russell had been waiting patiently on the floor board of Lenny's wooden wheeled cart. He jumped up and sat beside his friend as Lightning shot out of Aaron Burr's lane and headed toward home.

Lenny told his little buddy, "Hang on, Russell; Lightning must have got his second wind!"

They had considerable speed coming down out of Aaron's drive and continued gaining as they rounded the curve passing Junior's two lanes. Russell's black-and-brown ears were flapping in the wind. At the same place where Dusty had been hit earlier that day, Lenny realized he was no longer driving Lightning. The tall, dark horse seemed to be bent on going as fast as he could. As they came upon Noey's lane, Lightning showed no sign of slowing, and then at the last moment decided that he wanted to turn into the home place after all. Lightning made his turn just fine, but Lenny, Russell, and the wooden wheeled cart weren't quite able to. All three tumbled into the ditch. The last thing Lenny remembered was seeing Russell leaping into the air, stretching out his little legs, as if he planned to fly away. The next thing Lenny knew, he was standing next to Noey, looking at Davy's wrecked cart. Noey was holding Russell in his arms, and Ruth had her hands on her hips, scolding her husband, "That horse will be sold Monday at the horse sale!"

Noey chuckled. "That turned out pretty good."

Noey helped Lenny catch Lightning, and they got him un-harnessed and put away. Lenny told his uncle, "Sorry about that."

"About what?"

"That I let Lightning get away from me and wrecked Davy's cart."

Noey chuckled, his blue eyes as kind as Grandpa's always were. "Don't worry yourself about that. We don't need a horse like Lightning on an Amish farm. He was born to race, not pull a buggy."

Noey and Lenny stood looking at Lightning for a time until the older man spoke again. "Leonard, would you mind checking on our fat cattle? Just go out along this fence line that heads toward the river. They will be grazing that edge of the river bottom and up on those wooded bluffs."

"Sure. I know where they are, but what do you want me to do?"

"Well, I usually had Davy walk that lower fence to make sure there aren't any holes in it. And from there, you can see the fence row up above, too. While you're at it, take note of the cattle if they all seem to be okay."

Lenny nodded that he understood and headed off into the woods with his sidekick, Russell, close behind.

Dusk hung heavy in the air as night sounds began to echo out of the river bottom. Lenny looked back and forth carefully as he walked, worried of what may be nearby. Trees in the distance stood still, but as he walked, it seemed the nearer ones were moving, giving everything an eerie feel. He saw something out of the corner of his eye and turned. He was sure he saw a shadowy figure that stood upright like a man but didn't have an Amish hat like every other human Lenny had seen in these woods. Immediately, Bigfoot came to mind. The most surprising thing was that Russell looked in that direction also but didn't bark or pursue the thing. The young man crept along stealthily until he reached the far end of the cattle pasture, hoping whatever it was didn't see him. From there, he could easily hear the English River thrashing and threatening to leave its banks and swallow up Noey's fields.

Lenny scanned the hillside, looking at Noey's cattle. They all stood perfectly still, staring back at him. A woodpecker knocked loudly on a tree, followed by a clicking sound, and then a screech-owl call. Lenny turned and started to trot back along the fence toward home. His trot turned to a jog, then a run. And finally, he was sprinting frantically. Russell outran him. Just as Lenny rounded the corner of the barn, something grabbed his ankle and sent him tumbling in summersaults. While still rolling, he remembered the concrete block he had hidden beside the barn and knew what had caught his ankle.

He headed to the house and slipped upstairs quietly, not wanting to wake Aunt Ruth. When he got into his room, he lit a lantern and saw his Bible lying on the dresser, waiting to be consulted. Lenny opened it, letting the pages flop where they may. Thunder rumbled overhead. He looked at the page he happened upon and read.

"Then he got into the boat and his disciples followed him. Without warning, a furious storm came up on the lake, so that the waves swept over the boat. But Jesus was sleeping. The disciples went and woke him, saying, 'Lord, save us! We're going to drown!

"He replied, 'You of little faith, why are you so afraid?' Then he got up and rebuked the winds and the waves, and it was completely calm.

"The men were amazed and asked, 'What kind of man is this? Even the winds and the waves obey him!'" (Matthew 8:23 –27)

The words seemed to roar at Lenny like lion. Another wave of rumbles sounded from an approaching storm and shook the house; windows were rattling. He shut his Bible. Everything seemed quite again. He blew out his lantern and put his head under the covers, listening for thunder but heard nothing.

Chapter 11

SLOW HORSE

Noey, Ruth, and Lenny rode to church together in their black top buggy. Big Red, harnessed in his Sunday leather, pulled them over sloping Iowan hills. Occasionally, those hills gave way to long stretches of flatlands. The three of them sat quietly, listening to their horse's constant hoof beats. Gentle breezes rolled like waves across farm fields, bringing with them distinct scents of growing corn and various natural fertilizers. Aunt Ruth broke through the rhythm of hoof beats with her kind voice, "Well... it sure is a fine Sunday morning." Noey and Lenny both mumbled an acknowledgment to her words but stayed silent, both knowing this was the way Ruth opened up a sermon of her own.

"Let's not set our hearts on our troubles. Davy made his own choices. He easily could have made a few changes about what he wore and some words that he used, and he could still be here. We need to remember all of our blessings in life; God has been very good to us. Let's go to church with those things on our hearts and in our minds."

Noey replied by quoting a verse, "Whatever is good, whatever is right, whatever is pure, fix your mind on these things."

Lenny was quiet. He was happy they both wanted to focus on good things, but all he could think about was a few things he could have done differently himself. How he should have told Davy W. about Leah. Maybe then he would have been willing to make some changes.

Jonah

Morning church services started out as normal. Lenny didn't look over at the women until Herbie nudged him and nodded at the older girl section, where all four of Harold's daughters were seated there among them. Lenny felt his heart skip a beat on seeing Leah's face. Ruby, Rachel, and Della gave a slight smile when they saw Lenny looking at them. Leah didn't change expression; she was still clearly avoiding eye contact. Ruby glanced over occasionally, as if trying her best not to look in Herbie's direction but unable to resist. When she did, Herbie got all fidgety. On one such occasion, Lenny poked Herbie's side, and his buddy's face turned bright red. He looked over at Ruby and could see from across the room that she was blushing. Lenny wished he could get that reaction from Leah.

After long slow singing, preachers stood one at a time and spoke. One of them spoke a scripture reference, and Lenny turned quietly to read it. It was the beginning of the book of Jonah. Lenny knew the part about Jonah being told to go and warn a certain group of people that if they didn't change, trouble was coming. And how Jonah went the opposite direction and tried to run from the Lord by getting in a ship heading to another land.

"Then the Lord sent a great wind on the sea, and such a violent storm arose that the ship threatened to break up. All the sailors were afraid and each cried out to his own god. And they threw the cargo into the sea to lighten up the ship. But Jonah had gone below deck, where he lay down and fell into a deep sleep. The captain went to him and said, 'How can you sleep? Get up and call on your god! Maybe he will take notice of us, and we will not perish.' Then the sailors said to each other, 'Come, let us cast lots to find out who is responsible for this calamity.' They cast lots and the lot fell on Jonah. So they asked him, 'Tell us who is responsible for making all this trouble for us? What do you do? Where are you from? What is your country? From what people are you?' He answered, 'I am a Hebrew and I worship the Lord, the God of heaven, who made the sea and the land.' This terrified them and they asked, 'What have you done?' (They knew he was running away from the Lord, because he had already told them so.) The sea was getting rougher and rougher. So they asked him, 'What should we do to you to make the sea calm down for us?' 'Pick me up and throw me into the sea,' he replied, 'and it will become calm. I know that it is my fault that this great storm has come upon you.' (Jonah, chapter 1)."

Lenny drifted off into a light sleep after reading and began to dream that he was Jonah and was supposed to go speak to Davy W., but he went and did the opposite of what he was told. He wanted to finish his dream and see how things would end but woke up instead. When he opened his eyes, he could see a fly walking around on Herbie's hand. Lenny waved his hand at it, and it only walked over onto Herbie's other hand. Lenny went to shoo it again, but Herbie pushed his hand away as though protecting his little friend.

Lenny gave Herbie the look. "What is going on here?"

Herbie leaned over and whispered, but his voice wasn't that quiet as he said, "I pulled his wings off."

Lenny looked at the fly again, and what Herbie meant sank in. The non-Amish guy couldn't help himself sputtering out loud. He laughed at Herbie's words as much as at the fly. His buddy had said it so seriously, "I pulled his wings off."

The fly walked contentedly on Herbie's hands and couldn't fly off. Herbie didn't laugh. After Lenny quieted down, Herbie leaned over and whispered loudly again, "I forgot my sister's long hair." Lenny felt like his chest was going to burst as he leaned forward and tried to hold back his laughter. After a time, Lenny recovered his composure and glanced in Leah and Ruby's direction. Ruby seemed to be enjoying the fact that young men were struggling to keep from laughing; Leah, on the other hand, looked at them without any expression. Even then she looked beautiful.

After the service, Noey, Ruth, and Lenny rode home in a peaceful silence. Something about listening to Big Red's faithful, steady hoof beats seemed comforting. Lenny thought about how willingly horses comply with all that is asked of them without complaining. At first, it made him mad at Davy W. for being so stubborn that he hurt Aunt Ruth like he did. Then he remembered that he wasn't any better himself.

Singing

On his way to the Singing, Lenny enjoyed the quiet ride behind Nelly. He examined neighboring farm fields with rich green growing crops. He thought about Noey's cornfield having just been planted a few days ago, and his beans were not even in the ground yet. Red-winged blackbirds swooped off telephone wires, attacking Nelly as she trotted past. She ignored them as though it was a plan to discourage the birds from bothering her. They rumbled through a low place where a field creek gurgled loudly because of the spring runoff. As they passed under a clump of trees, a catbird meowed repeatedly. Lenny searched the limbs for a little gray bird but didn't see it. He thought of Leah.

"Nelly, I have to tell Rebecca that I'm not taking her home from the Singings anymore. I don't want to get Noey and Ruth in trouble with Mose, especially now that Davy got sent away. I just can't cause more trouble. Besides, Leah won't even talk to me because, as she says, 'You're dating my friend.'" Nelly's ears turned back, listening to the young man's voice. Lenny added, "I have to tell Leah about Davy for Ruth's sake. I just have to!" Nelly shook her mane and rounded the top of a hill. Just ahead of them, a line of buggy horses trotted into a lane, toting their cartloads of young passengers to a Singing.

A long Quonset hut building housed the Singing. Corrugated tin arched over them like a tunnel and reverberated, the sound of their singing saturating the air with rich beautiful sounds. Lenny sat in the midst of his cousins Sam, David, and Perry and near Herbie, Howard, Henry, and Harvey. He enjoyed being surrounded by all of his favorite guys. It seemed like a perfect world as he listened to a few hundred young people singing four-part harmonies. He wished he was really one of them. While they sang, he determined in his heart to stay all summer and help Noey farm; it was the least he could do since it was his fault that Davy W. was gone. More than that, he didn't have any desire to leave this place. With a background of hymns being sung, he thought about being in the fields working with his colts. He imagined more hay days at Alvin's and Harold's farms. He didn't want to leave his little buddy Russell behind. Most of all, he wanted to be wherever Leah was, even if just as a friend. He decided that he would find a way to talk to her soon, maybe even that very night.

Young Amish men gathered outside in the darkness, waiting for girls to come and join them one by one. Lenny stood in a semi circle that included his cousins and neighbor buddies. Perry teased, "I wonder who in this group is brave enough to take the bishop's granddaughter home from the Singing?"

Herbie said, "I only know one guy that brave!" Everyone laughed but Lenny.

One by one, Amish girls stepped out of the glow of lantern light into the darkness. A shadowy figure would disappear from the circle of boys and join one of the girls, and the couple would slip away on a horse-drawn cart. Lenny saw Rebecca's slender silhouette exit through the veil of light into a yard of darkness and fireflies. He tried to sneak away from his friends discreetly, but Henry said, just loud enough for him to hear, "Horse Pull Lenny is one brave guy." The other boys all let out catcalls.

Rebecca led the way to Old Nelly, as Lenny struggled to find his way by firefly light. He didn't know how Rebecca and the rest of the Amish did it. Nelly was tied to a fence down in a ditch beyond Vernon's barn. Rebecca was happy and talkative as they climbed on their two-wheeled open cart. Nelly pulled them, jostling up out of the ditch, and trotted off at her usual pace. They headed into a dark night, one of the first couples leaving. It was a lovely evening, with warm breezes passing over the young man and woman, bringing delightful scents of mown hay. Lenny could barely see the outline of Rebecca's pretty face as she started to say, "What are you planning to do ... " But another horse and buggy were catching up to them, so she asked, "Can't you get this old horse to go any faster?"

Lenny clucked and shook his lines, but Nelly continued on as though she hadn't heard him or felt the lines shake. Moments later, the other horse came near, breathing down on their backs so close that Lenny could have reached back and touched its nose. Then it veered around them, rumbling past, and the other boy called out, "Slow horse!"

And his girl passenger said, "I thought it was stopped."

Lenny and Rebecca listened to the other couple laughing as they disappeared into the darkness ahead of them. "That was just embarrassing!" Rebecca moaned. After a few moments, she restated her earlier question. "Are you planning to stay on at your uncle's for the rest of the summer then?"

Lenny watched old Nelly slowly trotting for a few moments as he contemplated an answer. Just as he opened his mouth to speak, another horse came trotting up, overtaking them with ease. This time, Lenny recognized the horse as Smoky. Herbie and Ruby sounded like they were having fun. Their laughter echoed off a steep bank that ran along the gravel road beside them.

Rebecca chided Lenny, "Use your buggy whip on that old mare. We're going to get passed again!"

"That's useless," Lenny reasoned. "There's no way Nelly can keep up with Smoky anyway."

Rebecca looked embarrassed as Smoky romped past. Herbie teased, "Is your buggy broke down, or why are you stopped in the middle of the road?"

"No, we are enjoying a nice Sunday evening drive. Are you two on your way to a fire, or what's the hurry?" Lenny quipped.

Herbie teased back, "Oh, it's not the buggy that is broke down—it's that broken-down old horse."

"Sophomore," Lenny called back at him.

After Smoky rounded a curve and out of sight, Lenny got around to answering Rebecca's question. "Yeah, I think I'm staying on at least until the end of the summer, and then we will see from there."

Before Rebecca could reply, hoof beats sounded behind them as a third horse began to overtake them. This time Lenny knew it was Henry's black horse—it had a white diamond marking on its nose that could be seen even by starlight. He hated to have Henry pass him, especially with Leah. Lenny pulled his buggy whip out of the holder and gave it a crack with care, trying not to touch Nelly with it.

Rebecca looked disgusted. "It wouldn't hurt to give her a little tap you know!"

Henry and Leah came up beside them, and Henry said, "Hey look! It's Slow Horse Lenny. What's wrong? Is that old mare going lame?"

"She's not as lame as your jokes!" Lenny replied.

Henry retorted, "Oh, your response is faster than that old nag."

Lenny heard Leah say to Henry, "Be nice to Nelly; she's a good old mare."

When everything got quiet again, Rebecca asked, "Why don't you drive Lightning now that Davy W. is gone?"

"I tried driving him, but he ran off with me. I just don't trust him."

"Everyone calls you 'Horse Pull Lenny' like you are a big horseman, and then this."

"And then this what?"

"And then I'm humiliated by taking a ride home from a boy who's afraid of horses."

Lenny was quiet. He planned to tell her that he couldn't take her home from a Singing again and was trying to think of how, as they pulled in her lane. Before he even got Nelly to a complete stop, Rebecca had jumped off his cart and turned, facing him in the dark. "I don't think we should date anymore," she announced.

"Okay," Lenny answered, wanting to tell her that they never really were dating in the first place. However, he didn't say it.

She continued, "You're not really Amish, and we just aren't a good match."

"Okay," Lenny said again and sat quietly, waiting to see if there was anything more to breaking up than that.

"Don't you have anything else to say besides 'okay'?"

"Well, I think you're right."

Rebecca let out an "errrrr" and hurried into her house. Lenny sat quietly on his cart for a few minutes, not sure what had just happened. Fireflies glowed here and there, moving about silently. A few crickets chirped merrily in tall grasses nearby. Lenny gave a cluck to Nelly, and she quickly trotted out of Rebecca's lane.

Like a Thief

As Nelly pulled him away from Rebecca's, Lenny told her, "Well, I'm glad that's over with." Nelly let out a little nicker that sounded like Rebecca's giggle. This made Lenny laugh out loud. They hadn't gone far when he told Nelly, "I think we should swing over by Leah's place. Maybe it will work out for me to talk to her. I have to tell her about Davy. I just have to!"

Nelly began to turn at the road leading to Leah's, almost without Lenny even pulling on the right line. They passed by Web's place and turned into the woods near Harold's lane. Lenny had been by there enough times that he knew there was a wooded field entrance at the top of the hill. He tied Nelly to a woven wire fence and climbed over it, sneaking up toward the house.

Lenny hid in the trees not far from that place where he had stumbled with a container of flour and spilled it all over himself. He chuckled as he thought about how silly he must have looked in front of Leah and her sisters. Whenever he thought about that night, his memory of Leah, with her long-flowing hair, came back to mind. She was such a sweet girl; her personality was shining through her dark brown eyes. He was intrigued by her beauty when she was wearing an Amish covering. When her hair was down, Leah was stunning. He drew in a deep breath and released a sigh, and then scolded himself out loud, "What am I doing?" He winced, hoping no one heard him, and whispered to himself, "Leonard, you came here to tell Leah about Davy W. Quit thinking about her that way!"

He squatted down, leaning against a large oak tree, wondering how long he would have to wait for Henry and Leah to come out. He knew that Henry may spend an hour with Leah before leaving. It may be impossible to see her, but Lenny was determined to finally do the right thing. Both Herbie and Henry's horses stood at the hitching rack, waiting patiently while their owners courted Amish girls.

He was just thinking through what he was going to say—if he got the chance—when he heard the screen door creak open. Lenny could feel his heart beat in his chest. He wasn't quite sure why he was so nervous. He felt like a criminal stalking Leah, but he reassured himself that he was trying to do the right thing. It was difficult in the darkness to see if the couple left the porch or not. Lenny tried to focus and listen. It would have been difficult to know what they were saying if they had been talking in English, but because of their Dutch it was impossible.

All at once, Henry's horse spun and chugged out of the Yoder's lane, trotting at top speed down the hill toward Web's place. Lenny couldn't believe his luck. He could see Leah standing under the windmill, watching the buggy go. Lenny tried to make himself speak or move, but he felt like a person having a dream and trying to run but can't. He saw Leah turn and walk in the direction of her house. All at once, as if he had emerged out of water, he found himself lunging forward and calling, "Leah!" The girl slipped into the shadows of her porch, no doubt startled. Lenny tried again, this time in as loud a whisper as anyone could use. "Leah, it's Lenny.

Come here, I want to talk to you!" He kept moving in her direction and whispering, "Leah ... it's Lenny!"

Suddenly, she appeared, walking toward the windmill, which was also toward him. "Leonard?" she also whispered, as loud as a whisper could be. "What are you doing here?"

They met at the base of the windmill. A slight breeze caused the face of the windmill to change direction, and the blades began to turn slowly with a rattle. "I need to talk to you Leah?"

Leah didn't answer but turned and looked at her house for a long time as though she would be able to tell if a family member might be looking out a window. After a prolonged silence in a sea of dancing fireflies and a few crickets chirping, she turned and whispered, "Let's go over there under that oak tree." They quietly slipped like shadows across the yard and under the tree where Lenny had been waiting earlier.

"What?" Leah asked in a no nonsense way. She obviously wanted to get to the bottom of why Lenny would appear in her yard like a thief.

"Why did Henry leave so soon?" Lenny had to ask. He couldn't see the girl's face because of darkness. A firefly lit up beside them, and he could tell that she stood, arms folded, as though disgusted. He wished he could see what expression she was making but guessed he was getting an angry look. He tried again, "I'm sorry. I know that is none of my business. It's just that I was thinking I may have to wait a long time before he left, and I really am dying to talk to you. It can't wait any longer."

Leah surprised Lenny by answering his question. "Well, if you must know, Henry and I broke up."

"What?"

"Yep, we decided that we are not going to date."

Lenny was shocked. This was the last thing he expected, and he began to think of a bunch of questions he wanted to ask but didn't know if he should.

While he was evaluating what to say in his head, she asked him a question. "While we are snooping in each other's business, where is your little girlfriend? Why aren't you at Rebecca's house?"

"I...we...well." Lenny hesitated, trying to find a good way to say it.

"Well, what?"

"We broke up, too!"

"I guess it's a good night for breaking up," Leah said, and they laughed together for the first time in years.

Leah said, "Can I ask why?"

"You tell me why you broke up first," Lenny insisted.

Leah was quiet, but he had a feeling her dimple was popping even though he couldn't see it. And he liked it. She leaned back against the oak tree, and he could tell she was looking up away from him as though embarrassed. "He told me that he didn't feel we were a good match and that we shouldn't move ahead unless we thought we may want to marry sometime."

Lenny felt a bit sad and happy at the same time. He tried to cover the happy part and said, "Leah, I can't believe he said that to you. You're such a nice girl. What is he thinking?"

A short giggle came out of her, and then she replied, "No, it's okay, really. We both knew the whole time that we were just dating because Herbie and Ruby wanted us to."

All at once, Lenny remembered what he had come to say and tried to force himself to do the right thing. He knew that she really liked Davy W. and that if he told her, maybe they could send word to him and he would come back to the Amish and to Noey and Ruth. Just as he got ready to spill everything, she spoke first.

"So, it's your turn. Why did you and Rebecca break up?"

Lenny laughed quietly, embarrassed and not sure what to say. "We . . . well."

"Well, what?"

"Well, first of all, we never really were dating!"

"Shhhh, do you want to wake up my parents?"

"Oops, sorry," Lenny whispered again. "We never really were dating. She told me almost the same thing Henry told you; in fact, I wonder if they are planning to date each other."

They both laughed as quietly as they could in the darkness under the oak tree. Then Leah surprised him. "Maybe you could give me a ride home from the next Singing; that would take the sting out of getting dumped." Lenny's heart started pounding again; he wanted to kiss her so badly he almost did. His conscience stopped him. "So, what did you come to talk to me about?" Leah's voice sounded coy and cute. He got all mixed up inside and thought of another way to explain himself.

"Leah, I'm thinking about sticking around longer than I first planned. My uncle Noey and Aunt Ruth want me to think about staying for the rest of the summer. So, I may give it a try."

"Lenny, that's so good to hear!"

"Shhhh, you're gonna wake up your parents," he teased her.

"Oops, sorry." They both laughed quietly again.

"If I do stick around, I really want us to be friends! Can we please be friends?" he pleaded.

"Of course we are friends," she stated emphatically.

Lenny didn't shy away this time but challenged her, "Leah, friends talk to each other."

"We will talk when you bring me home from the Singing next time!"

With that she headed back up toward the windmill. Lenny leaned against the tree where Leah had been standing and sighed. He watched as she disappeared into the sea of fireflies and shadows near her house, and then headed back to old Nelly, who was waiting quietly where he had left her. She let out a warm nicker when he got next to her, and Lenny rubbed her soft nose and told her, "Thanks for waiting, Nelly. It went good! Oh, uh, except that I still didn't tell Leah about Davy W. What is wrong with me?"

Nelly snorted a short snort as Lenny climbed aboard his two-wheeled cart. As she clip-clopped merrily past Web's place,

Lenny's mind alternated between bliss and agony as he thought about Leah and then about what he should have said. As he crossed the creek, he met a car barreling toward him, narrowly missing his cart as it raced past and left him in its dust. Lenny said to Nelly, "Those crazy English people! Huh, ya know what, Nelly Girl? That car was an Impala, about like mine." Nelly continued trotting through the quiet night toward Noey's. Lightning lit up the sky off in the southwest followed by a deep rumble a few moments later. "Looks like that storm is way down south; I hope it stays there, too!"

Chapter 12

ACCUSATIONS

L enny woke to the sound of crows fighting. The sound came from one of the four oaks that sprawled out above Noey' s house whose branches hung over Lenny's room. The young man didn't get up immediately but lay there listening to their cantankerous calls. He imagined that one of them had a small piece of bread and three others were trying repeatedly to snatch it away, having witnessed similar fights while plowing Noey's fields. All at once, he heard wings flapping as the big black birds took their battle to a more distant tree—their angry calls grew faint. Freddie, the rooster, crowed, and Lenny sat on the edge of his bed and pulled on his work pants, looping his suspenders over his soldiers.

"Time to get up, Russell."

The little mostly white dog lay snuggled in his usual blanket nest where Lenny's feet had been. Russell didn't move but opened his eyes and watched the young man button up his shirt. "What mischief are you going to get into today?" Lenny asked, which seemed to remind the dog of some ornery plan he had made. Russell immediately jumped down and stood, waiting for Lenny to open his bedroom door, and then scrambled downstairs.

Aunt Ruth called from the kitchen. "I think that dog needs to go outside."

"I'll let him out," Lenny answered. He took in a deep whiff of coffee as he headed to the porch and pulled on his boots. As soon as Russell got outside, he chased a robin into flight. The small bird had been pulling a worm out of the yard, but it tore in two as the Robin flew off, barely escaping with its life. Lenny was greeted with a deep nicker as he neared the barn. He let his horses in and began the morning ritual of feeding, grooming, and harnessing his fleet of draft animals.

"I went to see Leah last night," he told Train as he brushed his huge friend. "No, I didn't tell her about Davy. I fully intended to, but I failed again. Every time I go to tell her, I look into those sweet brown eyes and melt. All my good intentions escape me, and I don't say what I know I should. Instead, I try to woo her for myself." Train listened quietly, as if he understood Lenny's dilemma. "Should I help someone else get with the girl that I love for Uncle Noey and Aunt Ruth's sake?" While he was currying Tug, all the horses lifted their heads, clueing Lenny that Noey entered the barn.

"We can finish up our planting today," Noey seemed happy to announce. "If you plant that lower section with horses, I think I can finish the top of that field with a tractor. It's not as wet as it was on

Saturday, and that higher part drains better because of the lay of the land."

Lenny used Stone and Jim on the planter. Tug and Train took a day off, having made hay the last several days. Stone reminded Lenny a little of Train and Jim of Tug. They were both well-broke, trustworthy horses. Lenny watched them walk steadily, pulling the small corn planter. He was glad that Stone and Jim would be around when Tug and Train went back to Alvin's.

Lenny pulled his horses up under his massive oak resting tree. They didn't need a long break because corn planters were light and comparatively easy work. He walked around the front of his team to look at their harness.

"Stone, I'm glad you'll be here to help me with training my colts; you, too, Jim. I need a good quiet team to hitch those colts with until I am sure I can trust them." The young man looked his horses in the eyes and adjusted their harness even though it didn't need it. "Well, I guess it's over between me and Rebecca." He sounded out his feelings to his horses. "She is a really nice girl, but we just weren't right for each other. But if I can get Davy to come back, who will I take home from Singings?" A horse fly continually landed on one horse and then the other. Lenny watched it carefully until he had a chance to smash it against Stone's thick neck. Just when he did, he heard a giggle. He looked up and there was Fannie Ella.

"What are you laughing at, girl?"

"I'm laughing at you! What are you doing, killing flies?"

Lenny didn't like a little girl making fun of him. He tried to explain himself, "Yeah, I don't like those flies bothering my horses. I know it's silly."

"I don't really think it's silly; I did the same thing for Dusty all the time." The little Amish girl's face got sad when she said it. Then she smiled and said, "In a couple of years, you could take me home from Singings."

Lenny laughed, his face getting hot, because he realized that Fannie Ella heard him talking about Rebecca.

He told her, "I couldn't ... "

"I know—because we're related ... but I asked my mother, and she said that it is okay if a person dates their second cousin."

Lenny stood looking at Fannie Ella, his mind working hard. Then he asked, "What are you saying? Are we second cousins?"

Lenny was standing in front of his horses, so Fannie Ella climbed up on the empty planter seat and sat down. She rested her chin on her palms and elbows on her knees, looking cute in her little Amish dress and white apron. She smiled as though pleased to be able to tell Lenny something he didn't know. "You didn't know that we are second cousins?"

"No, I had no idea!"

"Yep, your dad, Jake, is my dad's first cousin."

Lenny was almost mad. "Why didn't anyone tell me this before!"

"I guess we all thought you knew it. After all, this is a small community. Don't you realize that most of us have some family connection to each other?"

"Nope, I didn't think of that at all. So, I guess that means that I'm Herbie's second cousin, too?"

"Yep! And there are no rules against having your second cousin for a best friend either!" Fannie Ella laughed and climbed off the planter seat. "You better get back to work if you want to be a real Amish man."

Lenny picked up a dirt clod to throw at her, and the little barefoot Amish girl disappeared through the trees between her home place and Noey's.

While his horses faithfully pulled the planter, Lenny watched a bank of dark clouds build in the southwestern sky. At first, he thought they may pass by to the south, but instead they hung in place, churning and boiling. Birds swooped into limbs over Lenny's head, chirping wildly, as though arguing. And then, suddenly, they all took flight. Squirrels scurried around the base of Lenny's shade tree, chasing each other, clucking and scolding each other, tiny claws scratching against the bark as they swirled around the trunk. Lenny lowered the row marker on his planter and put his team back to work. On top of a rise, he could see Noey on his small steel-wheel tractor. He watched his uncle for a while, knowing that the older man was struggling with back pain. Noey continued his work faithfully even though he had no son to pass down his farm to. That is, unless, Lenny could go to River City and find Davy W. and talk him into coming back to the Amish. He knew he had to try.

Horses for Sale

Aunt Ruth rang the dinner bell, and Lenny hurried his team into the cool barn and tossed some hay into their feed bunk. Russell started barking as a rattling-rumble of a diesel engine pulled into Noey's lane. Lenny stepped out of the horse barn to see what was up. A huge white pickup with a fancy horse trailer was pulling up near the house, which wasn't an everyday occurrence at Noey's place. The sound drew everyone out to see what was going on. Even Aunt Ruth stepped outside to take in the sight. A tall, well-dressed man who didn't look like a horseman climbed out of the truck. The man was clean shaven, with no hat, and wore a polo shirt that read, "Harris's Hitch," which was also written in large letters on the side of the horse trailer. By the time Lenny got close, another man had come up and had a matching dark blue polo shirt. The man who had been riding as a passenger reached out a hand to shake with Uncle Noey and spoke, "Hello, I'm Kevin Harris. Have you heard of Harris's Hitch before?"

Noey looked down at the ground near his feet as though searching around for a something to remind him of those words. "No, can't say that I have."

"We have top quality show horses. We tour all around, with our six and eight-horse hitches going to horse shows and fairs. Last year, we took first in the eight-horse hitch at the state fair and up at the big show in Brighten. You probably heard about that?"

Noey told them, "No, I don't keep up with that sort of thing." The men in polo shirts seemed baffled that someone didn't know about them and their fancy horses. They looked at Lenny, and he shook his head, indicating that he hadn't heard of them either.

"Well, I'll get to the point. We have a special bloodline of horses. My older brother used to be my partner, but we got into an argument and went separate ways. His gambling habit got him into debt and he sold off all his horses at the Bulltown Sale Barn a few years ago. He sold a stud named San Hosea, and we have been looking for him for a while. We discovered that your neighbor had him. I just went and bought him from—what's his name?—Junior?"

"Junior sold you his horse?"

"Yes, he did. We paid a handsome price for him, too! He happened to mention that you have a couple of colts here that he sired. Would there be any chance that we could have a look at them?"

"Sure, I don't see why not." Noey looked at Lenny to see if he had any objection. Lenny didn't say anything but headed off to get them. Being in a hurry, he came running out with both colts trotting. Both Mr. E and Misty had their heads held high, nostrils flaring.

The strangers stood, eyes wide with amazement, when they saw the colt and filly prance out. "These colts are both out of San Hosea?" the one man asked, and Lenny nodded that they were. The man looked at Noey and told him, "I would be willing to give you top dollar for this team of colts."

"You will have to talk to Leonard; they belong to him."

The man pointed at Lenny, and Noey nodded. "Young man, I would be willing to write you out a nice check for that team of colts right now."

"They're not for sale," Lenny said.

The man who had introduced himself as Kevin Harris got a sinister grin on his face. "Every horse is for sale—if the price is right." He looked at Lenny as though sizing him up. "Does ten thousand dollars sound like a lot of money to you?"

Lenny took in a deep breath and let it out as a whistle.

"Well, you think about that, young man. In the meantime, we have a couple of colts of our own that need some work. Would you consider using them on the farm to help break them in?"

Lenny looked at Noey, and Noey looked back at him. Neither of them gave an answer.

Kevin said, "Junior's barefoot son told me that Leonard is the best person to train horses he knows of."

Lenny laughed, "He must have been joking around."

"No, he was definitely serious when he said that. He told me that most Amish are satisfied to throw harness on a horse and somehow keep the horse in check enough to get a job done. But that Leonard isn't comfortable unless his horses are thoroughly broke."

Lenny wasn't sure how to take that. He told the men, "I guess we could work with them a little. What do you think, Noey?"

Noey scratched his beard and answered, "I don't see why not?"

"Great!" The Kevin-fellow grinned. "We'll come by the first of next week and bring our colts. You think about our offer on these fine colts."

Lenny nodded and took his colt and filly back inside.

Something Big

A horse and buggy pulled in Noey's lane late in the day. Noey drove his tractor out of his bean field and parked it near the house. Lenny continued planting beans; however, he tried to see if he could tell whose buggy it was. The horse had one long white sock, but Lenny reasoned to himself, "That wouldn't be Bishop Mose, now that Davy W. is gone." A deep rumbling sound rose out of the southwest. Dark ominous clouds began banking up higher, growing in intensity, turning black. Lenny told his horses, "Something big is about to happen; I can just feel it."

Noey never did come back out to the field even after the buggy pulled out of his lane. Lenny and his horses finished planting soybeans against a backdrop of thunderheads, which rose higher until they covered up the sinking sun. A dark shadow crept up, slowly covering Noey's house and buildings, and moved steadily across his fields, finally sweeping over Lenny and his horses, leaving everything in darkness. The young man hurried his horses inside and quickly un-harnessed and released them into their pasture. He wanted to get inside before a storm hit.

Ruth and Noey were quiet during supper, which seemed really odd to Lenny. Instead of talking, they all listened to deep rumblings coming from the heavens. Everything felt heavy—even what came through Ruth's kitchen window was pressing into the house and onto the people. Aunt Ruth must have felt it, too, because she went over and slid the storm window shut. She sat back down, and they bowed for silent prayer. Ruth got up and quietly began to clear away everything from her table. She slowly and carefully washed dishes while the men sat without words. Lenny waited for his uncle to speak. Finally, Noey cleared his throat and began to talk.

"Bishop Mose came here with some serious accusations this evening."

Noey and Lenny didn't look at each other while he spoke, but both looked at Russell, who sat near Ruth's feet with his head on his paws. The little dog's eyebrows were twitching as he looked at Noey for a bit, then at Lenny.

Noey continued, "I don't believe all the things Mose is saying about you, Leonard. I told him that I would talk to you about it, and if it is all true, that I would ask you to leave. That is what he wants me to do."

Ruth washed dishes as if she didn't realize the men were there. Russell listened quietly to Noey talking, and then looked at Lenny, waiting for a response. Lenny didn't speak.

Noey began again, "Mose is telling me that you have been pursuing Amish girls even after he specifically told you that you should stay away from them." The older man briefly glanced up at

Lenny. Lenny shook his head no, denying that accusation. "Mose is also saying that you took his granddaughter to a wild party with English young people and got her drunk."

Ruth stopped washing dishes but left her hands in her dishwater. Without turning away from her work, she said quietly, "That is ridiculous. When would Leonard have had time to do such a thing?"

Ruth went back to washing dishes, and Noey continued, "Further more, Mose is telling me that you pulled your car out to the road with horses and drove it. That on the same night you took his granddaughter home from a Singing, you drove your car to Harold's place because you were after Leah."

Lenny surprised himself and Russell by shouting, "That is not true!"

Russell stood up and barked once, then sat back down quietly and resumed his eyebrow twitching, looking first at Noey and next at Lenny. The men sat without another word, watching Ruth meticulously cleaning each dish until everything was towel dried and put away. When she was done, she carefully dried off her own hands, and then turned and calmly said, "Leonard, I think that dog needs to go outside before you take him upstairs." She began to untie her apron, which, Lenny knew from his time in their home, was a clear signal that the kind woman had finished her day's work and was heading off to bed. Noah and Lenny sat for a while in Ruth's clean kitchen, both watching Russell watching them.

Thunder sounded and rumbled deeply, and then the rain began to pour. Noey and Lenny sat listening to the rain steadily pounding on a window by the kitchen sink. An occasional stroke of lightning lit up the window, and the threesome sat waiting to hear deep rumbling that always followed. It sounded like low voices mumbling long sentences. Lenny wanted to say something, but he didn't know what. He looked up at the plaque on Aunt Ruth's kitchen wall: "The voice of the Lord is over the waters; the God of glory thunders, the Lord thunders over the mighty waters.—Psalm 29:3"

After a while, Noey stood up slowly and began to head out of the room. He stopped in the doorway without turning back and spoke, "We'd better get some sleep; we can talk about this tomorrow."

Lenny listened to the floor creak under Noey's feet. When the sound of his uncle's footsteps had faded, followed by a bedroom door closing, Lenny stood up and spoke to Russell. "You better go and do your business."

Russell jumped up and waited at the porch door until Lenny let him out. The young man watched rain falling against dark windows. Every time lightning flashed, the windows lit up. Lenny could see Russell running in circles outside. Lenny called and Russell ran back inside, dripping wet.

"Come here, buddy. Let me dry you off."

He took a hand towel from beside the washroom sink and dried Russell off thoroughly, and they headed up to bed.

Dreams

In his bedroom, Lenny's thoughts began to race. He thought about everything Mose had accused him of. It was true that he had driven his car; he wished he hadn't, but he wasn't really Amish. He whispered to Russell, "I didn't drive my car on Sunday, and I didn't take it to Leah's place."

Russell looked in Lenny's eyes as though he believed what the young man was saying. Lenny thought about how it must sound to Noey and Ruth that he went to see Leah after taking Rebecca home from the Singing. He couldn't think of how he could explain everything that had happened over the past couple of weeks. He didn't want his kind aunt and uncle to hear all of that. He was sure he didn't want them ever to find out about how he had failed to help Davy W. and Leah get together. He hoped to take that secret with him to the grave.

Lenny told Russell, "Now Mose is going to send me home, and just when I really want to stay here more than anything. I want to keep Mr. E and Misty and drive them as a team. I want to take Leah home from the Singing next Sunday. I don't want to leave my best friends Herbie and Perry. And ... I can't leave you behind, Russell."

The little dog shinnied across the covers on his belly and licked Lenny's face. A rumbling above reminded Lenny of Noey's other troubles. He could hear and almost feel huge raindrops falling on Noey's house and farm, further saturating already damaged fields. He lay back on his bed listening to a continuous rainfall drumming on the roof. Russell curled up by Lenny's feet. When lightning flashed, he could see that his little dog's eyes were open, looking at his friend with concern. When the young man drifted off into a light sleep, troubling dreams came to him. He dreamt he was at Noey's church. Preachers stood one at a time, speaking deep, rumbling Dutch sentences, yet somehow Lenny could understand what they were saying. And it was all about him. They were repeating over and over all the awful things he had done. Thunder rolled on and on, along with waves of heavy rain, waking Lenny up often. He went over everything Mose had said again. His head felt dizzy; everything seemed blurry. He slipped in and out of more dreams, trying to explain himself to Noey and Mose.

In one of his dreams, Noah came into the room and said, "Leonard, get up. I need your help. The river is out of its banks, and our place is flooding." He rose up from his bed, pulled on his work clothes, and followed his uncle outside. Cold rain splattered on his face, and Lenny realized he wasn't dreaming; he was outside following Noey toward the barn. Lightning flashed, reflecting off pools of water everywhere around them. There were short moments of darkness, but an almost continuous electrical display in the heavens illuminated one end of the sky, then the other end. Lightning reflected off every leaf and tree limb; they were all glistening wet because of the deluge that was upon them.

Noey hurried into the big barn, calling in his horse herd. Lenny could see the horses just beyond the large door swirling and circling as a group. Noey poured grain into their feed bunks, enticing them in a few at a time, while Lenny quickly slipped on their halters, not sure what his uncle was planning to do. Once they were all tied, Noey told Lenny, "I'm going to open up the mow doors. You start bringing up a few horses at a time, and we will tie them up there."

Everything felt dreamlike. He untied Tug and Train first, being least afraid of leading those two. He led them out into the stormy night, and as they followed him outside, a lightning bolt shot across the sky. Lenny could see his horse s' black silhouettes prancing around him. He tried to calm them. "Easy, boys, easy." They followed him up the earthen ramp into the hay mow while Noey headed down to get another team. It was difficult to see inside the hay mow, but Lenny knew the layout well and found a center beam, He tied Tug and Train, all the while talking to them. "It's okay, boys. Easy, boys. This is a good safe place for you, boys." Thunder rumbled, covering over Lenny's voice. Noey came up the ramp, leading his buggy horses, and Lenny headed down and untied Stone and Jim. They were almost as trustworthy as Tug and Train. The white dapple stars that covered their bodies seemed to twinkle every time lightning flashed. They also pranced nervously as Lenny led them. Winds drove rain against all three of them—man and horses—and seemed to slap them in the face as they came around the barn. Jim reared up, but Lenny tightened his grip as though he meant to hang on. "Easy, Jimbo, easy. We are fine, Jim. Let's get up here in the mow where we can be safe." Stone was less easily rattled and walked calmly into the mow, which made it possible for Lenny to focus on Jim.

It was dark enough in the mow that Lenny walked right into the black sides of a large horse. It didn't budge, and the young man knew instantly that he had collided with Train. Both Train and Lenny were startled, but they recovered quickly because of the trust they had in each other.

Uncle Noey brought up his crossbreds, Mack and Jack, which left Lenny's colt and filly. Lenny told them, "I'm gonna take you up first, Misty, then I'll come back for Mr. E. Lighting flashed, and he could see that Mr. E was sidestepping nervously in his tie-stall. Lenny didn't feel like he could handle both colts at the same time. In the next lightning strike, Lenny made a split decision to untie Mr. E, hoping that he would follow Misty around the barn. Misty was prancing and sidestepping as Lenny led her around the barn. Lightning again lit up the sky, and she rushed forward, bumping into her master, almost knocking him off his feet. Mr. E seemed to be right behind as Lenny and Misty went up the mow hill and inside. It was so dark that Lenny began wishing for another lightning strike just so he could see again. When the next flash occurred, a long row of tall horses could be seen, glistening wet and rain-soaked.

Noey came up the ramp leading Gracie. Lenny stood behind a row of horses, watching, as his uncle pulled on his cow's lead rope. He could barely see them as they walked past but could almost feel their presence in the darkness. He concluded that Noey was tying Gracie opposite the horses.

"Noey, I'm not sure if Mr. E is up here. I untied him, but it was all I could do to hang on to Misty. I think he followed us up here, but I'm not sure."

Another lightning bolt revealed that Noey was beside his line of horses. Lenny couldn't tell if Noey was seeing them or feeling, but he heard his uncle taking a roll call. "Stone, Jim, Tug, Train, Jack, Mack, Big Red, Nelly, Lightning, Misty..."

Lenny waited in pitch blackness, hoping to hear Noey say Mr. E, but it didn't happen. The young man stood, biting his lip, staring out the open mow door, waiting for another lightning strike or for Noey to speak. Both happened at once.

Noey said, "Mr. E isn't here," just as a flash of light revealed the form of a horse trotting off a distance from the barn in ankle-deep waters.

"Oh no! I see Mr. E out in the barnyard. Is he gonna be okay out there?" Lenny asked.

"We may be able to catch him yet," Noey said. "He may come up here on his own, too. We have a job ahead of us tonight. We need to haul some water up here."

"What is going on?" Lenny had wanted to ask but finally felt there was a moment for his question.

Noey hesitated, and then answered soberly, "We're having a flood."

"How bad?"

"Junior stopped in an hour ago and said that there were flood warnings out tonight. Someone told him that the weatherman was predicting the English River will be out of its banks way above flood stage."

Lenny still didn't know what that meant for them.

Aunt Ruth's voice surprised Lenny. "Here are some dry clothes for both of you in these plastic bags, and I brought along a box of food that will keep." Lightning flashed and lit up Ruth's silhouette and revealed the supplies she had brought out.

Noey told her, "Thanks, you better get back inside before things get any worse."

"I will be praying for you," Ruth said and disappeared into the blackness and rain.

Uncle Noey said, "Well, we may be hold up in this place for a few days."

"What about the house? Will it be okay?"

"Oh, I think so. It's on higher ground; it will be fine.

Then Lenny asked quietly, "And what about the corn crib? Will it stay above water?"

"I sure hope so." Lightning flashed and concern was clearly visible on his uncle's face.

Lightning continued to flash in a dark black sky while Noey headed down the ladder into the horse stalls area. Lenny followed his uncle. "We need to get all of our harness up into the mow before it floods," Noey told his nephew.

Lenny got busy carrying collars and harnesses up the ladder. Noey rigged up a pulley above the ladder hatch. He came up with a plan to hoist buckets full of clean water up into the mow where Lenny would dump them into a water tank, which they had dragged up earlier.

All night, Lenny worried about Mr. E. For a stretch of time, there was only the sound of steady rain beating down on Noey's barn, and

Lenny dozed off. Deep rumbling thunder shook Lenny awake from time to time. His first thought was of the colt. He strained his eyes to stare at the row of horses below his hay bed, hoping to see that Mr. E joined the others. At one point, the young man climbed down the wall of hay and quietly slid one wooden door open, peering out into a dark night. With every flash of lightning, Lenny searched for his colt. Flood waters had risen enough that everything looked like a lake where it used to be a pasture. Trees glistened when lightning flashed, being completely water-soaked. A long, brilliant flash of lightning gave Lenny enough time to locate his horse. Mr. E stood in knee-deep water, head down, rear to the wind. Lenny fixed his eyes on that spot, waiting for another lightning to flash. His view alternated between utter blackness and moments where everything was completely lit up like daytime. In those bright moments, he could see that Mr. E hadn't moved but stood like a statue.

All through the night, Lenny wished for daylight to come. But when sunrise came, it was less than he had hoped for. Everything remained dim like a late evening; it was so dark out he couldn't be certain about the time of day. The torrent continued with only one variation: sometimes it poured; other moments it drizzled. Occasionally, heavy storms rolled in with lightning and crashing thunder, winds and hail.

Chapter 13

NOEY'S ARK

Rumblings continued in the heavens above until morning. When Lenny woke, it was the first thing he heard: deep rumbling thunder, and then rain. Looking up at a wooden cathedral ceiling of rough-hewn timbers and layer after layer of wood laths that resembled the skeletal structure of a whale, Lenny eerily felt he had been swallowed by one. Pigeons flew from rafter to rafter, cooing and shuffling their feet until they found a dry spot to perch. Grace let out a long mournful moo, drawing Lenny's attention down to the animals below. His bed of hay bales stacked in a small mountain gave the young man an upper-loft view. He spoke to Russell quietly, so Uncle Noey wouldn't hear, "It looks like we are in Noah's Ark doesn't it?" Russell crawled up from his bed at Lenny's feet to a place beside his head. Together Lenny and Russell looked down on a scene that belonged in a Bible story, not in real life. A row of giant draft horses were tethered at one end: a few were lying down, others were resting, with one hip sagging. Chickens scratched in straw, walking among the legs of enormous horses. Rain pounded continuously on the barn roof, sometimes slapping its sides in sheets.

Freddie crowed, urging Noey and Lenny to get started with makeshift morning chores. The older man milked his cow, Grace. The younger man brushed and fed the long line of Percherons and buggy horses. He also carried five-gallon buckets of water, offering a drink to each horse. He was stunned by how much they gulped down. Tug and Train each emptied all five gallons in one long drink. Noey scrounged up a breakfast out of the box Aunt Ruth had brought out. They ate scrumptious cherry pie with a sugary golden crust doused with fresh cream, which cheered them up considerably.

Lenny slid the haymow door open and stood looking at water that was lapping upon the earthen ramp. A bright flash drew his attention to the road nearest their barn, where a shiny black car was idling. Through the rain, he could see a woman with a huge camera pointing in his direction. Not having grown up Amish, Lenny didn't shy away but stared back at her. Her camera gave a series of flashes that hurt Lenny's eyes, and then she drove off. Through his camera-flash blind spots, he saw Mr. E standing in water. He tried calling him and whistling, but wind and rain seemed to drown out Lenny's voice. Mr. E hung his head and kept his back to the driving rain.

While Lenny was looking toward the corncrib, Noey came near and peered in that direction with him. "Do you think the flood will reach as far as your corncrib?" Lenny asked.

Noey's face seemed troubled. "I hope not."

Lenny wondered why Noey was so worried about the car. There really wasn't anything else of value in the corncrib.

Emersion

All day long, Lenny kept thinking about the story of Jonah he had read on Sunday. A torrential rain continued with lightning flashes and thunder rumblings. By evening, Lenny felt sure that God was sending this storm in pursuit of him until he confessed everything. He looked out at Mr. E again—still stranded in dark swirling water, which had risen to the colt's belly. He slid the haymow door open and called, "Mr. E, come here!" He whistled Grandpa's horse call but still couldn't seem to draw Mr. E's attention. Maybe it was because of the howling winds or rushing waters and pouring rains. Uncle Noey must have heard the whistling. He came and gazed at the scene beside Lenny.

"Noey, is Mr. E going to be okay out there?" The young man searched his Uncles face for a sign of hope.

"I think so. I'm a little concerned that if the water gets deeper, the colt may try to swim over the fence and get caught in it."

Lenny's heart sank. He could bare it no longer. His face was wet from rain that whipped in and lashed him as he stood watching his helpless, miserable-looking colt. He looked past Mr. E and saw Noey's fields flooded—all of their hard work plowing, discing, harrowing, and planting in vain. He thought of Ruth trapped in her house, alone. Kind old Noey stood beside Lenny without a word, watching his farm being destroyed by flood waters, and Lenny was sure that everything was his fault. His face was wet from rain mingled with tears.

"Noey, I have to tell you something." He didn't look at his uncle; he couldn't bare the sight of Noey's kind face.

"Yes, Leonard, what?"

"All of this is my fault! I'm a terrible person, and I've brought nothing but trouble on you and Aunt Ruth."

The most painful thing Noey could have done, he did. He spoke kindly to Lenny. "No, Leonard, you're a good young man. None of this is about you."

"It is, though. I did those things that Mose accused me of. I said I would leave the girls alone, but I ended up taking Rebecca home from two Singings. I took her on a hay ride with drunken English kids. I pulled my car out with a team of horses and took Herbie and Perry for a ride. I was the one that went to Leah's place on Sunday evening... I did all of that."

Noah was quiet. Lenny glanced over at his uncle. In an instant, he could see disappointment weighing heavily on Noey's face. The worst part was yet to come. He felt he had to confess everything.

"That isn't even all of it. I knew something that could have kept Davy W. from leaving the Amish, but I didn't tell him."

Noey's face changed from disappointment to shock. "What on earth could that be?"

"Davy told me that he wanted Leah, that if he could marry Harold's Leah, he would stay Amish. I also found out that Leah wanted him, too, but I kept it to myself. I was the only one that knew it, but I was so selfish I didn't tell him."

"Why ever would you do that?" Noey looked at Lenny with astonishment.

"Because I wanted her, too."

Noey didn't do anything; he didn't leave or speak. For an agonizing period of time, they stood watching destructive water slowly swallow up Noey's fields and lap up further and higher on his barn. It threatened to take Mr. E and suck him under its dark swirling current at any moment. Finally, Uncle Noey walked slowly away, fading into the darkness of his sinking barn. Lenny was sure his uncle was drowning in disappointment. All that he and Ruth had done for their nephew, only to be completely let down by him. Lenny thought about how Jonah told the men in his sinking ship that if they threw him in the water, the storm would cease. He looked at Train. Grandpa's horse was noble and trustworthy. Another lightning flash revealed Train's eyes, dark and shiny, honest and faithful. The young man had to look away; he couldn't take it. He fell down on his knees beside Train in the darkness. On the wet straw, he bowed and poured out his heart to God.

"Please, Lord, forgive me." He couldn't say any more for a while, but only sob in shame, so disappointed in himself. He couldn't look Noey in the eyes; he couldn't look Train in the eyes, much less look up into heaven. All he could do was lay there, bowed down and ashamed. Thunder rumbled deeply and shook the barn. He cried out all the tears he had in him, further soaking the straw he knelt on, and then looked up. Train's eyes met his, and, in that instant, Lenny knew what he had to do.

He crept quietly to the area he and Noey had stored all the harness and found Train's bridle. He snuck back and gently slipped the bit in Train's mouth, then untied him. He climbed up a bale near his massive horse and onto Train's soft back. The big door was opened just enough for them to fit through. Lenny kissed to his mount, and Train obediently headed out into the driving rain. They had only gone a few paces down the mow hill when Train stepped into the water. Lenny was worried his horse may refuse. Deep inside, the young man knew that Train would not refuse him anything. Together they sank down into the cold, dark, swirling water and headed in the direction where Lenny had last seen Mr. E. Lightning flashed and illuminated an eerie scene. Glistening wet tree trunks rose up out of swirling water, its rippling surface reflecting light. A bright flash and corresponding crash sounded, which normally would have made him jump, but he was focused on using the light to help him find his colt. Train turned even though Lenny hadn't asked him to. At the next lightning flash, the young man could see that Train was heading right toward Mr. E. "Good boy." Lenny patted Train on his thick, rain-soaked neck; it was warm. "You know exactly what we are doing out her, don't you, Train?"

"Leonard!" A voice rose above the tumult of storm and waters. "Leonard, come back!" Lenny looked at the barn and saw Noey, glowing in the light of a lantern he held up above his head, Russell by his side. "Leonard, please come back! It's too dangerous! Come back!"

Lenny started to pull back on Train's bit when he heard his uncle's voice, but Train ignored the tension on his mouth, obeying Lenny's heart and not his hands. They pressed forward through deep waters.

Lenny felt his body come off the big horse as water rose up under him. He took a firm grip on Train's mane, holding on for dear life with one hand, and reaching out and grabbing Mr. E's halter with the other. "Okay, Train, I've got him." Train turned and headed back toward Noey's lantern light. Mr. E followed his older teammate. Noey's voice could still be heard cutting through the sounds of pouring rain falling on rushing waters.

"Leonard ... Leonard!" It occurred to Lenny that Uncle Noey probably couldn't see them, his lantern glow not reaching that far out into the stormy night.

Lenny called back, "Noey! We're coming, Noey!" Just then, Train seemed to stumble on something hidden by floodwaters. Lenny felt his head go under completely, but he held onto Train's mane tightly with one hand and Mr. E's halter with the other. The momentum of both big horses moving in the same direction pulled him back up. He tried to keep his head above the waters, eyes fixed on the light.

He could almost hear Aaron Burr's voice: "When storms come, remember Him who spoke and calmed the storm and sea. When troubles rise around you like a flood, keep your head above the waters and look for your deliverer."

Lenny felt his body being pulled by the savage current; his fingers clung to Train's mane and Mr. E's halter. He couldn't see clearly; he had too much water in his eyes. But he could see light ahead of them. Train pushed on toward that light, and Mr. E followed. Lenny felt something under his feet and realized he could walk the last few steps up into the haymow and let go of his horses as they clomped inside. He fell onto the soft straw, feeling a floating sensation, and shut his eyes.

He woke up surrounded by brilliant light. He tried to focus. Squinting because of the light, he coughed, spitting out water. He tried to focus again and looked into Grandpa's kind blue eyes.

"You didn't go after Mr. E because of the money, did you?"

It was Uncle Noey's voice. Grandpa's eyes and Uncle Noey's voice. Lenny sat up coughing and looked at Noey. "No, I guess I didn't. They couldn't pay me enough to get into that water." They laughed.

Noey's face still looked old and sad, yet somewhere in his blue eyes, Lenny could see a glimmer of hope.

Confession Takes a Turn

After Lenny had dried off and changed into another set of clothes, he went and sat down across from Noey at their table made of straw bales. Noey didn't seem angry, but sadness hung on his features. The sight of it weighed heavily on Lenny's heart. Finally, Noey spoke as though laboring to make the words come out.

"I don't understand why you went to Harold's and crashed into his buggy with your car?"

"What? Now that I didn't do!"

"But you said that you did. Mose asked if you pulled out your car with a team of horses and drove it, and you said that you did."

"Yes, I did pull it out with horses, but I didn't drive it to Leah's."

Noey looked at his nephew for a long time before he added, "I asked if you went to Leah's on Sunday night after the Singing, and you said that you did."

Lenny's head felt fuzzy and confused; he almost wanted to doubt himself. Lightning flashed brightly. Looking Noey straight in the eyes, he confessed, "I pulled out my car with horses last Wednesday evening when Perry was here. We drove it over to get a hamburger and came right back home. That was the night Bishop Mose came to tell Davy he had to leave."

More flashes of light blinked on and off. A short time later, thunder rumbled deeply and shook the barn. Noey looked Lenny in the eyes, searching for truth. It was clear that he wanted to believe him. "What about Sunday after the Singing? Did you go to Harold's with the car?"

"No ... I mean, I did go to Harold's place, but I took Nelly."

Noey and Lenny sat on hay bales in the glow of a hissing lantern. They sat looking at eat other, both searching for something, but neither of them seemed to know the right question to ask. Lenny finally looked down at his hands and said, "This storm, this flood—it's all my fault."

"No," Noey said quietly, "I believe it is my sin that brought all this on."

Lenny wanted to ask, "What sin?" but he didn't dare. If Noey wanted to confess, he would.

After a long space of silence, Noey spoke. "When Bishop Mose came, he told me that if I didn't send Davy away, Ruth and I would be shunned. I told him that I would send him off ... but I didn't."

"But you did. Davy left that night."

"No, he's been living in the corn crib, with your car, and we've been hiding him there. I deceived the bishop, but I couldn't hide my sin from God. And now, as the head of this home, my sin has spilled over onto you."

Neither of them spoke for a while. Lenny thought about how he had been seeing a creature in the woods and realized that it must have been Davy W. Lenny asked, "Did you say that someone crashed into Harold's buggy with a car?"

"Yes. It was a silver car just like yours. Mose wanted to go look in our corncrib and see if your car had black paint on it. I talked him out of going down there because I was afraid he would find Davy in there."

"Would Davy have done that?" Lenny asked.

"Why would Davy want to damage Harold's buggy?"

"Well, he is mad at Leah because she won't date him."

Noey ran his fingers through his beard and mused on Lenny's suggestion. He asked, "So, it is true that you took Bishop Mose's granddaughter home from the Singing and afterwards went to see Leah that same night." Noey studied Lenny's face as though trying to understand his nephew. Lenny's thoughts raced; he could see how strange everything must sound to his poor uncle.

"Please, let me just explain everything to you." Rain continued pelting the side of the barn while Noey waited patiently for Lenny's version of the story. "I want to clear this up and be honest about everything." Inside, Lenny wished he could avoid it, but after what Noey had said about someone destroying a buggy at Leah's, he knew it was time to tell everything, and he plunged right in.

"When I stayed at Alvin's place two summers ago, I got to know Leah, Harold's Leah." He looked at his uncle, and Noey nodded. "I always was..." Lenny searched for the right words. "I was really fond of her and even took her home from a couple of Singings back then. When I came to your place, I didn't plan to pursue her, but inwardly I wanted to. Early on, right after I got here, Davy W. told me that he was interested in Leah, that he would stay Amish if he could get Leah to marry him. A few days later, Barefoot Herbie told me that he had heard that Leah had feelings for Davy but wanted to hide her feelings. She was sure that Davy wouldn't stay Amish, and if they dated, she would get her heart broke. I was the only one that knew that they both had feelings for each other, and I could have brought them together, but I didn't... because I was jealous. I'm sorry, Noey."

Noey looked kindly at his nephew. Lenny was surprised that his uncle didn't seem angry. Noey calmly asked, "Please tell me what happened on Sunday."

"Oh yeah, well, let me tell you first about Rebecca. Mose told me at church one Sunday to stay away from the girls, and I fully intended to. That first Sunday night, when I went to the Singing, I was on my way home by myself and came upon Bishop Mose's granddaughters who were walking down the road. They told me that their horse had died suddenly, so I gave them a ride home. Rebecca is a friendly girl and talkative; she sort of didn't let me out of becoming her friend even though I was trying to stay away from girls." Lenny looked up at Noey, who returned an affable smile. Lenny continued, "On that next Sunday, Rebecca insisted that I take her home from the Singing. I should have refused, but I didn't. I took her home, but on the way, we talked about it, that we knew we shouldn't date each other for a number of reasons. After I dropped her off, I headed with Nelly." He looked at his uncle to be sure he heard that. Noey smiled and nodded. Lenny went on with his story. "I went to Leah's because I was determined to do the right thing and tell her about Davy even though I thought that Davy had already left. When I got to Leah's, Henry was there; he had brought her home from the Singing. I waited for him to leave, hoping to get a chance to talk to Leah, and it so happened that she stayed outside when Henry left. I talked to her for a short time."

"Did you tell her about Davy?"

Lenny couldn't look Noey in the eyes. "No." For a few moments, he thought about how to explain himself. Then he finally forced himself to continue. "I was fully intending to, but we talked about how I was thinking about staying on at your place, and she told me that Henry had suggested they stop dating. Leah asked me to bring her home from the next Singing. I wanted to tell her about Davy, but more than that, I wanted to date her myself."

Russell sat on Noey's lap. Noey scratched his little dog behind the ears while he looked up with a grin and said, "Leonard, you and this here, Russell, sure know how to get yourself into a fix in a short time. I would never have believed things could get that tangled up in only a few weeks." He sat quietly, petting his dog for a few moments, then said, "Maybe you better explain about taking Rebecca to that English young folks' party?"

"Oh yeah, I will try to explain that." Lenny looked at Noey and saw that his uncle actually looked hopeful as though it was possible there was a good explanation for this, too.

"When Perry was helping us with fieldwork, that English boy who drives his huge red truck by here all the time got it stuck just down the road. We took horses over and pulled the guy out. That was the same night we drove my car to get hamburgers—me, Perry, and Herbie. When we were at the hamburger place, we met up with that guy with the big red truck. His name is Justin. He asked me to give a few of his friends a hayrack ride with horses. It just so happened that he was having a party near Hershey's garage on the night I was gonna be coming back from making hay at Alvin's. We set it up for me to stop by there and give them a short hayrack ride. Believe it or not, when I got there, Rebecca was already there. That Justin had given her some of his 'punch,' and she didn't know it had alcohol in it. She had been told by Alvin's girls that I was going to be stopping by there and that I could give her a ride home." Lenny looked his uncle in the eyes again to be sure his uncle understood him. "I didn't know those English kids would be drinking, and I didn't know Rebecca would be there, or that they would give her something bad to drink."

Noey looked at Lenny and said, "I believe you."

A soft rumble came from the heavens above and rain gently sang on the roof of Noey's barn. "It's late now, let's get some sleep and see what tomorrow brings," Noey said with a slight smile. Russell and Lenny headed up to their hay-bale loft and drifted into a sound, peaceful sleep.

Chapter 14

THE NOTE

Sunlight beamed down on Lenny's face and woke him up. He thought someone was shining a flashlight on him at first, but then realized it was the sun shining through a knot hole in Noey's barn. Freddie, the rooster, must have seen the light, too; he let out a loud cock-a-doodle-do that made Lenny's ears ring. Old Gracie gave a long cheerful moo. Lenny sat up on his hay-bale bed and looked around. Russell was still curled up in a blanket nest by the young man's feet. The little dog jumped up with Lenny, and they headed down for morning chores. Noey and Lenny cleaned up last night's manure, adding it to a pile on a plastic tarp in one corner of the haymow. Noey tossed some bales down to his nephew, so that he could feed the livestock.

Noey slid the barn door open and remarked, "Come and see this, Leonard." A huge rainbow glowed over their flooded cornfield. Translucent colors rose in columns that arched and met in the heavens above them in stark contrast to the gray-green storm clouds that appeared to be moving away.

"I think we still have time to plant soybeans in that field," Noey stated.

"Is the corn ruined?" Lenny asked.

"Yes, but we won't need to plow again. As soon as that field dries a little, you can disc and harrow it, and we can plant soybeans. It's too late for corn now."

Lenny hung his head, "All that hard work…for nothing."

"No." Noey smiled, his blue eyes twinkling like Grandpa's always did. "Hard work is good for your soul. And besides, you got those colts trained, and look what they are worth now that they're broke. More than that, you learned a lot, and we had a chance to get to know each other. Those experiences are worth more than a whole field full of corn. Like your grandpa always used to say, 'It rains on the just and the unjust, both good rains and flood rains. It is God that gives seed to the sower and brings forth the crops in their due season. He will provide.'"

A pair of mourning doves cooed in the rafters of the barn, drawing Lenny's attention. One of them held a small green leaf in its beak. All day long, the old river seemed to shrink back away from Noey's barn, exposing more of his gravel drive. Noey and Lenny had discussions about how soon they would be able to leave the barn.

Water had barely drained off their drive when a buggy pulled in. Lenny recognized Bishop Mose's dark bay horse with one white sock; it had been in the drive so often. Mose climbed out of his top buggy, heading toward the porch. Noey headed out of his barn to meet him, with Lenny following behind. The older men spoke a few words in Dutch. Lenny understood most of what they said to be a friendly greeting. Bishop Mose began to speak in English. "I think we should take a walk out to that corncrib and have a look."

Noey turned and headed directly toward his corncrib. Mose followed Noey, and Lenny followed Mose. Lenny concluded that after he and Noey had both repented, neither of them would try to hide anything anymore. Before Lenny got there, Noey was already sliding the corncrib doors open. All at once, a small white blur rushed past, and within seconds, Russell had Bishop Mose by the pant leg, growling fearlessly. Mose tried to shake the little pest off his ankle. While he shook his leg, he backed away from the dog and fell over a large tree limb that had washed up from the river. Lenny tried not to laugh as the old man hit the ground with a "humph."

Noey hurried over and took a firm grip on Russell and handed him over to Lenny. Then he helped the bishop back to his feet. Surprisingly, Mose was chuckling as he got up. "That little dog doesn't like me too much, does he?"

Lenny could feel the vibration of a growl in Russell's chest as he held him. After Noey slid his corncrib doors open, the younger man stood back, holding his dog and watching Mose's face to see his reaction. Lenny couldn't see in the crib from where he stood, but Mose didn't change expressions; it was Noey who had a look of astonishment on his face. The older men walked on inside, so Lenny went on toward the doorway. As he rounded the corner, he didn't see his car as he expected. Instead, there stood Smoky, quietly eating on a large pile of hay heaped in a corner of the alleyway. Noey had a piece of white paper in his hand. He held it up and said, "I'd better read this out loud." Mose nodded his approval, and Noey read the note.

> Lenny,
>
> I took you up on your offer. I know you were joking when you told me that you would be happy to trade your car for my horse. Davy and I decided to move to River City. I won't need Smoky anymore, and I think you could use him. If you want your car back, sell Smoky at the next horse auction and bring me the money, and I will give you your car. I'm not trying to tell you what to do, but I hope you stay on at Noey's and keep Smoky. Don't be a sophomore!
>
> Your best friend,
> Herbie

Nothing in the world could have surprised Lenny more. His face might have shown that, too, until Noey spoke and said something equally as surprising. "I believe it was Davy W. that drove Lenny's car to Leah's last Sunday night and did all that damage." Mose looked at Noey, stunned, waiting to hear more of an explanation. Noey continued, "I shouldn't have, but I let Davy move into this corncrib because he had no place to go. On Sunday evening, when Lenny was at the Singing, I heard something out here and didn't know what it was. Mose, when you came by and accused Leonard of pulling his car out with horses and also going to Leah's place, I didn't believe it, until Leonard confessed it was true."

Bishop Mose stood looking at Noey with a confused expression. Noey went on with his story,

"When Leonard and I were up in the haymow surrounded by flood waters, God spoke to us both … in the Lord's own way. Leonard came to me to make a full confession. He told me that he had pulled the car out with horses and drove it. However, he told me that he did it only once, and that was last Wednesday. He also confessed he had gone to see Harold's Leah, but he was driving our old mare Nelly, and he went to tell Leah that Davy W. was upset because he wanted to court her."

Mose looked at Lenny to see if he agreed with Noey's story. Lenny nodded. The bishop opened his mouth and surprised Lenny and Noey by what he said.

"I went to see my granddaughter, Rebecca, and asked her myself about what happened between her and Leonard. She told me that Leonard rescued her twice: once when her horse died and again when some English young people tricked her into drinking alcohol. Both times Leonard was innocent. I also went to talk to Harold and Leah. They didn't know who was driving the car that hit their buggy, but both were positive that it wasn't Leonard."

Lenny didn't know what to say. He just stood there holding Russell, trying to keep him out of trouble. Bishop Mose turned and looked Lenny in the eyes. After a moment, where he appeared to be reading the young man like a book, he spoke directly to Lenny. "If you choose to stay on here with Noey, that's fine with me. I only ask that you do everything just as we Amish do. And see if you can keep this little dog from ruining my pants!" He reached out his hand for Russell to smell. Russell took a sniff and then began to lick Mose's hand. All three men laughed.

Junior and Ruby

As soon as Mose drove away, Lenny told Noey, "I have to go see Junior's family. I still don't believe that Herbie left. It can't be true!" Lenny walked his normal path through trees to Junior's place. He dreaded seeing Junior's family and was afraid that if Herbie actually did leave, they may be blaming him. Nevertheless, he needed to see them and find out for himself if it was really true about Herbie. As Lenny and Russell walked past the chicken house, everything seemed strange. It was quiet. Normally, Blue and Tick would be sounding their alarm, a hound dog bugle, but they were nowhere to be seen. Russell beat Lenny to the house and up the steps. He joined Blue and Tick stretching out on the porch, with their heads on their paws. Both of Junior's dogs lifted their heads and looked Lenny in the eyes as he came up the steps. It was as if they had hoped it was Herbie. Once they were sure it wasn't their missing friend, they mournfully rested their chins back on front paws again.

Lenny walked the wooden porch boards, and they creaked. He had never noticed that before. Maybe because there was usually enough commotion on Junior's farm to cover those sounds.

Lenny made it all the way up to the house door without anyone noticing—that had never happened before. Everything seemed wrong. He knocked and Fannie Ella opened the door and, without speaking, stepped aside as though inviting her neighbor to enter. Lenny leaned forward, pushing himself through an invisible barrier. He wasn't sure if it was his own dread of facing Junior's family or the sadness that seemed to be flooding out of their home. No lanterns were lit inside. It took a moment for Lenny's eyes to adjust to the darkness when they did, saw Junior sitting in his chair. He looked exactly like the stone replica of Abraham Lincoln in Washington, D.C. His face was stiff and sober, and his normally cheerful eyes stared ahead blankly. The presence of Herbie's brothers could be felt; all were awkwardly sitting on couches nearby with long gangly legs. Lenny never remembered seeing them sitting down anywhere but at a table to eat or at church.

Their table was all set for a meal, but none of them seemed to be heading to eat anytime soon. It seemed curious that Herbie's place was set at the table, in the corner where he always ate. Lenny didn't look at Herbie's brothers; he came to speak to Junior and Ruby. All at once, Lenny realized that Ruby was sitting beside Junior in a straight-backed chair, pulled next to his overstuffed throne-looking chair. Immediately, a lump grew in Lenny's throat. He knew that he had never seen Ruby sitting still on a workday. Junior and his family had always made Lenny feel completely welcome in their home, as though he were Amish. At this moment, he felt like a complete outsider even though he stood there with suspenders on and straw hat in his hands. He wished he could have spoken to them in Dutch. He wanted so badly to say what he had come to tell them, but to speak in English at this moment seemed cruel. He hated the sound of his own voice and words, even as they left his mouth.

"I want you to know that I didn't want Herbie to leave ... I mean, I wanted him to stay Amish ... " Part way into speaking, Lenny found that although he had rehearsed what he wanted to say, it didn't seem right anymore. He doubted they could believe him.

Junior moved. He turned his head toward Lenny and opened his mouth to speak. Lenny was as surprised as he would have been if the statue of Lincoln moved and began to speak. Junior's voice echoed in the room, "We know that, Leonard. We don't blame you."

Lenny felt a wave of emotion come over him. He had to sit down, but not in a room full of Herbie's grief-stricken siblings. Without thinking or planning what to do next, Lenny turned and headed out the front door. He had to have some fresh air or he knew he would either get sick or pass out. He staggered out and sat down between Blue and Tick on the top step. He crossed his arms on his knees to make a shelf to set his forehead on and felt himself moan. As if a flood gate had opened, he began to weep and couldn't stop. It came from so deep within him as though it had to escape or he would burst. He would have run off if he could have, but his legs were useless. His whole body was limp. All he could do was cry.

Somehow, during his sobbing, he knew that Herbie's family had come out onto the porch and all stood quietly around him, listening to him weep. Lenny knew that Amish refrain from showing emotion, but Lenny wasn't Amish; he didn't grow up that way. Yet, even while crying, Lenny sensed that Junior's family needed his tears as though he was crying for them, letting out an emotion they couldn't express for themselves—except for Fannie Ella. When Lenny finally was able to raise his head, he saw she was beside him on the steps, covering her face with both hands, sobbing. He wanted to hug the little Amish girl, but that didn't seem like the right thing either.

One by one, Junior's family headed back inside until only Lenny, Fannie Ella, and the dogs were left on the porch. After Fannie Ella stopped sobbing, she looked up and their eyes met. Lenny looked at her tears. "You will really miss Herbie, won't you?" She nodded but didn't speak at first. A few moments later, she said, "I'm also sad because I know how badly you will miss him, too."

They were quiet again for a while. Finally, Lenny couldn't help but ask, "Why is Herbie's place set at the table?"

She explained, "When a young person leaves the Amish, their place at the family table will be set at every meal in hopes that they will return to where they belong." Lenny thought of Ruth and how she had been setting Davy W.'s place at her table, too. Russell had been sitting under Lenny's knees, with his chin on his fore legs. When Fannie Ella spoke, he hurried over and stood with his little hind legs on the porch and his front paws on her lap, licking tears from her face. She laughed even as she cried.

Lenny gathered his strength and stood up, walking away without looking back. Junior spoke through a screen window. "Leonard, we hope you will come by often!"

"Okay, I will," Lenny choked out and continued walking toward home.

Chapter 15

At Last

N oey and Ruth didn't speak during breakfast or on the way to church. It was obvious that they were grieving the loss of Davy W. and Herbie. None of them dared to talk about it. Lenny remembered someone sharing a sentiment when Grandpa passed away; he tried to recall the exact words. "When people really care deeply about each other, they are comforted without using words, but merely by the presence of loved ones who understand each other's pain."

Bright sunlight and warm breezes brought about some additional comfort as Big Red clip-clopped along a gravel road that cut through a beautiful green valley. Birds made a valiant effort to cheer them up with boisterous singing in trees along the way. They passed through a low-lying area drenched with the scent of honeysuckle.

Butterflies fluttered about them, floating up and down in a motion that emanated happiness and made it difficult to stay sad.

For the first time, Lenny felt completely at home sitting in an Amish church service. Bishop Mose sat on a bench with the elders to the left and at a right angle from the young men. That position made it easy for the older men to see every move in Lenny's section. One week before, that would have been agonizing for Lenny; this week it wasn't even an issue.

During the long slow singing of hymns, Lenny couldn't quit thinking about Herbie. In his mind, he went over all of his conversations with his friend and couldn't come up with anything Herbie had ever said about wanting to leave the Amish. A twinge of anger opened up inside of Lenny's heart, like a little weed seedling in a garden. He quickly tried to dig out the seed of bitterness by reminding himself that something possibly happened that he didn't know anything about.

A fly landed on Lenny's arm. Normally, he would have shooed it off immediately; however, this time he held still, hoping to keep the little friend with him as long as possible. If Herbie had been at church, that fly would have provided some kind of wonderful entertainment. Odd as it was, the fly seemed comforting to Lenny, and he watched it for a long time. The fly walked around on Lenny's shirt sleeve over folds at his elbow, as if he was climbing over tiny hills. Sitting on top of one of those hills, the fly rubbed his hands together furiously as though warming them over a fire. A sudden snicker came out of Lenny through his nose, and he feigned a sneeze. He was almost happy Herbie wasn't beside him at that moment, or they would have gone into laughing convulsions again. As it was, Lenny still had to struggle imagining Herbie's lighthearted grin.

One of the preachers who took a turn speaking was a younger man, possibly in his late thirties, which seemed unusual for the Amish. He spoke with a kind voice and such sincerity on his face it made Lenny frustrated that he couldn't understand more German. He watched closely as the man spoke and almost understood what he was saying. He continually spoke about walking in the light and having fellowship with one another. Lenny thought of a passage like that and turned in his English Bible to 1 John 1:5 –7.

" … God is light; in him there is no darkness at all. If we claim to have fellowship with him yet walk in the darkness, we lie and do not live in the truth. But if we walk in the light, as he is in the light, we have fellowship with one another, and the blood of Jesus, his Son, purifies us from all sin."

Something about those verses spoke to Lenny. He decided that he needed to talk to Perry and Leah about not coming back the past summer. It hadn't seemed like a bad thing at the time, but by the way they both acted, he knew he had hurt their feelings. He wanted to walk in the light and have fellowship with them both.

Perry

Shortly after Noey, Ruth, and their nephew returned to their peaceful home, Lenny went out and harnessed up Nelly. As he was hitching her to his two-wheeled cart, Noah came along; he didn't say anything but quietly helped.

"I think I should go see Harold's Ruby," Lenny told his uncle. Noey didn't look up but nodded his head. Lenny tried to explain, "I know it's really hard for her that Herbie is gone."

Noah tugged on his beard like Grandpa used to and motioned toward Nelly. "I guess it might be tough for Ruby if she saw Smoky coming in the lane."

"Yeah, I didn't think I'd better take Smoky this time, anyway." Lenny looked at Noey and their eyes met. Noey's blue eyes smiled as he nodded an approval of Lenny's decision to take the old mare and maybe even acknowledging his nephew's desire to go see Harold's family. Lenny gathered Nelly's driving lines and stepped into his cart. Noey backed away, so Lenny could leave, but stood by the hitching rack and watched Nelly walk toward the road.

Lenny and Nelly had only gone a short way when they came upon a lanky Amish man walking down the road. As they drew near Junior, Lenny looked at his dark eyebrows and beard and marveled once more at how much he looked like a living replica of Honest Abe. Junior spoke, "Ho, Nelly." She stopped and he took hold of her bridle, looking her over carefully as though wanting to buy her. He said to Lenny, "She's in good condition for her age." Lenny nodded in agreement. Junior looked Lenny in the eyes for a moment, and then said, "I think you should be driving Smoky; Nelly has already put in her time."

Lenny nodded. "Okay, I will." The older man let go of Nelly's bridle, but Lenny held her in check. "Junior, I have a question for you." Junior stood still, his kind dark eyes revealed sadness behind his heavy brow. Lenny hesitated, trying to think of how to ask a difficult question. "After Dusty was hit, did you feel bad that you didn't sell him to Milkman Tom?"

Junior's dark eyes glistened and a smile came to the corners of his mouth. "No. Dusty was like a member of the family. I felt bad about having to bury him, but I couldn't have sold him; he meant too much to us."

Lenny nodded his head in agreement and shook Nelly's lines. As the horse walked off, Junior spoke again, "Leonard, I'm really glad you didn't sell your colts." Lenny pulled Nelly to a stop one more time and looked back. Junior continued, "Herbie told me what that man offered for them. That's a lot of money, and I wouldn't have blamed you if you took it. But I think someday you'll realize that those colts mean more to you than money. You just can't find horses like that anywhere. And if you do, they won't be for sale."

Junior and Lenny exchanged a smile, and both went their way.

Lenny didn't mind how slow Nelly was; he enjoyed looking around and having time to think. Yoder Towers rose up before them as the old mare trotted on the flat pavement between the feed mill and Hershey's repair shop. Lenny looked at the pop machine. Bold red letters spelled out "Coca-Cola" with drops of water painted on the word, enticing a thirsty person and tempting Lenny to remember the modern world.

As Nelly pulled Lenny's cart to where the road split two hills, his heart was pounding. He wanted to talk to Perry but wasn't sure he would get a chance. Nelly tromped up to Alvin's hitching rack, and before Lenny could climb off his cart, his relatives appeared on the porch.

Aunt Lydia called, "Did Nelly have to swim outta your barn this morning?"

Lenny laughed. His cousins were also laughing as they came off the porch and stood in a semi circle watching him tie up Nelly.

Edwin looked up, eyes squinting in bright Sunday sunshine. "Tell us about the flood, Leonard."

Aunt Lydia scolded, "Let Leonard come on in and sit down, and then he will tell all of us about it. The little children hung around their older cousin like a swarm of flies.

Sam, David, and Perry were asleep on the living room floor. Alvin nudged each of them with his stocking foot. "Wake up, boys. Your cousin Leonard is here."

They all got up right away and took seats the way guys in town may act when they are about to watch a good TV show. Lenny knew they were expecting to hear a great story from him.

Alvin smiled. "We all heard about Noey's ark, but we want to hear the real story."

Lenny told them about how they had to take all the horses up into the haymow. He winced as he shared the story of Mr. E getting away from him while he led Misty out into the storm. They all watched wide-eyed as he relived with words, riding Train out into floodwaters to rescue his colt.

When they all had heard every detail, Sam and David began to drift off into their Sunday afternoon nap again. Alvin went back to what he had been reading when Lenny came in. Aunt Lydia and her older daughters swished in their long dresses as they cleared off the table. It was rare that they stopped that job in the middle, yet they had made an exception to hear Lenny's tale.

Perry quietly asked Lenny, "Should we take a walk outside?"

Lenny couldn't believe he asked. He was sure it was an answer to what he had prayed for on his way there. Perry was barefoot. Lenny had taken off his Sunday shoes when he came into the house, but as he went to put them back on, he had a thought. "It sounds kind of nice to step outside barefoot right now." Perry nodded with a grin, and Lenny pulled off his socks.

The two young men strolled off the porch and headed toward the pasture fence. Cool, soft blades of grass massaged Lenny's feet as he walked slowly, making sure he didn't step on a thistle. "Where should we walk?" Perry looked at his older cousin for an answer.

"I'd sure like to go see my old bean field."

"It's a cornfield this year." Perry's blue eyes were smiling, just as Grandpa's used to. They walked slowly past Alvin's big barn and made their way to that old familiar lane between fence rows. Lenny had so many good memories in that place. There were two dirt paths were tractors, horses, and wagons had worn ruts over the years. Perry walked in one; Lenny the other.

"Perry, there is something I have to say." He looked at his younger cousin. Perry glanced back out of the corner of his eye, waiting to hear what it was.

"I came here to ask you to forgive me," Lenny said.

"Forgive you for what?"

"Well, first off, for not helping you when the bees were stinging you."

"I don't blame you for keeping away … I would have done the same thing."

Lenny nodded. "I should have at least tried to help. But the main thing I want to ask forgiveness for … is for not keeping my promise. I told you that I would come back and help you when you were going to have your turn being the horse boy. I'm sorry that I let you down."

"It's fine, Lenny. Don't feel bad."

Lenny stopped walking and looked Perry in the eyes. "No, it's not fine. I'm glad that you are so nice about it, but I feel like I let you and Grandpa down. I asked God to forgive me, and I just couldn't feel right until I said something to you."

Lenny started walking again, but Perry didn't. He stood in the same spot until Lenny came back.

"Thank you, Lenny. This means a lot to me. If I'm honest, I have to admit I was let down when you didn't come back. Don't think that it's because I don't like you; it's because I thought so much of you. I almost feel like a part of Grandpa is here when I'm around you. And I really want to learn everything I can about how you and Grandpa handle horses."

Perry's words made Lenny feel great and terrible at the same time. They confirmed what Lenny had feared: he really had let his cousin and Grandpa down. However, Lenny felt a hundred pounds lighter, having everything off his chest.

"I'm just glad that you came back, Leonard; I'm really glad that you came back."

Neither of them said anything for a while. They walked on out toward Lenny's field. When they got to the top of the field, Perry looked at Lenny and asked, "How did it happen that you came back?"

Lenny winced, not sure if he wanted to tell Perry the truth. He concluded there was no use trying to cover anything up anymore.

"Actually, I didn't plan to come back. I was missing everyone, but I was afraid it would be awkward. I was on my way home from college and was just going to drive by and look around. I wasn't even planning to stop and talk to anyone. I guess God had different plans."

"Oh, you mean the storm."

"Yeah, if my car hadn't gone in the ditch, nobody ever would have even known I came by."

Perry was quiet for a moment, then asked, "Do Noey and Ruth know that?"

Lenny shook his head. "You're the only one I've told, but they might have guessed it by now."

The two young men stood quietly for a long time looking at Lenny's field together. Lenny was remembering Grandpa, and he assumed Perry was, too. Without a word passing between them, they both turned at the same time and headed back up to the house.

Perry and Lenny found Sam, David, Rosie, and Ruthie on the front porch. Rosie had brought out a pitcher of garden tea and poured a glassful for her cousin. They all sat together and reminisced about Barefoot Herbie telling funny stories about things he had done. Lenny had some good tales to share himself. After they all laughed heartily, they grew quiet. One by one, they each stated that they still couldn't believe he had left.

Lenny told his cousins, "I'm planning to stop over at Harold's place this afternoon. I'll see you all at the Singing tonight."

"Hope to see you there," Rosie spoke for all of them.

Ruby

Nelly trotted past the timber where Perry and Lenny had cut down a tree with Grandpa's help. He then crossed the Old Man's Creek and went past Web's messy farm. Lenny looked in, but there wasn't any sign of Web; he supposed the lazy fellow was inside watching TV. Nelly's hoof beats seemed to be thumping in time with Lenny's heart as they came to Harold's lane. Lenny wasn't sure what to say to Ruby and wondered if she was blaming him for Herbie's leaving the Amish. He was excited to see Leah, but that made him feel guilty because that wasn't why he decided to go to Harold's place.

Harold must have heard Nelly's hoof beats or spotted her trotting into the lane because he met Lenny at his hitching post. "Hello, Leonard, are you still putting miles on that old mare?" Harold's eyes wrinkled in the corners as usual. Lenny grinned back, happy that Harold was so friendly.

"Nelly still likes heading down the road."

Harold tied Nelly to his hitching post and stated, "I doubt this old girl even needs to be tied; she would probably wait here all day."

"Oh no, I think after about a half an hour, she would head over to that bush and start eating leaves off it."

Harold laughed and asked, "Will you come in and have some cold tea?"

Before Lenny could answer, he saw Ruby sitting on the porch swing. "Actually, I just stopped by to say something to Ruby. Thanks for the offer."

Harold seemed to vanish as Lenny stepped up onto the porch. It is very rare to see an Amish man outside without a hat and even more unheard of to see an Amish man inside with a hat on. However, Lenny wasn't sure whether it was appropriate to have his hat on or off at this moment. It seemed like the right thing to take it off, so he held it on his lap as he sat down next to Ruby on the porch swing. Ruby was such a kind girl. When Lenny had been staying at Uncle Alvin's for the summer, Harold's girls had always seemed so happy and easy going. Yet, at this moment, Ruby sat quietly, like a widow mourning a recently deceased husband.

Neither of them spoke for a while, but they rocked the porch swing, cooperating with how much they bent their knees to keep the swing even. Ruby's dark gray dress and white prayer bonnet looked cute on her even if the girl's face never changed expression.

Finally, Lenny took a deep breath, the way a person would before diving into deep water, and then spoke, "I'm awful sad about Herbie going away."

He glanced at Ruby and thought she nodded her head ever so slightly. Lenny tried to think of everything he had planned to say, but it was slipping away from him. "I hope I didn't put it into Herbie's heart to leave. He is such a good mechanic. He wanted to fix my car, so I let him. I never meant to encourage him to leave the Amish...you know that, don't you?" Ruby didn't answer. Lenny looked right at her, but she didn't say anything. Maybe she couldn't. Ruby looked so sweet and pitiful. Her light brown hair peeked out from under her white head covering in soft wisps, and her dainty eyebrows reminded Lenny of Leah's.

"I just found out that Herbie and I are cousins, second cousins. I wondered why we got along so good...we hit it off this summer right away..." Lenny started getting a tight feeling in his throat. Ruby must have been able to tell because she turned her face without changing expression and looked Lenny in the eyes. He could feel a tear welling up in the corner of his own eye. He was fighting it back when Leah came out and sat on the porch swing in the space between Ruby and Lenny. All three of them sat without speaking, pushing their feet at the same interval and working together to keep the motion of the swing steady.

Leah cleared her throat, and Lenny was expecting her to say something. But instead of words, she began to hum. Almost instantly, Lenny recognized the tune from "God Is Love." After she hummed the tune all the way through once, she began to sing the German words, "Gott isch De Leibe." Leah's voice was soft and sweet as an angel. Lenny glanced over at Ruby and saw a crystal teardrop brim over and stream down her cheek and onto her lap. The three of them continued their slow rocking motion for a while. Lenny nonchalantly wiped his own cheek with his shirtsleeve and stood up to leave. He heard Ruby's voice and stopped to listen.

"Leonard, you should drive Smoky to the Singing tonight."

He looked back at the pair of sisters still rocking on their porch swing and smiled. "Okay."

Finally

After the Singing, Lenny headed out with a group of boys. They stood in a semi circle making small talk, but all Lenny could think about was Leah. He couldn't wait to hear her voice and cute laugh. More than that, he was determined to talk to her about Davy W. once and for all. He made up his mind that he would not leave her house until it was done; he had to do it.

Lenny barely listened to what the others were saying. He tried to keep facing in the boys' direction, but under the cover of darkness, his eyes were fixed on the doorway, watching for Leah's silhouette to appear and head out to meet him. The boys were talking about good names for horses, something that Lenny would normally find interesting. A number of other girls stepped outside first; in fact, a few times it almost looked like Leah, making his heart skip a beat. At last, he was sure he saw her step through the divide between lantern light and darkness. Lenny strode toward her, barely able to see, and bumped into her as he got close. She giggled.

As they walked away, Perry teased loud enough for them to hear. "You know what would be good names for a team of horses? Lenny and Leah!"

The other boys laughed and let out cat calls. Leah laughed, too. As much as he liked the sound of it, Lenny knew he had to tell her about Davy W., which took the fun out of it.

Smoky was waiting, tied to a woven wire fence. He nickered quietly as Lenny untied him and helped his date into his open buggy. As they took off down a dark gravel road, Lenny couldn't help but smile about driving his new, fast horse and sitting next to the girl he wanted to take home from the Singing.

She teased him, "The others are going to have to come up with another nickname for you." He looked at her to see what she meant. Even though the sliver of moon and twinkling stars were the only light, she must have seen his puzzled look. "Well, now that you're driving Smoky, they can't call you Slow Horse Lenny anymore."

He felt hurt that she said that name and even more hurt when she giggled about it. Nevertheless, he loved her cute laugh enough that he couldn't stay mad.

"Leah, I want to ask you something." He looked at her, and she returned his gaze. "Will you please forgive me for not staying in touch ... I want you to be my friend?" She didn't say anything. "I know I hurt you by going away and not coming back like I promised." She looked to one side, her silhouetted face growing sober, and she gave a slight nod. Yet an agonizing silence hung between the two of them.

Leah quietly said, "I felt really bad for Perry; he likes you a lot. He seriously wanted you to come back and help him with the horses."

A tear came to Lenny's eye. "I already asked him to forgive me." She looked at him again just as his tear brimmed over. He quickly wiped it off with the back of his hand.

"Yes, I forgive you." She looked up ahead at Smoky while he looked at her. She still seemed to be avoiding looking him in the eyes. After a moment, he saw her smile as she said, "Yes, we are friends. You've been such a nice person all summer, how could I stay mad at you?"

"Nice person? We haven't seen each other or even talked. How would you know what kind of person I am?"

"A little birdie told me!"

"A what?" Lenny looked at Leah like she was crazy.

"A little birdie named Fannie Ella. All she can talk about is what a great guy you are."

Lenny laughed. "Fannie Ella is my buddy."

When they got to her place, Leah said, "Come on in for a while."

"Can we just talk out here?"

"Okay, but why outside?"

"I just don't want Ruby to hear us talking; I feel so bad for her."

"I see," Leah nodded. They walked beneath the milky twilight, stopping where they had talked the week before, under a tree.

"Leah ..." She looked him in the eyes. He could see reflections of that slice of moon shining in her sweet, dark brown eyes. "...there is something I feel that I should tell you. In fact, I've been trying to tell you this for weeks, but I just couldn't get it out." Leah stood there under the moon, a host of stars twinkling around her, waiting for him to speak. Lenny hesitated, still struggling to make the words come out. "It's about Davy W. ... he likes you."

"What? What are you talking about?"

"I'm telling you ... Davy likes you."

"Okay, so what's the point?"

He could see she was staring up at him even though it was really dark. He wasn't sure what he expected her response to be, but this wasn't it. "Well, I know you like him, and well ... now you know that he likes you. Maybe I could go find him and tell him that you like him, too. If he knew that, he may come back."

"What makes you think that I like him?"

"Herbie told me! You told Ruby, Ruby told him, and he told me."

"I never told her that!"

"Yes, you did. You told her that you wanted Henry to take you home from the Singing, so Davy W. couldn't. You said that you didn't think he would stay Amish anyway." Leah started laughing and Lenny asked, "What's so funny?"

She shook her head. "I told her that I liked Herbie's neighbor. I didn't mean Davy."

"What other neighbor was there?" Lenny stared at Leah, trying to see her eyes.

She looked down at her feet and said, "You don't catch on too quick, do you?"

"Oh, you didn't mean Davy."

"Well, if you thought it was Davy I liked, why didn't you tell me sooner?"

"I tried...I mean...I kept planning on it. Every time I tried to tell you, I couldn't, because I was jealous."

"Jealous of what?"

"That you liked him...I thought." Lenny looked at Leah. Branches swayed gently above them, casting moon shadows. In that soft light, he could see her fussing with her covering. He watched her, confused.

She said, "Leonard, why didn't you come after me? Even an Amish boy would've done that!"

"I thought you liked him. Uncle Noey and Aunt Ruth want him to stay Amish, and I thought..."

She asked, "Are all English boys as slow as you?"

"I didn't know how to pursue an Amish girl."

"I think us girls are the same everywhere."

He realized she was carefully taking straight pins out of her prayer covering and neatly pinning them on her cape dress. When she took her prayer covering off, Lenny knew what was happening. Leah set it down gently and stood up facing him. He reached out and put a hand on her cheek to help guide his face to hers. He could see her sweet lips in the moonlight, those lips that he had wanted to kiss for so long. He shut his eyes and felt her mouth gently touch his.

Under his thumb that still lay against her cheek, her dimple sank in deep; he knew she was smiling. After kissing her lips, he kissed that dimple he had wanted to kiss so many times before.

He whispered, "Catbird." She looked so sweet. He studied her face in the moonlight and saw a tear glistening as it ran down through her dimple. "What's the matter?" he asked as he brushed it away with his finger.

"I'm just happy."

She walked over to a tire swing that dangled from a large limb and climbed on. He pushed her in circles as fireflies danced around them. In not much more than a whisper, he heard her say with a smile, "Slow Horse."

Chapter 16

New Outlook

Noey told Lenny, as they headed out to do chores, "After breakfast, you should head up to Aaron Burr's and get our new harness."

"Do you think it's done already?" Lenny asked.

"I'm sure it is if I know Aaron Burr."

With chores done, Lenny and Noey sat quietly while Ruth finished scrambling eggs. Her kitchen smelled of freshly brewed coffee and sizzling bacon. Russell sat near her feet, watching her every move. Lenny noticed her purposefully drop a tiny piece of bacon, and Russell lapped it up before it hit the ground.

Noey cleared his throat and stated, "You know, the thing that surprised me the most out of what all Leonard told me was that Harold's Leah is interested in Davy." Lenny choked out of awkwardness but recovered quickly.

Ruth chuckled. "That's ridiculous."

"No, it's true!" Noey insisted, "That's what Herbie told you, Leonard, didn't he?"

Lenny felt his face heat up as he tried to think of what to say. Aunt Ruth didn't wait for his response but laughed out loud and said, "You men don't catch on too quickly, do you?"

Noey looked completely bewildered as he searched Lenny's face for some kind of explanation of what Ruth might be talking about. After looking at Lenny's blank expression, he went ahead and asked, "What are you talking about?"

"Well, it's as plain as the day is long that Leah is only interested in Leonard." She brought over a plate of eggs and bacon, setting it between the two men who were staring at her, waiting for an explanation.

Noey asked straight away, "How would you know that?"

"Ever since Leonard got here, Leah just hasn't been herself. Fannie Ella and I both noticed it."

Lenny looked down at the table; he could feel Noey and Ruth looking at him. His face began getting hotter, and his clothes started to feel itchy. He glanced at his uncle.

Noey's blue eyes were twinkling as he teased, "And I thought it was those big colts that were tugging at Leonard's heart. Maybe he has more of a reason to stay here than I thought."

"Noey, don't be so hard on him," Ruth scolded, her face glowing, obviously pleased at Lenny's reaction.

After breakfast, Lenny walked past Aunt Ruth, who was hanging out her Monday wash. He stood and watched her clothespin-clicking frenzy for a few moments as she hung pants up to dry, and then socks. When she turned and moved her basket of clothes, she made eye contact with her nephew.

Lenny asked, "Why did she act like that?"

"Leah?"

"Yeah, I just don't understand why she tried to avoid me and wouldn't even talk to me."

Aunt Ruth continued on with her task of hanging socks until she ran out of room on the first clothesline. While moving over to start on the second line, she smiled at Lenny and said, "She was afraid of getting hurt again."

"Huh?"

"Well, when you were here a few summers ago, Leah fell for you. After two years passed, and you didn't come back around, her heart must have been broken. This time she tried her best not to fall for you, afraid that you will leave and break her heart all over again."

"Thank you, Ruth."

"For what?"

"For explaining that to me. This is the first time all summer any of this has made sense to me!"

Ruth laughed and said, "Well."

Sunshine poured out over farm fields as Lenny rode behind Smoky toward Aaron Burr's place. Birds filled the trees along the way, all singing happy tunes, while the young man smiled as he remembered kissing Leah. He sang, "There were birds all around ... but I never heard them singing. No, I never heard them at all ... till there was you ... " He laughed at himself and said, "Sorry, Smoky, you'll have to get used to my funny ways. And you'll be hearing a lot about this Leah girl, too!"

Lenny eyed rows of green cornstalks standing in soil blackened by rains. He told Smoky, "I wish that Noey's cornfield was growing like this one." Smoky chugged up Aaron's lane. Suzanna, Aaron's wife, was hanging clean clothes on her wash line. She stopped her work to wave at Lenny and called, "Aaron is in his shop!"

Aaron's shop door creaked familiarly as the young man entered in, greeted by rich harness aromas. It took a moment for Lenny's eyes to adjust to Aaron's dimly lit workroom. When they did, he saw a brand-new set of harness hanging on hooks at one end of the room. Aaron was at his treadle machine, already working on his next project.

"I suppose you're looking for a set of harness?" Aaron Burr asked.

"Well, I suppose I am." Lenny walked over to the set on hooks, and Aaron stood beside him.

"This set should be just right for Stone and Jim; I hope it's not too late for this year's fieldwork?"

Lenny laughed. "We wish it were. Our cornfield got flooded out, and I'm going to disc it up today. We decided to put soybeans in because it's getting too late for planting corn."

"Good thinking," Aaron chimed. "That same thing happened to me and my brothers when we were farming those fields. I used to get mad, but my brother Jesse always reminded me that God sends rain on the just and the unjust; both good rains and flood rains."

"I found out that Herbie and his brothers are related to me."

"Yes, Junior and Jake are first cousins."

Lenny thought out loud, "I guess that means that Junior's dad is a brother to my grandpa?"

Aaron laughed. "Yes, I am."

"You are what?"

"Your grandpa's brother."

Lenny took off his straw hat and sat down on a stool near Aaron's workbench, stunned. "What are you saying? Are you Junior's dad and my grandpa's brother?"

"Yes, that is exactly what I'm saying."

"So, Burr isn't your last name?"

"Nope, I'm Aaron Burr Gingerich, and my son is Aaron Burr Gingerich Jr."

Lenny shook his head in disbelief, "So, all those stories about you and your brothers are stories about my grandpa and his brothers?"

"Yep, it was your grandpa that used to plow those same fields you are plowing and that was getting stung by bees when I ran away."

"Did you know who I was the whole time?" Lenny asked.

"When you said your name was Leonard, I knew right away you were my brother's grandson. Your voice and mannerisms are so much like him. I almost thought it was Jesse when you came here the first day. Until you said your name, then I knew. Jesse told me about you, about how good you were with horses. He was so happy you came and spent that last summer with him."

For a moment, Lenny was speechless. Then he found his voice. "I should have known. I loved coming here because you reminded me so much of Grandpa. And you give me such good advice like my grandpa did, too. Aaron Burr smiled, and then said, "You have been reminding me of Jesse as a teenager, but something changed since the flood. Now, you remind me of Jesse when he matured. If you really want to hear your grandpa's voice … listen to yourself when you are talking to horses."

"My brothers and I used to tease Jesse because he always talked to his horses. Not scolding them and shouting orders, but he told them everything on his heart about how he felt, what he was worrying about … just like you do."

"How did you know that I do that?"

"I've heard you myself, and so has my little granddaughter, Fannie Ella."

"Oh," was all Lenny said before he began to bit his lip, worrying about how much Fannie Ella had passed on about what all she had overheard.

Aaron Burr cleared his throat and added, "Over the years, I've learned that people who really talk to dogs and horses have the most success working with them. I believe that God gave animals a special gift, an extra sense; they can feel what you are feeling. But as odd as it may seem, they get even more out of a person that really talks to them. Some people only talk to animals to scold them or to give them commands. Horses tolerate that type of person because they are such kind creatures, but they flourish with people who show a gentle wisdom. You and your grandpa both have done that." Aaron laughed to himself and shuffled over to his seat in front of the heavy-duty sewing machine and went back to work.

Harness

When he got back home, Lenny couldn't wait to put new harness on Stone and Jim. He was even more excited about being able to use Stone and Jim's old harness on Mr. E and Misty, instead of their baling-twine-patched set. The young man quickly un-harnessed Smoky and carried in a brand-new set of black harness with shiny silver buckles and snaps. As he was hoisting Stone's up to lay it on his back, Noey spoke, startling Lenny, who hadn't noticed his uncle walk in.

"I'm kinda used to Stone and Jim's old harness."

Lenny stopped what he was doing and held the heavy harness in his arms. His heart sank in disappointment, concluding that Noey was going to let the new harness hang, saving it for trips to town. He turned to carry it over and hang it on a wall covered with older harness.

Noey spoke again, "Why don't you try that new set on Mr. E. and Misty?"

Russell sat between the men with his head cocked to one side, as if trying to figure out what they were talking about. Lenny felt as confused as Russell.

Noey grinned and added, "I think that team of yours ought to have their own set of harness. They are too good a team to have to wear a set of hand-me-downs."

Lenny didn't know what to say. He didn't want to let his uncle do this kind of thing, but he didn't want to argue with him either. He stood behind a line of huge draft horses, holding a new set of harness in his arms as though stuck in mud. Finally, he thought to say, "Well, it would be fun to try it on my team and see how it looks." Noey nodded, clearly anticipating how the colts would look all dressed up.

Noey watched while Lenny harnessed them up. They untied both horses and led them out into the wide hallway. Mr. E and Misty had always seemed like nice enough horses, at that moment, they looked amazing. They pranced out, heads held high, obviously feeling good in their new outfits.

Noey laughed. "I don't think we can take those new clothes away from those colts now; it'd break their hearts if we did."

Lenny couldn't speak. He just stood looking at his horses. After a few moments, Noey said, "Let's get these horses in the field and see how they look out there."

That snapped Lenny out of his trance like state, and he quickly got to work harnessing up all the other horses. In a short time, they were driving all six large horses out to hitch on the disc. Just then a big fancy pickup pulled into their lane towing a matching horse trailer. Lenny recognized them as the guys who had offered him so much money for his colts. The visitors stood by their big truck. Their jaws dropped as Tug, Train, Stone, Jim, Mr. E, and Misty came prancing out.

"I'm sure glad you Amish don't show horses at the state fair!"

One of them called, "We'd have to settle for second place if ya did!"

Lenny and his uncle grinned but didn't make any comment. The men came over closer, and Lenny said with a smile, "My colts are still not for sale."

"I wouldn't sell those colts if I owned them either! We brought out our colts for you to work with. Are you still willing?"

"Sure, if you still want me to."

"Yep. Everyone says, 'Hire that Leonard Gingerich.' They all seem to think that you and your uncle are the guys to bring them to if we want them trained right."

Uncle Noey replied, "We have awful nice neighbors. They are just worried about us because our farm got flooded out. The only way we can get back in those fields right now is with horses." Noey looked at the men soberly. "We could use more horse power if you have some horses that need work?"

"We sure do!" one of the men said while the other one hustled back to their horse trailer and started leading out a set of colts. Lenny felt his own jaw drop when a pair of shiny black colts came trotting around the horse trailer. They looked like they had never seen an open field before or even a speck of dirt, for that matter. They pranced, lifting up their front hooves just like Mr. E and Misty. "These colts are related to your colts, Leonard. Can you tell?"

"I sure can! Wow, they are awesome!"

"Well, they're not for sale!" he teased.

"I wouldn't sell them if they were my colts, either," Lenny replied, and they all laughed.

Noey got a business like look on his face and said, "I'll show you men where to tie these colts. Leonard here needs to get that big team on the disc; we have some fields to get replanted."

"By all means," one of the guys said, "don't let us keep you from getting that done." They stood and watched as Lenny drove his six-horse-hitch out toward the field.

Justin

Everything was going good in the field. Lenny couldn't stop admiring his colt and filly in their shiny new harness. They looked like completely different horses than they had last time when they were in harness. They seemed bigger, stronger, and even appeared to be working better. A catbird meowed at the field's edge, sending Lenny into another round of smiles. In his head, he went over everything that he and Leah had said to each other last night, wondering if that kiss had really happened, or if he had only imagined it. Just as he was reminiscing, a low growl came up from the woods off toward the east.

Lenny told his horses, "Okay, Mr. E and Misty, here comes that Justin with his big red truck. Easy now, easy." He turned his disc, so that his horses were facing the direction of the sound.

In the past, he had tried to turn his horses away, but Noey told him, "Horses want to run if something is coming up behind them. Turn them to face that sound, so they can see what's coming. They still won't like it, but at least they will be ready for it."

Noey's advice seemed to work. Misty shook her mane, and Mr. E sidestepped a little, but Lenny was able to hold them in check. Justin didn't roar past like he used to; instead, he rumbled to a stop near where Lenny and his horses were working.

"What does that bully want now?" Lenny mumbled, as Justin climbed down of his big truck and climbed the fence. Lenny drove his horses over toward him.

"I saw you guys got flooded out!" Justin called as they got closer.

"Yeah, we are going to plant soybeans here as soon as I disc out any corn that survived."

By that time, Justin had come up close and stood there awkwardly, like he wanted to say something but didn't know how to get started. Lenny looked at him and said, "What's up, Justin?"

"You're the only person that knows about my girlfriend, you know..." He looked at Lenny, and Lenny nodded that he understood.

"Well, I wanted to ask someone's advice about it, and since you're the only one that knows, I thought I should talk to you." He looked in Lenny's direction for a moment but didn't seem to want to make eye contact as he continued, "She told me that she is gonna give the baby up for adoption if I won't marry her, but I don't know what to do."

Lenny was stunned by Justin opening up like that. He sat speechless for a moment and uttered a silent prayer in his heart, "God, help me know what to say." Then he opened his mouth and started to talk without even planning his words.

"You know, Justin, my parents weren't married when I was born. I'm sure glad that they got married and kept me."

"I just don't know if I'm ready to settle down and get married."

"Yeah, I guess I can see how you feel." Lenny sat quietly for a moment, wishing he knew the answer. Then he had a thought, "Justin, you do like Barbie a lot, don't you? I mean, you weren't planning to break up with her or anything."

"Yeah, I like her."

"Well, then, it seems to me like you already made the decision when you and her...you know what I mean?" Lenny looked at Justin, and he nodded and grinned. Lenny continued, "That little baby is family to you. And if she is your baby's mama, then that makes Barbie family, too. Don't walk away from family when they need you most."

Justin looked Lenny in the eyes for the first time since they had met. The young man's face took on a calm expression. Justin reached out to shake Lenny's hand. "I'm glad I came and talked to you. I never thought about it, that the baby was family. I just thought of it as a big problem. You're right. If Barbie is having my baby, then she is family, too!" Justin got a big grin on his face, "This is kinda exciting! I'm gonna go ask Barbie if she will marry me!"

Justin took off running toward his truck, and Lenny called after him, "I'm glad you're excited, but please don't take off loud with that big truck or I'll have a runaway!"

Justin stopped at the fence with a smile, "I wouldn't do that to you, Bud!" Then he hollered loudly, "By the way, my uncle Web wants to know if you kissed that Amish girl yet!"

Lenny looked around nervously and put a finger to his lips, "Shhhh ...." then nodded.

Justin let out a loud, "Yahoo!" He climbed into his truck and took off as quietly as he could in his beast of a truck.

Lenny started his team, moving in the same direction as Justin's truck. It moved slowly up the gravel road. They all seemed calm enough and watched the big red monster go up the hill near Aaron Burr's place. Lenny bit his lip as he thought about his advice to Justin, wondering if it was the right thing. Off in the distance, a roar sounded on the main road as Justin finally let his excitement go to his foot, pealing out in the direction of his girlfriend's house.

Lenny laughed and prayed, "Lord, let Barbie say yes."

Fannie Ella's Secret

After discing for a stretch of time, Lenny called his team to a stop under their shade tree. The young man walked around front and adjusted Mr. E's new harness, examining it close. Fannie Ella appeared again, without any of the horses lifting their heads. Lenny asked her, "How do you sneak up on six horses like that?"

"I'll tell you a secret." The young Amish girl smiled and motioned Lenny closer, so that nobody would hear what she was about to reveal. "I don't sneak up on horses at all. I talk quietly to them while I'm a long way off. They have really good ears; they hear me even though you don't. I tell them, 'Here I come.' So, they know that I'm walking up and don't get surprised."

Lenny shook his head. "You've got to be kidding me? So, you're saying that when other people walk up, it startles them, they jump, and I get the clue that someone is coming?"

"Exactly! It works good for you because horses notice a person walking up before you do. So, they don't get a warning, but you do. When I am walking up, they know I'm coming." She giggled at how clever she had been. Lenny stood looking at her in disbelief.

"Hey, Fannie Ella, some guys came out this morning and brought us some show horses to break, those same guys who bought San Hosea from you dad."

"Yeah, they asked us if we could work with them, and dad told them to bring them to you."

"Why me? I'm not that good of a horseman."

"You're not a good horseman because of the amount of your courage."

"See, I know it's true that I'm not a good horseman." Lenny looked at his feet, and then at the little Amish girl.

Fannie Ella's face contorted with frustration. She said, "My dad tells people, 'Take an Amishman for what he means and not what he says.' It's true for Amish girls, too.'"

"Why that?" Lenny asked.

"Because English is not our main language, we Amish often say things backwards."

"Well, then, what exactly did you mean?"

"I meant that you are a good horseman, but it's not just about being brave; it's because you love your horses so much. And I'm sure that they can feel that."

"Thank you, Fannie Ella. That is the nicest thing anyone has ever said to me, in Dutch or in English." Their laughter echoed off the bluffs.

"I'd better get in to help Ruth." Fannie Ella got serious. "My mom sends me over to help because she feels bad that Ruth doesn't have any daughters. We don't want her to be lonely."

"Looks like your mom had enough girls for both of them," Lenny teased.

Fannie Ella laughed, and then showed a serious face, "My whole family is hoping you will stay on with Noey and Ruth; they really need you here right now."

"I'm not planning to go anywhere else soon. I know what I want to do ... I want to farm with horses."

Fanny Ella giggled and said, "That will make Leah happy, too!" Lenny watched as she headed off toward the white farmhouse.

He heard a catbird singing in the tree over his head. "Huh, that's unusual—to hear a catbird singing this late in the spring!"

He clucked and his horses stepped into motion, pulling the disc. Lenny smiled the biggest grin of his life.

The End

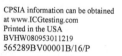
CPSIA information can be obtained
at www.ICGtesting.com
Printed in the USA
BVHW080953011219
565289BV00001B/16/P